Wawona Hotel

Other Books by Matthew McKay

POETRY:

Lucifer in the Resthome

The Yosemite Poems

NONFICTION:

Self-Esteem (with Patrick Fanning)

Thoughts & Feelings (with Martha Davis
and Patrick Fanning)

Prisoners of Belief (with Patrick Fanning)

Messages (with Martha Davis
and Patrick Fanning)

Wawona Hotel

A Novel

Matthew McKay

Boaz Publishing Company
Albany, California

Some of the poems in this novel appeared previously in the following publications:
"Your Father" in *Interim*
"Speeches So Small" in *Poet and Critic*
"Living With Strangers" in *The Little Magazine*
"Island" in *CutBank*
"Nature of Golf" in *CQ*
"Half Dome Turning Pink at Twilight" in *Lucifer in the Resthome* (Plum Branch Press)

Library of Congress Cataloging-in-Publication Data

McKay, Matthew, 1948-
  Wawona Hotel : a novel / Matthew McKay. -- 1st ed.
      p. cm.
  ISBN 978-1-89344-806-3 (alk. paper)
1. Women--Psychic ability--Fiction. 2. Married people--Fiction. 3. Man-woman relationships--Fiction. I. Title.

PS3613.C545175W39 2008
813'.6--dc22
                                    2008001857

Printed in the United States of America

DEDICATED TO JORDAN
AND BEKAH

All
our walls shake if we
listen
if we stop even
to rest a hand on them.

from "The Rock"
W. S. Merwin

When I know what people think of me
I am plunged into my loneliness.

from "The End"
Robert Creeley

And this is the room one afternoon
i knew i could love you;
And from above you how i sank into your soul,
into that secret place where no one dares to go.

from "The King of Carrot Flowers," Part I
Jeff Mangum, Neutral Milk Hotel

CHAPTER 1

There are certain occurrences in life that confound reason, that stand beyond all explanation. Yet we try to explain them anyway. We tell the story, over and over, hoping a listener's chance remark might somehow make sense of the absurd. I am doing it again, after years of silence. Perhaps because I have the time. Finally I'm writing it down, as if some overlooked detail, some stirred memory might illuminate what happened.

It begins, I suppose, in 1969, with Danielle about to turn south on Chowchilla Mountain Road. On her right were the lawns and white colonial-style buildings of Wawona Hotel. To her left was a golf course—Chowchilla Road cuts across its fairways to begin the switchbacked climb to Big Creek. Danielle was heading to a favorite picnic place where she planned to do a little unsuccessful fishing with her daughter. Annie, her little girl, was stretched out in the backseat playing with a puppet. No one later could recall whether Danielle gave a hand signal. Her 1947 Studebaker didn't have blinkers. What's known is that a twenty-year-old electrician's apprentice, on his way to rewire the gift shop at Glacier Point, decided to pass her at that exact moment. He hit Danielle broadside on the driver's door, just as she began her turn.

I remember the accident. I was on a tractor mowing the ninth fairway of the golf course. At the sound of the crash, I looked up to see Danielle's car spin violently, flip and slide on its roof thirty yards across the asphalt. The scraping metal made a roaring sound and bled a train of sparks. When I got to her, Danielle was crumpled against the ceiling of the car. Her nose and ear were bleeding, and a deep gash above her eyebrow was pouring blood into her hair. She didn't move.

Five-year-old Annie was screaming something I couldn't make out and pounding on the back window. Her door wouldn't open, so I reached through the broken driver's window to roll the back one down. When she crawled out, Annie stared briefly at her mother's bleeding face. Then she punched me hard in the leg with the hand that was holding her puppet, and started running, making a beeline across two fairways and into the pines by Meadow Loop Road. I remember it had rained that morning, and the sun had just broken through a high bank of cumulus to the east. I can still see Annie's blonde hair swaying as she ran, her yellow tie-dyed dress bright in the sun.

Maybe I shouldn't have done it, but I pulled Danielle through the smashed window. I laid her out next to the car, glass shards glittering around her. I wasn't sure, but I thought perhaps she was already dead. She'd wet her pants; her mouth had fallen open to reveal broken teeth and a badly lacerated tongue. Welling blood ran in a small river from the corner of her lips. Her eyes were closed. I felt for a pulse at the base of the jaw, but I couldn't tell if the beat I detected was my heart or hers.

I knew Danielle barely enough to say hello—we both worked for Wawona Hotel. Just the same, I held her hand. And then, for some reason, started talking to her. I told her not to leave her daughter, not to give in to whatever might be beckoning her away. I bent to listen for a breath or whisper.

Nothing.

I took off my shirt and put it under her head; I put a picnic blanket I found in the car over her. No response.

So I continued babbling—for forty minutes till the ambulance got there—about how beautiful the trees were at night, silhouetted against the moonlight. About the scent of pines, and the sound of Big Creek pushing its way over the cascades. I told her she would miss those things, that she would never know them again if she let go. I hadn't the faintest idea whether she liked nature or owned stock in a lumber company. I just kept talking, telling her about sunsets up in the sequoia groves, or borrowing John Muir's words to paint the granite cliffs and domes of the high country.

I wiped the blood out of her nostrils and off her cheek. But it started running again—perhaps a good sign. I was surprised at how important it was for me to still have hope.

While I was tending to Danielle, hotel guests who'd been sitting on the lawns and verandahs swarmed to the scene. Some helped the electrician's apprentice climb from his truck; the fool had careened into the creek that runs along the edge of the golf course. After a while there was a little crowd around us, including the electrician kid, who was repeating to anyone who'd listen that Danielle "never gave no signal." While he was bleating his story, I sent a couple of folks off to look for Annie. But she didn't turn up till much later—when it was almost dark.

It's odd, thinking back on it, how none of the bystanders came near Danielle. They kept their distance, murmuring among themselves. So I just stayed by her, looking for any sign in her face. I noticed then that she had lovely, high cheekbones and full lips, slightly downturned. Her skin was pale, her hair burnt umber, spilling in long tangles around her head. She was early thirties, I guessed, ten years older than me. Her face, despite the damage, held a sweetness and beauty I'd never noticed before.

When the ambulance screamed in, I reluctantly let go of her. As the EMTs checked vitals and taped Danielle's head to a board, they chewed me out for moving her.

"What you did could have paralyzed this girl, you know that?"

Obviously I didn't.

"Are you anything to her or just a bystander?"

I can't tell you why, but at that moment I felt a kinship with the woman, a bonding I've never experienced so suddenly or so deeply in my life. And with it came an anxiety, a fear of separation.

"I'm her brother," I said. In hopes, I think, that they would let me ride along in the ambulance.

"What's her name?"

"Danielle."

"Last name?"

Then I did my next crazy thing. "Kane," I said. I gave my own last name because I didn't know hers.

When they'd finally strapped her to the gurney and were lifting it into the rig, I touched Danielle's arm. It was warm—and beneath soft skin strongly muscled.

"You coming?" one of them asked.

The ride to Oakhurst was mostly hard turns and violent swaying. The driver punched the siren whenever he encountered traffic, then lurched left to pass the slower cars. In ten minutes I was completely nauseated. The EMT attending to Danielle gave her an oxygen mask and pulled back her eyelids. "One pupil sluggish," he said. He cut open her T-shirt and attached EKG electrodes to her chest. She wasn't wearing a bra, and I was startled to see her breasts. It felt suddenly like I was violating her in some way, invading this private place where she needed help and might be dying. I looked away, but heard him cut open each of her pant legs. "No apparent breaks or abrasions," he said, finally draping Danielle with a light blanket.

"Can I hold her hand?" I asked.

"If you can reach it without getting in my way. Don't go all nuisance on me, OK?"

Her arms were still strapped to her sides, and I had to stretch between the tech and Danielle to touch her hand. As I held it, I could feel the warmth and softness of her hips. Again, it felt wrong, as if I was taking something from her. An unearned intimacy. The tech was checking her blood pressure. He started an IV. I kept holding her hand, willing her to live.

"You gonna make the calls," the tech asked, "when we get to the hospital?"

"Did something happen? Did she…"

"It's OK, man. She's stable. Can't say about later, but we'll get her there breathing. I mean calling her family, telling her people where she's at."

"Yeah, no problem." I hadn't the faintest idea how I'd do it; I knew nothing about this comatose woman.

"Do you think she'll make it?"

"Want me to tell you straight?"

"Sure."

"This is a bad head injury. Could be internal hemorrhage from the looks of her pupils. She could make it, man. Or she could die or end up on the veggie ward. I don't know."

I held Danielle's hand more tightly, noticing for the first time the hard edge of a wedding band.

"She has to be all right," feeling in some crazy way like the responsibility rested solely on me.

"I know what you're sayin', man. When a thing like this happens, you feel like," he adjusted the air flow on the oxygen, "like love should have the power..."

"What?"

"To keep someone alive."

"Yes," I said.

He fiddled with the saline drip.

"Yes," I said again, looking at the crusts of blood on Danielle's face. "That's right."

CHAPTER 2

The next morning Danielle had surgery to relieve pressure from a cerebral hemorrhage. When I came to see her that afternoon I caught my first glimpse of her husband. Loitering near the nursing station, I spent a long time watching him. The man was tall and slouched, with a hard, wiry frame. His curly hair hung to the shoulder, swinging in a tight arc whenever he turned his head. Thin lips were nearly hidden by a bristling mustache. He wore a red plaid shirt, torn jeans, and square-toed boots.

Danielle lay, as she had from the time of the accident, in a deep coma. A thin sheet covered her; tubes and monitoring wires ran from the bed to various machines mounted on poles. Her husband was talking to her.

"Come on, Dani, come on now. Wake up time, Dani." He was pulling on the raised side rails, shaking the bed. "Don't be laying here looking like shit, Dani. Come on now, baby girl…for Christ's sake." He gave a particularly vigorous shove at the rail.

Now he was looking at the machines, reading Danielle's heart rate and blood pressure. He traced a finger on the electrocardiogram as it marched across the narrow screen. Then he touched the tape that covered the IVs on Danielle's hand.

"Come on, baby, don't lay here like a sack." He picked up the sheet and took a long look up and down her body. "Awe, they got all kind of shit coming out of you." He touched her—maybe her breast—and dropped the sheet. "They got all kind…" Tears shot sudden, glistening paths down his cheeks. He looked around in that scared-rabbit way men do when they fear some weakness might be observed.

His eyes found me—I think he knew I'd been standing there for a while. A few quick strides carried him to the nursing station, smearing the tears as he walked. His movements were controlled, catlike.

"What are you staring at? You think you're at the movies or something? That's my wife!" The word wife came out like a small explosion.

The sound of his voice startled one of the nurses. She raised her head out of a chart and pointed to me—I think she was trying to calm things down. "He came in with the patient yesterday. He's her brother." She looked puzzled. "Don't you know each other?"

"No, I don't." The big man's lips were pressed in a thin line. "I'm James McAllister, husband of your sister." As he made this pronouncement, he took my arm, digging his fingers into my biceps, and guided me out past the double doors of the ICU.

"What is this shit? Danielle doesn't have a brother."

I explained what happened. How I'd seen the accident from the golf course tractor and done what I could to keep her alive till the ambulance got there.

"Why'd you say you were her brother?"

"I felt she might still need me in the ambulance. The only way they'd let me ride is if I said I was a relative."

McAllister looked puzzled, but he released my arm. Up close I could see thin seams running down his cheeks. His breath smelled of cigarettes.

He stepped back and looked me up and down, in much the same way he'd done with his wife a few minutes before. Examination over, he turned away. A flush rose in his face. "I'm sorry," he said. "I'm in a state. I see her lying there…" He shrugged. "Thank you for what you did. Come over to Fish Camp and I'll buy you a drink sometime." His hand went back to my arm. "But you don't need to deal with this anymore. Go home. I'm with her now."

But that wasn't really true. I was sitting in the hospital parking lot, trying to fathom the sense of responsibility I still felt for

Danielle. Trying, actually, to let go of it, when I saw James McAllister climb in a Jeep and drive away. No more than twenty minutes after our conversation.

During the next three weeks, Danielle's condition remained unchanged. She lay without movement. Monitors glowed above the bed while unknown medicines dripped into her veins. A tube was put in her nose for feeding.

I learned through the grapevine that McAllister worked for the Sugar Pine Railroad on the weekends, so that's when I visited Danielle. I continued talking to her as I had done on the day of the accident: describing beautiful scenes; inventing lovely moments she could have with her daughter. Between visits, I made lists of places I'd been that I wanted to describe to her. The trail to Merced Lake in the high Sierra, Going-to-the-Sun Road in Glacier, Glenwood Canyon, Ruby Canyon, the grove near Santa Cruz where the monarch butterflies gather. Then I'd pour all of it out on Saturday and Sunday.

It feels important to me now to understand this—because it was the beginning. Because all that followed seems, somehow, the necessary outcome of those visits. I was not in love with Danielle, but, oddly, I loved the damage in her face. The forehead wound, the broken teeth, the swelling. I will admit that I watched the curve of Danielle's breasts under the thin sheet. And the outline of her thighs and hips. But I was twenty-two; a woman's body held great fascination for me.

The core of what I felt was that Danielle had somehow been entrusted to me. And I believed I was the only one who could reach her. It felt like I was shouting into a cave, but somewhere, miles away, she could hear me. And I was all she had there, lost in that place.

Never before had I felt essential, or even important, to anyone. If I were to describe my childhood, it would be the life of a ghost. Drifting like smoke through the rooms of my house. A vapor that cannot be hit or hurt. Or caressed. So now, feeling wholly responsible for Danielle's life, I was both terrified and excited. I was at the center of something. I was indispensable.

As I write this, the morning light casts long shadows of pines across the lawn. Their scent inhabits me, becomes a code that tells everything I have ever known about loneliness. I inhale, and listen to it speak.

It was on the fourth Sunday that I realized I didn't know the color of Danielle's eyes. I decided, finally, just to look, lifting the lid to find a brown iris. The pupil contracted with the sudden light, but when I moved my hand back and forth, the eye remained fixed, lifeless. Like I was examining a cadaver. If Danielle was in there, I began, for the first time, to doubt that I could reach her, or had ever reached her.

The nurse came in and hung a new IV. "We're moving her tomorrow," she said. "Long-term care unit. This floor is for acute patients. The way she is now could conceivably go on many days or weeks."

"Till what?" I asked.

The nurse looked searchingly at me for a moment. "Till she wakes up or she dies," she said softly. "I'm sorry. But it doesn't do any good to avoid the truth. You have to be prepared for it."

After the nurse left, I remember telling Danielle a long story about her daughter's next birthday—her sixth. In the scene I painted, Annie and her friends were playing a tag game and Danielle could see the joy on the girl's face. Then the scene shifted to ripping open the packages, Annie's bright eyes as she saw each present. And then the darkened room, the candles, Danielle placing the cake before her little girl. I'll admit these are stock images, but what I wanted Danielle to hear was her irreplaceability.

While I went on about all this, I was holding Danielle's hand—the one without the IV in it—feeling the tendons and the calluses, rubbing her slender fingers. It was then, for the first time, that I sensed the slightest pressure back.

Two days later, Danielle's eyes opened. And the nurses called her husband with the good news.

When I heard, I was setting sprinklers on the seventh green. My boss told me. After he'd gone, I remember kneeling and looking up the fairway. It's narrow and steep, cut right out of the forest. On some level I was greatly relieved. But I was also suddenly empty. I ached to see her, yet I knew Danielle had no need for me now.

CHAPTER 3

*I*t was a good month before Danielle came back to work. And during that time I never saw her. I heard that she was having trouble focusing, getting her eyes to work in sync. She was also rumored to have a limp due to weakness in one of her legs.

It was a period of sadness for me. While Danielle was in the hospital, I had discovered something. Instead of the usual search for small pleasures, for satiety, I had found a meaning. I had learned to forget myself. And now the old life seemed less bearable. As if I could never again be satisfied with chasing some minor object of desire.

The golf course, and my job as greens keeper, became both solace and a place of isolation for me. I drove my tractor down the fairways in the afternoons and evenings, pulling hoses, setting the sprinklers on their tracks. I cut the rough, I mowed the putting greens, I raked the traps. It was a Tao, a focus on the moment. I let the evening's coolness rub my skin, the mist from the sprinklers settle on my face. But the whole while, I was alone. Golfers sometimes waved. My boss drove by to check on me from time to time. And finally I would go home to read, to drink port in my room.

About a week after Danielle came back to work, I saw her walking down the road from the hotel—toward the spot on Highway 41 where the accident occurred. She stared for a while at the intersection, then kicked at something in the weeds by the apron of the road. She walked a little farther before pausing and picking something up: a piece of cloth.

Danielle looked out across the golf course. She ran her fingers through her dark, center-parted hair. And, to my surprise, she headed toward where I was working on the first tee.

"Harper?" She looked uncertain. I noticed simultaneously her lovely, downturned smile and that her front teeth had been capped.

"Hi, Danielle. How are you feeling? You're not taking up golf, are you?"

She smiled and held up what had once been a puppet. "Annie said she lost it when I had the...accident."

"It's good you found it. Children miss things."

Silence.

"I wanted to thank you for what you did for me," she said. "People told me. How you pulled me out and covered me. And held my hand the whole time till the ambulance came."

Her brown eyes searched my face. I wondered what she was looking for.

"You're welcome, Danielle. I'm glad for whatever help I could be."

"Are you upset?" she said. "You seem..."

I started to speak, but nothing came out. She kept looking at me. With unnerving intensity.

"Are you..." her eyes narrowed, a look of curiosity, "afraid of something?"

"Yes," I blurted.

"What?"

Silence.

"Tell me, Harper."

"You, I guess. I was afraid...we'd talk. And then..."

It was instantly the craziest conversation I'd had in my life. I had no idea what I was going to say next.

Danielle waited. She touched a finger to the corner of her full lips, rubbing slightly.

"We'd talk, and then what would happen?" she prompted.

"I don't know."

"We'd walk away?"

I nodded.

"And that would be the end of it?"

"Yes."

She went back to studying my face.

"The nurse at the hospital told me about my brother's visits. 'A very nice young man,' she said. Always telling me about beautiful places, about things to live for. Are you that young man?"

"Yes," I said. "I felt…"

I noticed her T-shirt had a daisy on it. I was trembling slightly. She waited.

"I felt some kind of connection to you. From the moment I pulled you out."

She briefly touched my arm. I could feel the calluses on her hand.

"And you don't want to lose it."

"I think I already have."

She nodded. "Did you ever talk to me about Annie? About a birthday? I have a picture of that in my mind."

"Uh huh."

She didn't say anything for a good while. We stood there as the dusk began to chill us.

"Then I think you did help," she said, and turned and headed back to the hotel.

CHAPTER 4

I learned much later from Danielle—from something she wrote—what I'm about to say now. But I feel it must be kept in the proper order. There's no other way to ensure that some thread, some fact hasn't been lost that might shed light on things.

When Danielle and I spoke that day on the golf course, the conversation was at first unsettling. She saw things about me. She finished my thoughts. She sensed the feelings I hadn't yet found words to describe. And, as we talked, this very odd feeling of relief came over me. As if something had happened that I'd been waiting for. Even craved. As if, for one brief moment, I no longer had to be the ghost.

James McAllister had a different response. When Danielle woke up in the hospital, he embraced her. Her lips were still painfully tender, so he kissed her on the cheek. Then he brushed her hair across the sutures on her forehead.

"Dani," he said, "you're back." Over and over.

She was frowning, looking at his hand.

"Was it hard to come back, baby girl? Were you lost in there?"

"No. I don't know where I was. I can't remember any of it."

He touched her cheek, but looked away. "We'll get the tubes out of you and get you home, baby. Won't that be good?" He smiled broadly.

"James?"

"Uh huh?"

"You seem…"

"What?"

"I don't know. You seem…unhappy."

"What are you talking about, Dani? To see you wake up like this—it's the happiest day of my life. Except when we got married. How can you say that? Have the docs got you whacked out on some drug?" He was smiling again. "Let's get a hold of somebody in charge and find out how to bring you home."

"James," she was giving him an X-ray stare, "I'm sorry. I just feel…a distance in you. I don't know why."

"Well, I don't know either." His voice had an edge.

"It's like…you lost something. Something you miss," she said. "I can feel it."

"You can feel it?" Mocking. "You woke up. How could that take anything away from me? How, Dani? Are you crazy? We should be celebrating here."

"I can't help it."

"For Christ's sake." He was loud now, and one of the nurses came in. "There's something wrong big time here."

He took the nurse by the arm and propelled her out of the room. "Something's happened to her. The coma's done something. She's talking weird as hell. I've known Dani eight years, and she's never talked like this."

He was right. Something had happened to Danielle while she was unconscious. And what that is no doctor has ever explained. In the first hours after opening her eyes, Danielle had a new awareness that was disturbing, but still indistinct. She could feel things around her, things she'd never sensed before. Emotions. Intentions. Things she hadn't yet found language for. While McAllister talked to the nurse, Danielle sensed something she hadn't recognized in all their years together: Her husband's words were disconnected from what he felt.

Sometime during her second week home, James stood naked behind his wife, kissing her neck, while she did the exercises to strengthen her leg.

"Do you want me to stop, James?"

He pulled her shirt out of her pants and ran his hands under it to cup her breasts.

"Yeah. I'm going to take off your clothes. Is that OK?"

She nodded and he opened the belt on her pants, letting them drop to the floor.

"I love you, Dani," he said, as he began rubbing her pubis through her underpants. "You're the best."

He was erect now and pushing against her from behind. It was at this precise moment that Danielle began to sense the violence. She felt, rather than saw, a woman being stripped; she felt tearing. She sensed the rage, the demand for acquiescence in every thrust, though James was only just now beginning to pull down her underpants.

James knelt to kiss one cheek of her buttocks. He turned to kiss the other. He ran his fingers down the cleavage to her anus. "You're the best," he said again.

Now she sensed…contempt. She had the image of a woman lying face down on a table, her legs spread—as James lifted and carried her to the bedroom. Danielle got a rush of fear. She'd no idea where these images came from. Were they her own, or was she somehow picking them up from James?

"I missed you," he said. When they were lying down, he opened her legs. Then he was inside. Hands on her shoulders, pulling her down on him. She let it happen. The images continued.

When it was over James lit a cigarette. She could see the seams on his face deepen as he sucked in the smoke.

"That was nice," he said.

"Uh huh." She pulled the blanket up to her mouth, dabbing it like a napkin on her lips.

"You don't seem too sure about it."

"There's something happening, something weird," she said. "I see…too much."

An old man in a cook's hat is smoking behind the kitchen. His foot is on the rail. Jays in a nearby tree get raucous, but fly off when he throws something at them. His smoke drifts toward the four sequoias planted by John Muir.

CHAPTER 5

*W*awona Hotel began as a way station on the road from Mariposa to Yosemite Valley. Galen Clark, consumptive, failed miner and furniture maker, built it in 1857 as a place to wait for death. Instead he lived to the age of ninety-six, and became Yosemite's first guardian.

The Washburn brothers bought the place in 1874, and built a white, two-story hotel with wide verandahs and huge, rough-hewn posts supporting a peaked roof. It has always seemed to me a lovely bit of architecture—simple, utilitarian, with beams and railings framing tall, slender windows. Over the years, the Washburns erected a half-dozen other buildings—some as big as the original hotel, some merely cottages. They range around a vast, sloping lawn shaded by cedar and sugar pine.

On the far side of Highway 41, just opposite the hotel, is an expanse of meadow. At the west end is the golf course that I tended; at the east, separated by a split-rail fence, is a wildflower-covered field. The Washburns once raised cattle there, and in the twenties built a narrow landing strip across the pasture. By the time I worked at Wawona, the field was again wild, and I loved to go out in it at night to watch an oblique moon brush the grass with light and shadow.

The room behind the hotel's front desk is the nerve center of Wawona. Edward Washburn labored there as head accountant until his death in 1911. And it was from this room, fifty-eight years later, that our paychecks were still distributed.

Danielle stood at the pay room door, waiting for the manager to find her checks. She'd been home from the hospital two weeks, but wasn't yet strong enough to return to her duties as a maid. According to a journal she kept during that time, it was a warm July morning, with a susurrant wind pushing the upper branches of the pines.

James and Annie hung out on the back porch. The plan was to take Danielle on a short walk to build up her strength. Then they would head home to catch the radio broadcast out of Cape Kennedy, to hear Walter Cronkite describe the first steps on the moon.

After Danielle got her checks, the family drove along North Wawona Road to the trailhead next to Chilnualna Creek. They parked where the road dead-ends, climbed from the jeep, and started up the rutted path. The forest is thick there, leaning above the granite boulders that twist and drop the creek down noisy cascades.

James was a live wire, full of tense enthusiasm. "We'll get you right now, Dani. Smell the air; listen to the water. That's what you need. We got to pull you out of the house more, that'll get you right."

"We'll see, James." Danielle stopped walking and looked doubtfully at the steeply ascending trail.

"Damn straight, baby girl. I always got the cure for you. Don't I?"

Silence.

"Don't I, Dani? Don't I got the cure, baby?"

"Yeah, James. This trail's gonna cure the hell out of me."

"Don't be negative now, baby." There was a warning edge in his tone. He put his arm around her waist, and began rubbing her backside.

"Let's get going then." Danielle moved away.

"Not letting me touch you? Is there something so special about your ass that I can't touch it?"

"No, I just thought...we were going."

"We are, baby girl." He was bright and glittering again. "We are, baby. We're getting you some mountain air."

As they moved out on the trail, James and Annie walked ahead and quickly fell into conversation. Annie pointed toward the creek, a patch of Queen Anne's lace, some manzanita on the hillside above. Danielle watched them, but moved more slowly; her right leg was still weak and dragging slightly. In less than five minutes James and Annie disappeared around a bend, their voices drifting back to her as distant murmuring.

Danielle sat down to rest. The voices were soon lost to the water and wind sounds. Eventually, she half walked, half slid the thirty yards to the creek, where she perched on one of the massive gray boulders. Removing a shoe, she dangled her foot in the water. The pool below her was the color of jade. Upstream, two boulders cut the creek into a trio of small falls. The roar was constant, inlaid with splashing sounds.

After a while there were voices again. Coming toward her. Annie and James appeared on the trail above.

"Mama, we waited and you never came." Annie's voice was high and complaining.

"I was tired, sweetie. I had to rest."

"It's better up there. It's got more waterfalls up there." She pointed upstream.

"I couldn't walk any farther. Come down here, sweetie. Maybe your daddy will show you how to skip stones."

"I don't like it here. Come up there, Mama."

Danielle could feel her daughter's frustration—ratcheting toward anger. And sensed how it momentarily erased their relationship.

"James, please bring her down. There's a nice pool here. She can wade at the edge."

"I don't want to. I'm going back up there." Annie turned, but James snatched her up and held her under his arm like a football.

"Down we go, Annie Banani. Let's do what your mama says."

The girl started screeching.

When they reached the water, Annie wouldn't look at her mother. James got her engaged in finding stones of the proper shape, and they went on to have a rather lengthy skipping contest. With Annie upset that most of hers sank.

Danielle watched all this while rubbing her foot, which had gone numb in the snow-fed water.

"James?" She had to repeat it several times. He was holding Annie by the ankles so she could throw upside down. "I don't know why, but you seem annoyed with me."

"You've got me mixed up with Annie, baby girl. She's the one not talking to you."

"I know about Annie, but—"

"You'd better clean up your crystal ball, or whatever you're using. You're not reading me worth shit, Dani."

"I keep feeling like I'm holding you back from something. And it's irritating you."

"Oh, for fuck sake, Dani. Put all that to rest, will you? You're getting paranoid, baby girl."

Danielle was twisting her bare foot in circles, trying to get the blood flowing again. No one said anything for a while. The sun's reflection cut a glittering swath down the middle of the pool. Annie took off her shoes and began wading in the shallows. She kicked at the water, making plumes that arced and fell across the sun path.

Danielle finally spoke, her voice soft and faraway sounding. "I'm tired. I'm ready to go home."

Annie screamed, "No." She was involved in a target game with her father, throwing rocks at tree trunks and boulders. "We're having fun. You can rest *here*."

Once again, Danielle felt herself disappear to her daughter. "Come on, time to go." Said with an edge.

"No." But Annie walked toward her mother, maybe willing to cooperate after all.

"Ready to head back, sweetie?"

Annie picked up Danielle's shoe and threw it across the creek. It landed in the shallows on the far side. "I said no."

The child walked back to her father. He was laughing.

"I guess she means it, Dani. Why don't you relax? We'll play a bit more, then we can go."

"James, I need to lie down."

"Lie on that rock. It's pretty flat."

"James, could you go over there and get my shoe? I need to start walking back now."

"I'll get it in a while." Father and daughter were throwing rocks at some unfortunate water-skippers by the edge of the pool.

"Could you get it now? Please?"

"Get the damned shoe yourself, Dani. We're doing something here."

"It's too deep for me."

"If you want it that bad, you'll find a way. Take off your clothes and swim over. I don't care."

Danielle had the sensation of shrinking. She lay back on the hot granite and listened to the stones splashing. After a few minutes, she pulled off her jeans and T-shirt and threw them up the bank. Then she slid into the freezing water. The cold made her cry out involuntarily.

Annie looked back at her mother. "Mama's in her underwear," she screamed.

The trip across the creek was treacherous, with the water washing high on Danielle's chest. She lost her footing on the slick bottom rocks several times, and Annie and James cheered when she righted herself again. After she returned with the shoe, Danielle stood for a moment in the shallows. She had nothing to dry herself with.

"Now ain't that a sight to make a man happy. God got it right with you, baby girl."

A group of hikers passed above. Looking down, Danielle could see the dark triangle of pubic hair visible through her underpants. She didn't move.

"Going to stand there and drip dry, Dani?"
Annie laughed.

"All right, baby girl, I'll help you." James came over and began drying Danielle's legs with her T-shirt. Then he held her pants out for her to step into.

"Arms up, baby girl."

Danielle raised her arms above her head, and James pulled the wet T-shirt over her. He kissed her cheek.

"We'll get you home now, Dani. All good times have to end."

CHAPTER 6

*B*y the time the family returned from Chilnualna Creek, the moon landing was already in progress. From the speaker of the old plastic Philco came Neil Armstrong's voice, announcing the changes in altitude as the landing module descended. A cheer could be heard from several homes in Fish Camp as Armstrong finally stepped from the ladder and said the words he's remembered for.

That night, in the darkness of their bedroom, James lifted Danielle's nightshirt. He bent to kiss the nipple of one of her breasts. I don't know the reason—particularly in light of the scene at the creek—but Danielle says in her journal that she put her hand at the base of the same breast, pushing it up, offering it to him. A gesture identical to that of a nursing mother.

"Have I said how beautiful you are, Dani? These tits could launch a world war." He laughed and began moving his kisses lower, down to her stomach. "Know what I'm going to do now?"

The picture that came to her was of a woman, helplessly opened, being stimulated against her will. And then the shame of her orgasm—as if it were a tacit acceptance of the violation.

"What are you going to do, James?"

"I'm going to make you come."

"Look at me." She pulled his head up.

He arched away from her hands. "What?"

"I feel something strange. I don't know where it's coming from."

"What's the matter this time, Dani?" He reached back and began feeling around the night table for his cigarettes.

"What do you want, James? Right now. Tell me." Her voice sounded frightened.

"All I want is to turn my wife on. I want to kiss her. I want to touch her. Is something wrong with that?"

"I feel maybe there's something else." She raised both her hands in a gesture of uncertainty. "I can see a woman who's helpless, who's at your mercy. In my mind I see her. Why is that?"

"I got no idea, Dani."

"Am I seeing your intentions? Things you want to do?"

"Do what—hurt somebody? Hurt you? Is that what you're asking, Dani? Listen, have I ever touched you in a way that hurt you?"

"No, but—"

"Then what is this? Judge me by what I do, not the crap you imagine."

"James, when you were kissing me, what did you want?"

Silence.

"Tell me. Did you want to hold my legs open? To control me? Shame me?" She was pointing at him. "Was that coming from you? Was that what you imagined when you kissed my breast?"

Without warning, Danielle felt a bolt of shame. Sharp, searing. And with it a deep sense of worthlessness. In a few seconds she knew something else: the pain didn't belong to her.

James rolled away from Danielle and stood up. He walked out of the room. After a while she heard the toilet flush, and his steps come back to her in the dark. The pain, which for a few minutes had diminished, got worse as soon as James returned to the room. Danielle was starting to get it, that she had somehow become a receiver for her husband's emotional turmoil. The pain, she noticed, now had an imploding effect. As if her body had become empty, a vacuum, and her skin was collapsing inward. She recognized a need—James's need—that seemed both strange and very correct.

The need to be punished. Danielle drew her knees up, trying to soothe herself. It didn't help.

James walked to Danielle's desk. He picked up one of those snow-flurry paperweights. Just then she felt his rage. Pure. Merciful. Instantly it filled the emptiness.

"You're not someone I'd do that to." James was speaking in a whispery voice.

He dropped the paperweight, bent, and, with a single motion, swept the desk clean. Everything clattered as it hit a wall and fell.

"No. You are not." He swept the top of the bureau. "You are not." He yanked the covers from the bed, exposing Danielle's curled-up body.

"You are not," he whispered, spinning in a tight circle and flinging the blankets back at his wife.

Annie's voice could be heard in the other room. Crying. Calling for them.

Danielle started to get up, but James held up his hand for her to stop. He listened another moment, then went to Annie, closing the bedroom door with an exquisite carefulness.

When at last he returned, the anger was gone. James sat on the bed, pressing his mustache with his fingers. Like it might come off.

"The anger saved you. Didn't it?" She made a reaching gesture, almost touching him. "I never realized how that worked before. How important it is."

Silence.

"It saved you," she repeated.

An owl started hooting by the lake. Marking the unseen distance.

CHAPTER 7

*A*nnie's sixth birthday was celebrated on a Saturday, about a week before Danielle returned to work. Her journal describes how James decorated the living room of their rented house with balloons and streamers. Then he dispensed a bag of party favors to each of the five little girls who showed up at noon.

The party had the usual fare of a piñata, pin the tail, and musical chairs. Annie was ecstatic. Laughing and prancing around the other children. Her energy had a whirlwind force that Danielle sensed might have been driven by all the uncertainty following the accident. During musical chairs, Annie was particularly frenetic. Each time the music stopped, she dived for a chair, squirming and pushing the other girls out of the way. The last chair was a doozy: Annie's effort to win literally knocked her competition to the floor.

Danielle whispered to her daughter, "Sweetie, be respectful to your friends. You don't have to win that bad."

"It's my birthday. I should win on my birthday." Annie was pulling away, but her mother held her arm.

"Let your friends enjoy the game too." But Danielle felt Annie's indifference to her companions. It seemed wrong, and it was starting to embarrass her.

Annie ripped away from her mother, and ran to where James was organizing a last game before the cake and ice cream. This contest was waged with blocks. The idea was for each girl to build the tallest tower possible without having it fall down. Two of the girls over-built and their towers collapsed; two others created teetering structures that managed to stay up.

Annie was the last to try. Her tower had elaborate reinforcements with a tapered, Empire State Building design. At a height somewhat above the other towers, Annie ran out of loose blocks. To Danielle's horror, her daughter pulled blocks from the bottom of the other towers and giggled, "All fall down," as they collapsed. Then Annie continued building. When the last block had found its tenuous balance, the child stood. Her eyes held an incandescent energy.

"I won," she announced.

"No, you didn't," Danielle snapped. "You should apologize. You're so busy trying to beat everybody that you destroyed—"

"Relax, Dani. It's a game." James wanted to smooth things over. "How many little girls here are ready for some chocolate cake?"

Danielle watched the sudden jumping and screeching and raising of hands.

"Come to the table then," he said. "But give me a minute to light the candles."

Danielle fought an impulse to leave. During the tower game she'd had the feeling she was actually inside her daughter, seeing things through Annie's eyes. The other children had seemed like empty holograms. Without real feelings. Makers of sound, of movement, but essentially only stage props for the event.

A surge of weakness hit Danielle—not unusual since the accident—and she retreated to the far end of the living room. From there she watched the party. Light filtered through the pines, illuminating the yellow madras bedspread she had cut and sewn into a curtain. The room in front of her held a thrift-shop selection of overstuffed chairs. Two Aztec-style lamps, cast off from some institutional waiting room, graced either side of a powder-blue couch. The floorboards were painted a chocolate color, with a small green hook rug accenting the dark expanse.

After the girls began digging into the treats, James came over to sit by Danielle.

"What's the matter with you, Dani? She's a six-year-old. Kids get excited. They get lost in the good time. Don't spoil her fucking birthday by getting bent up over a game."

"I can't help it. I feel this awful selfishness in her sometimes. It shocks me. The absolute…disregard. I think it—"

"All children are selfish. That's the beautiful thing about childhood. You don't have to give a shit about anything but yourself."

"It scares me, James. I'm not kidding. It feels like something's wrong, like something's missing in her."

"The only thing wrong here, baby girl, is that you got a bump on the head. And all the ordinary things, the things everyone takes for granted, look weird to you. It's like a scene lit by a black light. All our faces have an eerie glow."

Annie was lifting globs of cake and ice cream on her fork, then bombing her plate with them. "All fall down," she said as it dropped and splattered. "All fall down."

Several girls started imitating her, joining in the all-fall-down mantra.

"We'll need a hose to clean this place up." James was laughing. He put a hand on his wife's knee.

Danielle stood. "I'd love to go back to when I saw just…the surface. And nothing underneath. I'd love that. It would be a relief."

"OK, so look at Annie. She's just a little girl playing. That's all there is. Look at her smiling. She's happy being the star, the center of things. See her bending to whisper to the girl next to her; they're giggling. That's all there is, Dani."

From where she stood, Danielle could see across Highway 41 to the tiny lake that was stocked each summer with bass. Two fishermen sat together on the far bank, poles waving above their heads like insect antennae.

"James." She turned to him. "Imagine this. Imagine that for the first time you could see color. You see that these lamps are an ugly bronze. You see that this couch is blue, stained with wine and coffee. And this curtain's yellow and doesn't match the couch. But James— you can't go back to the way it was. You can't not see that. You can't pretend it's all just black and white."

"It's not a matter of pretending, Dani. Forget the shit about the couch and the curtain. Just look at your little girl; she's six today. She's riding a high wave."

The stair post is broken, its crown knocked off to reveal the ancient, rotting wood inside. Beyond is a scattering of pines. Deer graze between the saplings, then wander into some tall grass. A buck in velvet steps delicately across the remnants of an old foundation.

CHAPTER 8

*A*fter a few switchbacks, the pavement on Chowchilla Mountain Road turns into a rutted dirt track. This is the old toll road built by Galen Clark to link Wawona and Mariposa. A mile west of the Wawona golf course, the road stops climbing and opens onto a plateau of red dust and manzanita. From there it descends back into a dense forest, twisting until it crosses the old log bridge over Big Creek.

It was the day before Danielle would return to work. Her journal says she and Annie were perched on the log bridge, fishing lines dangling into an emerald pool shaded by aspen and leaning pines. Upstream they could hear the faint sound of rushing cascades. The day was windless, with a fragrance combining tree sap and the musk of river sand. Annie was bored. Danielle could feel her restlessness. Along with something that seemed like anger. A sense of being trapped.

"You want to eat now?" Danielle put an arm around her daughter's shoulder and leaned to kiss the top of her head.

"I don't know." Annie reeled up her line to check the bait. The salmon eggs were gone. "How come the fish can eat the eggs without ever getting caught on the hook?"

"They're smart, I guess. I don't really care if I catch anything; I just like sitting here."

"But we *never* catch anything. I don't think we have the right bait."

"Want to put on a spinner?"

"No. We need something good. Like worms. Something that wiggles."

"You'd have to put them on, Annie. I can't stand sticking a hook in something that's alive."

"Fine. I'll do it." Annie was whirling the end of her rod, spinning the hook and sinker in a tight circle. "How long are we going to stay here?"

The tension inside Annie was growing. Danielle smoothed back the child's hair. "You used to love this place. What's wrong, sweetie?"

"Nothing," said defiantly.

"Yes, there is."

"No. It's the same as always."

"The same as what? What's it always like?"

Silence.

"Come on, Annie, what's it like when we come here?"

"You know what it's like, Mama. We sit up here. And the fish never bite."

Danielle felt hurt. "You mean you don't like coming here? I thought this was our spot. Where we could just be together and talk. We were coming here the day we crashed. Remember? I've been looking forward to sitting on our bridge and having everything feel…normal again."

Annie carefully placed her hook over the bail and reeled in slightly to make the line taut. She stood up. "I guess we should eat lunch."

A moment later they were off the bridge, climbing down to a sandy area at the stream's edge. Hundreds of small white butterflies fluttered above the wet bank, landing occasionally to drink, then setting off in random patterns above the water. They found a place where the sand was dry and leaned against a dome-shaped boulder. Annie opened her lunch box—one of those metal ones—with a picture of a Jupiter rocket on the lid. Danielle had a sandwich in a paper bag.

"So you don't like it here, Annie? You never liked it?"

Again she sensed the trapped feeling. Very intensely now.

"It's nice. I like the…butterflies."

Danielle could tell she was lying. "What's it like when we come here? Tell me, Annie. All these times we come and fish or have a picnic. Is it boring? Do you want to be home?"

"There's too much jelly on this." Annie opened the sandwich and held it up to her mother.

"I see. I'll be careful on the jelly next time. But, Annie, please answer me. Is it boring? Would you rather do something else?"

"Yes." Annie turned away and looked up at the bridge. She shrugged. "I don't know."

"What would you rather do, sweetie?" But Danielle knew the answer already. She had a flash of a neighbor's tree house, and then Annie's bedroom—her puppets arranged in a complicated stage set.

A minute or two went by. Danielle watched a monarch land on some milkweed. Mica sparkled in sand that lay just beneath the surface of the water. A car rumbled across the bridge, changed gears, and ground up the hill above them. Dust boiled from the tires—and after the motor sound had died away still drifted through the trees.

"We should go, sweetie," Danielle said finally.

According to her diary, the place was ruined for her.

CHAPTER 9

I've never believed much in destiny, or things happening for a reason. We live, as Camus suggested, in an absurd world. Beyond the basic law of cause and effect is a great chaotic blundering, a universe governed by accident. By chance. So the fact that Danielle had developed a friendship with a sixty-year-old widow named Lara, or that Lara's room was two doors from my own, has never impressed me as having any meaning. But random or not, there are crossings and collisions that spin enormous consequences in our lives.

I was reading in an old wicker chair in front of my room. It was a Saturday morning, maybe around ten o'clock. In those days, the second floor above Wawona's main lobby was employee housing. The Curry Company, owners of Wawona, later realized that those rooms could generate thousands more in revenue each night, and the employees were promptly banished to tents and outbuildings.

My room was in the back, facing uphill toward the white cupola of Moore Cottage. The late-August sun forced slanting shadows of the rail and balusters across the porch. The air was heavy, gathering heat. A guy on the first floor was arguing with his kid—something about her hanging around boys from the campground. "You don't know them; you don't know their agenda." The word "agenda" drawn out and carrying a lot of bitterness. Then the voice of a bellman explaining the importance of getting dinner reservations. "And never leave food in your car. The bears will open it like a tin can."

I closed my eyes. A few minutes later I heard Lara's voice. She had moved to Wawona in May, just as the dining room opened for the season. Rumor had it that she was a lot better off than most Curry Company employees. Lara's husband had apparently died a few months before her arrival, so she just packed what she needed and left everything else behind. Perhaps hoping to recover in a place where nothing reminded her of the past. The woman was slender and tall, with steel-colored hair, cut shoulder length. And she carried herself with a certain dignity—which is why she was immediately tapped for the maitre d' job.

Lara's voice was getting nearer, and she was in the middle of some story about a psychologist she once worked for. "He was researching how children get damaged. He'd observe them right in their homes—record the family's conversations—and I'd transcribe it. We listened to a lot of cruelty on those tapes, I'll tell you. But that isn't the big thing that twists kids."

"What does, then?" It was Danielle's voice.

My eyes snapped open to see the two of them dragging chairs to sit in front of Lara's room.

"When certain things happen in a family, and a child feels help-less to stop them—"

"What sorts of things?" Danielle interrupted.

Lara lowered her voice and I couldn't catch the answer. Eventually, I heard Danielle ask how long Lara had been involved in the research.

"Eleven years. Hardest thing I ever did. And the most interest-ing." There was pride in her voice.

The conversation meandered from there. To a children's book Lara was trying to write, and finally to Danielle's accident.

"You were so fortunate to come through that," Lara said. "To be able to go home to your family instead of languishing in some hospital."

Danielle nodded. "Yes, I'm thankful. Physically, I'm recover-ing." Her voice sounded tentative. "Physically, I am better," she repeated.

Lara looked out toward the sequoias before turning to study the younger woman's face.

"Has something else changed? Something that isn't physical?"

Danielle said something I couldn't hear, then patted her chest gently. "I feel...lost. Everything looks the same from the outside. James is still kidding around. My girl plays with her puppets. The puppets are always fighting." A little laugh.

"But now they both seem so...transparent. Feelings and desires I never saw before. It's as if they've become other people. People I don't know. But in reality they were always those other people." She stretched out one leg and studied her tennis shoe. Then ran a finger across her cheek. "In a way, they were always...strangers."

Lara touched Danielle's hand. "Honey, you seem very sad. Very alone with this. I didn't know."

Danielle shrugged, looked at her watch. "Almost eleven," she said. "You'll have to go down and work lunch in a minute."

The older woman nodded. "We'll talk soon?" She was still holding Danielle's hand, looking into her eyes. "Yes?"

"Sure." Danielle gave her friend a little push. "Go to work. I'll see you later."

After Lara had gone downstairs, Danielle just sat. Her back had been toward me during the conversation, but now she turned to look out at the lawns. Tears cut a glistening path down her cheek.

"Danielle, are you OK?"

She jumped at the sound of my voice. "Harper!" But she couldn't think of anything else to say.

"I could see you were crying and I, I admit I heard..."

She stood up and started looking around like she might have left something lying on the floor.

"I thought maybe you still needed to talk." I spread my hands in a gesture of surrender. "But if I'm intruding..."

"I didn't know you were there, Harper." She rubbed the top of her thigh, then put some unnecessary effort into tucking in her shirt. "I'm just getting worked up over nothing."

"I don't think so."

"Whatever it is—big or little—I can't talk about it now. Thank you though."

She waved vaguely in my direction and headed down the long verandah toward the stairs. I watched her lovely hips as she walked, the muscles strong and defined. When I'd held her hand in the ambulance, I'd felt their warmth. I thought of Danielle's breasts, revealed when the medic had cut open her shirt. But then I resisted the image, feeling somehow that I had no right to her beauty.

All of this flashed very briefly through my mind, because Danielle had walked no more than twenty feet when she turned around.

"All right, fine," was all she said as she grabbed a wicker chair and set it next to me. Her voice had a slightly defiant edge. The chair creaked as she settled in, and I opened my mouth to say something.

Danielle held up her hand. "Give me a second?" Her eyes commuted from my face, out to the trees and lawns, and back to my face again. "OK," she finally said.

"OK?"

"Yeah. I had to feel…what you wanted."

"What do I want?"

She traced the outline of her belt buckle. Then she nodded once. "Not to be alone."

That shut me up.

After a while she said, "I can feel this energy in you. Do you want to get something going with me? Is that it? 'Cause I'm not available, Harper. Not for that."

I felt an instant shame. "I don't think that's what it's about. I told you before, it's something that happened while I waited with you—after the accident."

Silence. She nodded again, still fiddling with her buckle. At that moment, oddly, I felt myself let go. Of any attempt at control. Any facade. She could read me anyway; what was the point in pretending anything? I would just tell the exact truth as it came into my mind. Whatever I felt, whatever I thought, I would simply tell her.

"Is it," she said, "like what certain cultures believe? That if you save a life, you are forever responsible for that life?"

"No. That's some kind of obligation. What happened to me is simpler than that. I just connected. I somehow…belong to you."

I felt, as I said the words, a rush of danger and excitement I'd never experienced before. Like when coaster cars have clacked all the way to the top and are paused on the highest chute. That feeling. Multiplied.

"So what am I going to do with a—what, an eighteen, twenty—"

"Twenty-two."

"A twenty-two-year-old kid who's decided he belongs to me?"

"You can talk to me—if you want to. That's all. Talk to me and I'll listen."

"About what?"

"Anything. About what's making you cry. I probably won't have answers, but I'll still listen."

She started rubbing the top of her thumb, like there was something she was trying to get off. Then she picked at a few loose pieces of wicker. Finally Danielle took a breath, and gave herself a while to let it out.

"James could always make me laugh," she said without preamble. "He could make the most ordinary things seem like high hilarity. I came from a family of dour, self-sacrificing people. Their idea of a good time was reading psalms. So when I met James, I felt like I'd come to life.

"And it wasn't just laughter he taught me. It was pleasure. The perfume of the high mountains. Watching sunlight sparkle on a stream. The cold, fresh-melted water. Then there was food, music— his collection of Appalachian and folk is incredible. He taught me how to drink so you stay in the high. Not sloppy, not falling asleep. 'Maintenance,' he calls it.

"Before James, I didn't understand pleasure. I didn't trust it. He showed me how…to surrender to it. To just step in the river and let it take you."

She stopped for a minute. "Why am I saying all this?"

"Because you need to make sense of something."

"Maybe. Or maybe I'm just indulging myself."

Silence. I let her pick that one apart for a while. I didn't know what to say anyway.

"But now I see his…" She paused, folded her hands. The corners of her mouth pulled down.

"Say it."

She looked at me, nodded. "Cruelty. I see his cruelty. Not on the surface. But deep in the cracks. Where he lives. And I'm not saying he wants to do harm. But there's a part of him that would enjoy it. I feel that. And the more I know about that, the more I can't stand it. Can't stand his jokes, his banter. It all seems like window dressing for…I don't know. For something that's very hard, very cold."

"Does he know you see him?"

"By now he does. It makes him ashamed. Then he gets angry."

"What do you think will happen?"

Danielle answered quickly. "I'm going to lose everything."

She stood up and walked over to the rail. Rubbing her eyes. A minute later she pointed: "There's Colonel Hall. Do you know him?"

"Sure, I see him every day on the golf course. He and his wife limp around together. Never a word between them."

"Did you know they married here—in 1913?"

"No. I hope they enjoyed each other better then. A half-century of silence could really wear on you."

Mirthless laugh. "I'd better go."

"Is there more?" I felt my usual need to help her.

"You mean like discovering my kid, my Annie…" Tears again. "I don't even know what my kid is. That's the problem. I thought I did, and now I look at her, her disregard."

"It feels like Annie's changed too?"

"Not changed. She's the same. Just the same. I just didn't know."

She returned to the wicker chair and sat down heavily.

"They're all fine. They're all just the same. I'm the one who's gone crazy." Danielle looked at me. She delicately wiped her cheeks, smearing the tears. "I try to…be normal. I try to smile, and let him touch me. But I want to scream the whole time because none of it's right. I saw it all so differently before.

"James said to me the other day, 'I'm surprised when Neil Armstrong got to the moon, he didn't find you there already.' He was making light of how totally out of it I've been. Just a silly joke, like a thousand that he's made. And I laughed. I made myself laugh.

Because I wanted to be normal again. I wanted it to be the way it always was."

She put her hands on the arm of the chair. Very formal. "But you can't force laughter. It sounds weird."

I touched my hand to hers. Squeezed gently for a moment to let her know I got it. Then let go.

"Of course, Richard Nixon does that," she said. "He's the master of the phony laugh. And look where it's gotten him."

CHAPTER 10

*T*he problem was I had nothing to give Danielle. I felt that as soon as she was gone. I was too young to possess any great wisdom about men and women. My yearnings were simple and undifferentiated—without interest to anyone. And I lacked stories. There seemed nothing that I could share about my past that would either comfort Danielle or balance her vulnerability with my own.

Then I got a letter from my father. It was short. Exquisitely vague. And, like all of his communications, it was addressed to some generic offspring—not me.

Dear Son:

I have been thinking of visiting you, and seeing that old hotel. Maybe do a round or two on the golf course. I haven't been feeling well lately, and I was finally diagnosed. Something unpleasant that one prefers not to think about. I was looking at late August. Would you let me know? Have been following the Giants avidly this year. Willie McCovey is having one of the truly great seasons.

Dad

He arrived on the twenty-first of August. Liver cancer was the thing too unpleasant to mention. Eyes sunken, well into the wasting process. At meals, we spoke about his great life passion, songbirds. Their markings, their habits, their music. He did dozens of falsetto renditions of warblers and juncos. And the joyous *de-DE, di-di-le-de, de-de* of the white-crowned sparrow.

I told him about witnessing Danielle's accident. He asked not a single question; we were back to the subject of birds in no time. I told him about the strange and immediate bonding I'd had with Danielle, how I'd felt compelled to hold onto her in her coma. My father responded that he had decided not to do chemotherapy.

We golfed twice—nine holes each time. He slumped in the electric cart, rousing himself with great effort for each shot. After the last hole he went to bed. It was like we'd been shouting to each other through a dividing glass.

My father left after three days. I borrowed a car to drive him to the bus pickup in Yosemite Valley. He talked about the demise of passenger trains. And how the brown-headed cowbird steals the nests of other birds.

At the window of the bus he waved several times, gray hair puffing from a jaunty beret. Then the bus pulled out. As I drove home, I felt liberated from a long confinement. As if an airless room had finally been opened. Yet when I watched the dark, brutish clouds of a storm move in, I again thought of my father. I could imagine him staring at the lightning through the Greyhound's panoramic glass. Rapt. Counting the seconds between bolt and thunderclap. Waiting for the inevitable. I would never see him again.

That night I wrote a poem called "The Nature of Golf."

Two men approach the second green.
The mountains are early morning purple.
On the left, a split rail fence
succumbs to meadow.

One man takes out a number 8
and practices the chip,
over and over, brushing the grass.
The ball flies well, or not,

to the green, or over, or away.
Death waits out of sight.
My father holds the pin.
How thin he is. We putt.

The next tee marks a long par 5.
We go around preserved
by one spare challenge at a time.
Our spiked shoes leave tiny holes.

He is too sick to play at the end.
The idea is not to be afraid,
to concentrate. On the second green
mosquitoes disappear in the lips of dragon flies.

CHAPTER 11

I *am leaning against the rough bark, my fingers pressing into one of the shallow cracks that ascend, in a lattice pattern, to the top. The shadows at the forest edge are cool, concealing. Out where the meadow starts, hard sunlight presses on the lupine and wild mustard. I write without thinking. If I am to learn, to discover anything, not one word can be false.*

It was late afternoon—middle September—and a dark bank of cumulus was stacking in the east, above the sequoia groves. Bursts of wind fluttered my shirt sleeves and carried the chilled fragrance of rain. I was doing something on the third fairway, maybe cutting the rough, and I could see a pair of hikers through the trees shrouding Meadow Loop Road. One red coat, one tan. Where the pines thinned a little, the red coat waved. It was Danielle. Walking with Lara.

I climbed up through the saplings and high grass to say hello. There was a minute or two of desultory pleasantries. Lara mentioned that she'd be going home in less than a week; the season was almost over and the hotel was due to close. Danielle said nearly nothing. I was afraid that her vulnerability three weeks before—the morning we'd spoken on the porch—might have left her feeling awkward, even ashamed, in my presence. The wind was catching loose tendrils of her hair, wrapping them around her face and throat. She pulled at them ineffectually with one hand. The other was touching her thigh, gently, as if fingering a bruise.

When things wound down, Danielle gave a little wave and turned. I watched her stride down the road, studied the architecture of her moving body. Lara looked back once, saw me watching. I was embarrassed, quickly making my way down through the undergrowth to the clipped grass of the fairway.

An hour later, the clouds had captured the sky above Wawona. The course was deserted. I was changing the location of the hole on the first green, drilling in the short, delicate grass, when I saw Danielle again. She was alone, walking on the shoulder of the highway that parallels the golf course. To my surprise, her steps hesitated, then she headed toward me through a thin stand of pines.

"Lara pooped out and went back before we got halfway around the trail. I finished anyway; just got done." A note of pride in her voice. "I'm getting stronger. No way I could have done the four miles even a few weeks ago."

Danielle picked up the aluminum pole and flag that usually sits in the hole. "What are you doing?"

I explained how we kept moving the holes to protect the greens and give the golfers new putting challenges. Danielle nodded, looking distracted.

The wind seemed to be swallowing our words, so I moved closer to her. Leaning on the drilling tool.

"It's getting cold," she said.

I nodded. "Least I don't have to drag hoses around today. It's going to rain soon."

She was pulling her sleeves down, trying to cover her hands with them. "I appreciated your asking how I was a few weeks back. That was nice. I think I gave you a bit of a hard time, and I didn't mean to. It was just strange. You asking like that. Being concerned. I'm not used to it."

"I understand. Anybody, when they're in a raw place, they—"

"Right. I was nervous, I guess. That you could see. But I'm better now. I feel better."

"Really?"

Danielle looked at the grass. A dragonfly hovered briefly near her face, and she waved it away. "Well, maybe not better. Different. Things keep happening, new surprises."

I was intrigued, but she hunched slightly, as if the wind was really cutting into her. Then she smiled warmly, yet with her lips pulled by some private irony. A signal that the topic was closed.

"And you, Harper? How are you?"

I don't think Danielle expected much more than the required mumbling that I was good, with maybe a small, self-deprecating joke to leaven it. But this time I actually had something to talk about, maybe needed to talk about. That old birdwatcher; that master of intimacy. My father.

I told her about the visit. His letter, his frailty, the golf. Meals where we seemed to be shouting across miles of tundra. And she listened, despite the obvious fact that she was cold. Hands in pockets, huddling deeper into the jacket—but all the while nodding, keeping her eyes on me.

I knew she'd read it if I dressed the story up, if I made it false in any way. So I told it straight. Letting her see my anger, my emptiness when the bus finally took my father away.

When I was finished, she touched my arm. Brief, glancing. "He'll be dead a long time before you can forgive him."

"For what?"

"For not paying attention. For knowing nothing about you." She paused and started rubbing her hands. Blowing on them. "For your loneliness."

I felt a surge of something that, looking back, I can only describe as exhilaration. It was like a feeling I used to have as a boy when someone would do something very nice for me, very unexpected. It would start as a kind of electric sensation in my chest, and spread to my face and arms and groin. I got it once when my sister—out of the blue—offered to give me a haircut. And once when my dad drew me a lovely picture of a robin. Or when a boy who often made fun of me helped me, one rainy day, to pull on my galoshes.

I didn't know what to say to her. I smiled, stuck my hands in my pockets. We stood there. After a few moments I asked if she'd like a lift on the tractor back to the first tee. She nodded and we climbed aboard, each sitting on half the seat, our hips touching on the slow drive down the fairway.

When we arrived at the footbridge, where she could walk back to the hotel, Danielle started to get off. But then she pivoted to face me, feet on the running board, steadying herself with one hand on the steering wheel.

"Have you ever ridden the Sugar Pine?" she asked. "That little tourist railroad just outside of Fish Camp?"

I said I hadn't, but that I knew her husband worked there.

"Yeah, he's a fireman on those old steam engines they use. Works weekends when they run four or five times a day."

Danielle stopped talking and began rubbing her finger on the fuel gauge. Cleaning the glass. She seemed to be trying to make up her mind.

"Something happened there—at the Sugar Pine—and I haven't told anybody. But I don't know…"

Now she was fiddling with the reverse lever.

"You might as well tell me. If you've gone this far."

"Promise you won't talk about it? If I tell you something, it'll stay between us?"

I nodded, killing the engine on the tractor.

"Every Saturday the railroad has what they call a 'moonlight special.' Bunch of tourists show up for a barbecue and choke down some leathery steaks. Then they pile on the train and chuff down to the far end of the line. There's a little outdoor theater there, and this trio croons 'em a bunch of folk ditties and old sing-along stuff. Then it's back to the train, and this 1913 Shay they have puts on quite a show—the steam and smoke just exploding out of the stack as it pulls a 7 percent grade back to the station."

"What's a Shay?" I interrupted.

"It's a geared locomotive, mostly used for steep logging lines. It can pull a helluva lot, but slowly. Maybe five or ten miles per hour. The Sugar Pine's got two of them."

I held up my hand. "You were starting to tell me something that happened, and I got you off."

"That's fine, I'm an expert on the Shays 'cause James talks about them nonstop. Want to know more?" She was smiling. "Invented by—"

"No, it's OK."

"Ephraim Shay, 1878. Built by Lima Locomotive Works in—"

"Really, it's OK."

"In Ohio. Over 2,800 were made between 1878 and 1945."

"Danielle."

"They came in three-truck and two-truck, three- or two-piston designs."

She was laughing. A sweet, light sound. I wondered if she was regretting starting her story, was maybe planning to use the laughter as an excuse to change subjects.

"Let's get back to the moonlight special," I prompted her.

Danielle pushed her fingers through her hair. Then did a little thing where she let her body fall back, and caught herself by grabbing the steering wheel. Despite the apparent playfulness, I could see the muscles in her jaw rippling with tension.

"Annie and I went last Saturday—to the barbecue and train ride. James is always trying to get me to go because it's free to employees. I've done it a few times, but I don't really…Anyway, we went because Annie wanted to, and it's the last run of the season.

"It's good for Annie to see her dad looking important. Pulling levers, opening valves, waving to her from the cab. And Bill Fagan, the engineer, gives her a lot of attention too. She loves that 'cause Fagan's kind of legendary in Fish Camp. He's an expert archer, won all kinds of tournaments. A few years back, the railroad set up a target near the track, and every run Bill leans out the cab and fires his crossbow at it. They make a big deal about it over the PA on the train. And the tourists go wild when he hits the bullseye."

"It's good marketing, I guess."

"Yeah, everybody loves Bill. He's funny as hell. And James says the guy never misses. Anyway, we do the barbecue, then ride the train down to the amphitheater. But when the train stops and everybody heads off to sing 'Home on the Range,' I see James walk the opposite way. Right into the woods.

"I'm curious because he seems so odd lately, so distant. So I quick ask one of the folksingers to keep an eye on Annie for me.

And I just follow him. The pines are all second growth there—spindly and dense. There isn't really a path, but James is using a flashlight, and I just walk toward the glow. The branches scrape my arms. I have the feeling I'd be lost in there if the light went out."

A strong gust blew Danielle's hair across her face. She stepped off the tractor and turned her back to the wind. "Winter's coming," she said. "You can feel it."

"Yeah, this storm's gonna be ugly."

She seemed to be hesitating.

I leaned toward her, propping myself on the high fender that covered the back wheel. "Please finish. Tell me what happened."

She turned to face me. "OK, but it's got to be fast. It's too cold. I don't know if I should have started this." Her lips were stretched with annoyance. And something I thought might be fear.

"So, OK, I keep blundering along. After a couple of minutes the light gets very dim and I think I'm losing James. But it turns out he's just reached a little clearing. When I get there, he appears to be bending, inspecting something with the flashlight. I can't really see much, but I—this is the same weird thing that keeps happening to me—I can *feel* him. I can feel his excitement."

Danielle stepped back up on the running board and leaned in toward me, making very deliberate eye contact. "You know what I mean? I'm sick of it. I'm sick of feeling shit that isn't mine. So anyway," a deep breath, "anyway, I creep around the edge of this postage-stamp meadow, full of ferns or something. I'm trying to see what James is doing. When I get nearer to him, he's on his knees, looking at the leaves of a marijuana plant. Kind of stretching them out. Tenderly rubbing them.

"Now some off-key sing-along is drifting through the trees. I'm crouched there, thinking, 'So this is what gets him excited. Growing weed.' And I'm starting to shift my weight so I can stand up—maybe talk to him, maybe just walk away—when there's a *thwump*. And eighteen inches above my head is an arrow, still vibrating in the trunk of a pine. Instantly, I pitch forward and begin to crawl frantically—deeper into the forest.

"A man screams, 'You're dead, you little shite.' Not James's voice—higher, full of rage. Then *thwump*, another arrow. Can't see it, but I can feel it passing over my head, the air parting.

"'You're a fooking corpse! Ya hear me?' the guy's screaming. And I can feel I'm wetting myself. I'm scraping through the undergrowth, and a flashlight is playing on the trees above me. *Thwonk*. All I can think is to get further from the light, and then play dead. Don't give them a sound to follow.

"Above the strains of 'Yankee Doodle,' I can hear two voices arguing. James and—then I know who it is—Fagan. King of the crossbow. And I lie there absolutely still, my face crushed into the twigs and pine needles. James is shouting for Fagan to stop. 'Are you crazy? You gonna kill someone over a few fucking plants?'

"'No,' Fagan screams, 'but I will over my fooking job and my fooking freedom.' The flashlight's still dancing across the low branches. 'You hear that, you little shite?' he says. 'I don't mind killing you. Now or later. You say one word to your brother, and you'll be a friend of the maggots.' *Thwonk*.

"That's when I got it. The two brothers who built the railroad also own the Swiss Melody Inn. It's a little chalet that sits right next to the Sugar Pine station. James is always complaining how one brother is OK, and the other sneaks around. How he hides and suddenly pops up to threaten people. He's got everybody scared—the maids, the gardeners, the brakemen, the ticket takers. The whole lot is afraid he'll see something, and they'll be out of a job."

"So he was actually trying to kill you—thinking you were that guy?"

"Maybe. But I don't think so. What's happening is that Fagan and my husband started a little marijuana farm. The clearing they use is a perfect place. Hidden, accessible only by train. There's even a little stream. One of them can walk in to check it every time a load of tourists gets treated to a sing-along.

"Fagan saw someone follow James into the woods. It was too dark to tell who it was. So he got paranoid, made a lot of assumptions, and headed after me."

"But not to kill you? To scare you?"

"I guess. But that's my problem. I want to tell James it was me who followed him, me who got shot at. And I want him to get clear of the whole business. Just walk away. Let the damn plants die or leave them to Fagan. But I suspect he'll tell Bill Fagan what I said. Fagan will know I was there, that I want James out of it. And…" She hesitated.

"And you aren't absolutely sure what Fagan would do. If he saw you as a threat, as someone who might start telling people about his little farm."

"I don't think he'd hurt me."

"But he's for sure capable of threatening you."

"Yeah."

"So it's a dilemma: you can't stop James without making yourself vulnerable."

"Or Annie. Fagan might…He's hotheaded. The way he was screaming that night, and how close he came with his arrows, I don't know what he could do."

She stopped talking. The clouds were over us now. Roiling and dark. I felt the pinpricks of the first drops on my hands.

"Could you tell James," I asked, "and make him swear that it would stay between you, that he wouldn't put you at risk?"

"Maybe. I'll think about it. Is that your advice?"

"Not really. Just a question."

"Harper, I don't know the answer. They're friends. Good ones. And they're in a business that requires people to hide. I don't know what James would say to Bill if he had to explain pulling out. He just might say I'm a nosy bitch and tell him the whole story."

She held her hand palm up. "The jeep's got no top." She shrugged, looked at me a fraction longer than necessary to make the point.

"Your husband's full of surprises," I said.

CHAPTER 12

*A*nd they kept on coming—the surprises. I learned later that Danielle stumbled on something else a few days after our conversation.

James had left a message for her at Wawona that he'd forgotten he had to work, and would she come home early to meet Annie after school. It was unusual for him to be called in on a weekday, and Danielle began to wonder if it pertained to his new interest in agriculture.

After meeting Annie at the bus stop, she drove the child home for some milk and graham crackers. On the way, Annie told Danielle about her school day—how every child had to tell the class a funny story.

"I told how you wet your pants."

"Great."

"Everybody laughed, even the teacher."

"That's just wonderful, Annie. I love having the whole world know about that." Danielle was smiling, but she wasn't liking the moment. She sensed Annie's pleasure in her discomfort.

"Why did you?" The child wouldn't let it go.

"It just happens sometimes. Since the accident, sweetie."

"I told the class something scared you."

"Why did you say that?"

"Because it did. Remember, I asked how come you were breathing so hard?"

"OK, sweetie, I got scared. You're right. I walked into the woods, just to feel what it was like in the dark. And a funny thing happened—I got lost for a few minutes. I couldn't find my way. It scared the heck out of me. Finally, when the singing got started, I followed the voices back."

Danielle hoped the elaborateness of the lie would satisfy Annie. But it didn't. The child continued to pepper her with questions. Annie's interest seemed to be a kind of one-upmanship, as if she'd become temporarily more powerful by forcing her mother to explain something embarrassing. Hoping to shift the focus, Danielle said it was time to pick up the house.

"Why did you want to be in the dark?" Annie persisted.

"Because I'm an idiot, Annie, OK?" Danielle felt in her daughter a strange weave of alarm and satisfaction. "Are you trying to upset me?"

Danielle didn't like how she was reading this: the impression that Annie enjoyed pushing her off balance, enjoyed, perhaps, embarrassing her. And something else. That Annie knew there was danger in pressing this too far, and perhaps welcomed it. A small excitement that was, in itself, pleasurable.

"So is that it? You're trying to see how far you can push this?"

Annie didn't answer at first. Then asked, "Push what?"

"I don't know." Danielle felt a wave of guilt. After all, it was perfectly normal for kids to enjoy it when adults made fools of themselves. She recalled laughing helplessly once when her father smashed his thumb with a hammer. And, of course, children's cartoons were endless variations on the plot where evil or incompetent adults make huge messes that kids have to fix.

While Danielle wrestled with the great question of what's normal, she was also tidying the living room. As she emptied a wastebasket, her eye caught the distinctive letterhead of the Swiss Melody Inn. It was a note in Fagan's handwriting.

Jim

That storm did some damage. We'll need to start immediate track work down by the loop. We'll take the Plymouth [a small diesel engine used for maintenance of way] *and get to it tomorrow, 1 p.m. We'll all be home before 5:00.*

See you

Zigzag

"Let's go pick up Daddy," Danielle announced after reading the note.

Ten minutes later, they were driving down the steep entrance road to the Sugar Pine. One of the Shays was steaming quietly across from the station. Its complement of five narrow-gauge flatcars, converted to rough passenger service, was strung out behind. About a quarter mile south, the low profile of the Plymouth squatted next to a row of rotting boxcars. It was coupled to a maintenance-of-way gondola that contained a very busy Bill Fagan. He was heaving over-stuffed garbage bags into the waiting arms of James and a slim, dark-haired woman. These two were transferring the load to Fagan's camper-covered pickup.

Danielle guided the jeep down the rutted dirt track that paralleled the rails. As they approached the train, Annie pointed to the woman—fumbling to keep her grip on a huge bag—and said, "There's Tara."

"Who's Tara, sweetie?"

Annie shrugged.

"I mean, how do you know her?"

"She's a friend of Daddy's."

At that moment, James approached the jeep. Mouth compressed, pulling off his work gloves. "What are you doing here, Dani?"

"Thought I'd pick you up, do my husband a favor."

He looked uncertain, and glanced back toward Fagan and the girl. "Bill, you still need me?"

"No, big boy," Fagan shouted. "You can toddle off. We're almost done here."

James motioned for Danielle to shove over to the passenger seat. He waved to his companions, but only Fagan, who was retrieving his crossbow from the diesel, bothered to wave back.

"What's in the garbage bags?" Danielle asked.

"Garbage."

She could feel his anxiety—and something else. Something hard, isolating. The emotional equivalent of an ice hut.

"That's a lot of garbage."

"Dani, a tree fell across the tracks. The storm toppled it. We cut it up and hauled out all the debris and branches."

She could feel him crafting the lie, offering just enough information. Her reaction was to feel slapped. Humiliated. Like she was too stupid or too unimportant to deserve something better. The truth, or at least a falsehood that took more effort, more cunning.

"Why haul it out? No one ever hauled anything out of that forest if there wasn't a profit in it."

Silence.

"We're hauling it out because it's ugly and tourists don't want to look at it. For Christ's sake, Dani. Is this a favor you're doing or a kick in the ass?"

A minute or two passed while James maneuvered up to the main highway.

"What's up with a girl working maintenance of way?"

"The old man uses whoever he can get."

"Annie says…" She wondered if she should pull her daughter into this. "Annie says she's a friend of yours."

"Well, I know her. She's a maid there at the Swiss Melody Inn. Tara's really more Bill's friend." He was whispering now. "They're fuck buddies."

James stepped on the gas, and for a moment they were all pressed back against the seats.

"Faster, Daddy. Make it windy."

He kept accelerating until Danielle's hair streamed back and the sharp autumn air roared through the cab.

"How come," Danielle shouted over the wind, "Annie knows

Tara?"

No answer. The jeep swayed heavily through a half-dozen curves.

As they slowed down again, entering Fish Camp, James leaned toward Danielle. "Don't put your finger in the wringer, Dani. I hung out some with Bill and Tara while you were in the hospital. That's all."

Danielle could feel the shame. And then James's anger. As if anger could debride the wound. As if it made things clean again.

James pulled into the driveway. "Why'd you fucking bother, Dani? I could have got myself home and been a lot happier for it."

CHAPTER 13

*O*ver the years, I've thought a great deal about the nature of pain. The singularity of each person's response; the endless varieties, in style and damage, of the emotional shivs. I've thought about James McAllister. About what might have happened in him as he became aware of each new sign of Danielle's disapproval.

We use words like shame to describe a profound sense of exposure. A public undressing of our physical or psychological flaws. But such definitions fail to open the curtain so we can see how the shame really works. How it derives from the meaning we give to a look, or gesture, or silence. How it feeds on memory. How it makes us run. And, finally, how resisting it crushes us—how the rage, the brittle pride, the lies, the numbing addictions only make it worse.

I think about James as he first discovered his transparency— when Danielle confronted him in the hospital for his emotional detachment. And, worse yet, when Danielle exposed his private fantasies. All this had blown a hole into James McAllister. Nothing inside of him was safe from observation, from judgment. I wonder what he did with it all. And what he saw in that mirror Danielle was holding up for him.

In some small measure, I've sought the answer in an event Danielle wrote about that happened very shortly after the incident with Tara and the garbage bags. Danielle woke up very early one morning with James's hand between her legs. Her first reaction was to tighten her thighs and twist away.

"Don't, Dani. You're somewhere else lately, you know that? You're gone. I need you to come back to me, baby girl."

Danielle stopped moving. Unbidden, a stream of images raced through her head: the arrow snapping into the tree, Fagan's voice, Tara's young, pouting face. And then, oddly, the smell of James's body when he first undressed with her. His voice, flecked with laughter, telling a story of how Half Dome stole his shirt. The time he pulled her, by one hand, up a rock face she'd slipped on. Quite suddenly she felt an acute longing for those early days. For being normal. And in that moment, her recent discoveries about James seemed less ominous. Seemed, perhaps, ordinary—the flaws you'd expect in those strange, permissive times. She opened her legs.

"That's the way, baby. Let it feel good now. Let it feel good." James kept murmuring—sweetly, hypnotically while he touched her—the familiar phrases from when his words had power, when they were well-learned cues that would always trigger her arousal.

But Danielle kept waiting for something else: the pictures. Of women controlled and helpless. Women ashamed.

"You can let go, baby. You can let it happen." His voice was soft. "There it is now. There it is." But getting louder—like a preacher building to the "Lord, God Almighties," where everyone opens his wallet.

Then it was over. Danielle wanted to ask what happened—because the pictures never came.

"I kept thinking of the strangest things," she finally said. "Trains. Track curving into the forest."

James said nothing.

"Were you—"

He held up his hand. "I wanted to make you feel good. To have something nice, you and me. And not upset you."

"So you tried to think...of other things?" Her voice was high, incredulous.

James shrugged.

A blend of hurt and sadness washed over her. Danielle touched his chest. "Look, don't do that."

"Do what?"

"Get hurt."

"Why not? Why shouldn't I?" Voice scalpel sharp.

"Because I didn't mean it that way. I was just surprised that you would try to hide your thoughts."

"What choice do I have, Dani? You tell me. You fucking look right through me. So I can let you do that, right? And then what? Then you see what I think about to get off. And you're sickened. That's great, right? Making my wife sick?"

"No, I—"

"Or I can try to hide, right? So you tell me what I should do, Dani."

Danielle sat up in bed, looked away from him. Then rubbed her eyes with the bottom of her T-shirt.

"I'm sorry. That's all I can say." Silence. "I wish I could go back. Truly, James. And not know these things. Or...react a different way."

James reached to get a cigarette.

"I'm sorry," she said again.

"Is that it then?" James was hardening. "Is that how it has to be?"

Footsteps padded toward them in the hall.

"I don't know."

Annie pushed open the bedroom door.

CHAPTER 14

*O*ak and bigleaf maple lean from the bank. The pool is narrow, the ripples pushing blades of light. I touch the emerald water, mottled by the changing depths, the various colors of the sunken rocks. Moss climbs the vertical cracks of boulders, joins the roots of fir and cedar. On both sides of me, water slaps and roars down falls—so loud it becomes a silence. So loud it becomes forgetfulness. Drifting, drifting, like the white foam swirling by the edge of the rocks—before it rushes through the next cascade.

From both Danielle's journal and what she told me, I know this story. Danielle and Annie were in a neighbor's tree house. The narrow floor was squeezed between two great limbs of a black oak; redwood planks formed the walls. Due to a slight lapse in taste, the roof was corrugated tin. Mother and daughter sat on a gingham tablecloth with a teapot and two tiny cups. There were also small plates for the cookies still sheathed in the picnic basket.

Annie sipped her tea, making an elaborate pantomime of smacking her lips. "Tasty," she said. "I like chamomile."

"I know. Let's get our dessert out." Danielle used two hands to scoop the still soft oatmeal and coconut cookies onto their plates.

Annie broke off a tiny piece, and with her pinky extended in a caricature of blue-blood femininity, took a bite. "Ah," she said, voice high and supercilious, "delightful."

Danielle leaned over the cups to kiss her child's forehead. "Yes, Mrs. Twaddle," one of several silly names they used, "it's lovely in the extreme."

"Yes, Miss Fussbudget, we must do this more often. I've always liked the view from here." Annie twisted to look out the open window. "That beautiful lake."

The two looked down at the fly-speck fishing pond—across from a gas station.

"Beautiful," Fussbudget simpered, and they both cracked up.

Danielle was doing something different now. She was using her newfound awareness to better recognize—moment to moment—Annie's desires. She could tell when the child had lost interest in something; when she was bored or scared or frustrated. She could read, with increasing accuracy, the first moment in a conversation when Annie started to get angry, or had the first squirrelly sense that she'd done something wrong. Or the sudden pairing of anxiety and wanting—when Annie became conscious of a new desire.

Danielle's perspicacity cut two ways. On one hand, she was able to create happier times with Annie. There was less frustration, less anger. Danielle was able to ask her child, "What shall we do?" and already sense the answer. And she could quit while she was ahead, stopping activities at the exact moment Annie's pleasure was wearing off.

On the other hand, Annie's moods and reactions—seen with such clarity—begat a sort of tyranny. Danielle so feared the moment when she felt Annie turning from her, felt herself disappearing beneath her daughter's anger, that she'd do anything to fix it. Which is what happened next at the tea party.

They were sipping and cooing at each other in their Fussbudget and Twaddle voices when Danielle felt an emotional shift.

"I used to come here…when you were gone," Annie said. Voice flat, words spilling in slow motion.

"Yeah? Was that nice? Was Cherie," the girl whose father built the tree house, "here with you?"

But something had changed. Annie was withdrawing. Sudden annoyance, distance.

"Is something wrong, sweetie?"

"No."

Yet Danielle could feel the child's desire to climb down, to have this moment over.

"Did you feel bad when you were up here? Did you miss me?"

Silence.

"Were you lonely, sweetie, when I was in the hospital?"

"Daddy told me to go play, then he locked the door. That's when I came up here."

"He locked the door?"

"When Tara came."

Danielle pretended to sip her tea. Then wiped a smudge off the lip of the cup. "You mean when Tara and Bill visited?"

"No, just Tara. Let's go, Mama."

Danielle looked out toward the steep ridge climbing up behind Highway 41. Smoke from three or four chimneys drifted through the trees. She heard the distant sound of a woodpecker.

"Let's go," Annie repeated. Danielle could feel her daughter's distress. Or was the pain her own? An ice pick puncturing—James and Tara while she lay unconscious in the hospital. Annie was starting to climb down the ladder.

"Were you scared, sweetie, when you couldn't get in the house?"

No answer. Danielle followed her daughter down.

Some cobwebs from the tree house were attached to Annie's hair; Danielle started to comb them out with her fingers. But Annie turned away, anger surging.

"Why are you angry at me?" Voice high and complaining. "It was your daddy who locked you out."

Annie started walking toward her house, ponytail swinging with her quick strides.

Danielle watched her go, leaning on the ladder, feeling a tidal wave of exhaustion. After a long time she climbed back up to gather the tea set and tablecloth, laying everything away in the picnic basket. While Danielle worked, a parade of images pushed through her mind. She understood now why James had seemed disappointed in the hospital. As soon as she woke up, the chance to spend time with Tara would be lost. He'd need to be home full-time, nursing and taking care of his wife. The affair would have to be put on hold, or abandoned altogether.

Danielle remembered James's detached endurance when, during her first weeks home, she sometimes wet the bed. He helped her, doing what was required. Not annoyed, not particularly involved. A man going through the motions.

She remembered something else. Her first shower, after the hospital, James had gone in with her. He'd held her with one strong arm around her waist, and with the other he'd soaped her body. Lingering on her breasts and pubis. Her hips. When she hadn't responded, he sighed and seemed to drift off. Somewhere else. He dried her and helped her dress, then parked her in a chair. A moment later the screen door banged as he went out, seeming grateful to get away.

Danielle was still lost in this unpleasing review when she climbed the steps to her front porch. Through the window she could see that Annie had arranged her puppets in a stage set, all of them slumped in miniature chairs around a table. As Danielle opened the door, she could hear Annie giving the puppets voices. Some gruff, some high and whining. The child's fingers danced around the little table, helping the puppets nod and gesture.

"Sweetie," Danielle said, smoothing her daughter's golden hair to get the last of the cobwebs out, "would you please talk to me? Were you scared when Daddy locked the door? Is that what you're upset about?"

"No." Annie shrugged. "He was…I looked in the back window—where the curtain doesn't cover. They didn't have clothes on. They—"

She didn't finish because she saw her mother was crying. And Annie, too, started to cry.

Mother and child looked slightly away from each other. No effort to touch. Nothing said. After a while, they heard footsteps on the front porch, then stamping sounds, as if to shake off mud. Annie winced and moved closer to her mama.

In that moment, Danielle understood Annie's anger. She had been left with James. Left unprotected from the lockouts, from a sudden untouchable aloneness. She now held Danielle responsible for all that had changed, all the terrifying uncertainty. The day of the crash had been a boundary—between the world before and the world after—and would never let things be the same again.

Tumblers turned in the lock. A blade of cool air. James stepped through the open door.

CHAPTER 15

*T*he next night James McAllister took up residence in a caboose. In his discussions with Danielle, he'd taken the less-than-sensitive position that a man, facing an extreme crisis, has the right to any comfort he can get. Namely, schtupping Tara.

"I thought it was over," he told Danielle. "All those tubes coming out of you. I was freaked, baby; I needed someone. And you weren't there."

He went on to explain how his dad, a tail-gunner on a Flying Fortress during the war, spent every leave with a girl in London. Even though he wrote twice weekly to his wife in San Francisco. "He needed that girl," James said, "to face what he had to do. To climb into that glass turret."

Danielle didn't go for it.

James's first night in the caboose was a doozie. I heard about it from Tara months later. It was after dark when James finally picked his way along a string of ancient boxcars and gondolas. He'd been hoisting a few, and now stumbled occasionally on the loose stones of the roadbed. The caboose was coupled to a rotting snowplow, both bearing the faded lettering of the West Side Lumber Company.

James climbed the steps to the rear platform of the car; with a trainman's brass key he unlocked the door. The interior had a musty smell. Pools of water occupied the low spots in the concrete floor. Our friend had come prepared—with a sleeping bag, kerosene lantern, tin coffee cup, and gallon jug of Red Mountain wine. He attended to these necessities in reverse order, pouring wine in the dark, then lighting the lantern, and laying out his bedroll on a dusty bunk. For the first time, he noticed the cold. But a check of the stove revealed an empty oil reservoir and a rusted-out firebox.

James climbed a short ladder to the cupola. One of the windows was shattered, and he had to pick shards off the leather seat before he could sit down. This was the brakeman's roost, where he watched for hotboxes on the snaking log trains. On his left, James could see the rails shining in the moonlight. On his right, the forest stretched unbroken to the bare granite peaks forming the spine of the Sierras.

The first stirrings of wind feathered through the ruptured glass. James stuck his hand outside, feeling the cold air brush his open fingers. In front of him, the cab of the snowplow was dark. He tried to calculate when it was last used.

"Here I am," James said out loud.

The wind was starting to get worse. He looked below, where the amber light caught a battered desk, a pair of Bank of England chairs. James climbed down to retrieve his wine, then pushed his long body back up to the cupola again.

"This is great," he said, and tried to light a cigarette. The wind forced him to cup his match. "Like fucking Siberia."

Now the wind was searching down the chimney of the caboose, making a faint moaning sound.

"This is great," he repeated, and began to exhale in a breathy imitation of the wind sound. He put his face to the jagged glass, moaning into the night. A long, low plaint. As if each breath could undo the loss. Soothe it.

"This is great," he shouted. "This is fucking great. I love this fucking place. I...love...this...place." Over and over. Till his voice was hoarse. Till it hurt.

Still he kept shouting, as if there was someone he could persuade. As if someone was listening.

During the first week of their separation, James and Danielle worked out a simple arrangement for taking care of Annie. James would meet Annie's school bus, and watch her the rest of the afternoon until Danielle got home from Wawona. The exchange was awkward, mostly silent with a few tense remarks about the child. Danielle quickly found herself dreading the event each day. Sometimes she would linger at Wawona, chatting with friends, or stop the Jeep at a turnout with a peaceful view, just to put off, for a few minutes, seeing James.

Toward the end of the second week, James informed her he was seeing Tara again.

"I didn't think you'd ever stopped."

"Of course I did." Danielle sensed a wave of shame, followed by images of the caboose. And now a leaden feeling. "I took care of you. I let that all go and took care of you." Now the first flickerings of anger. "I was there for you, I waited on you, I was your boy." The word *boy* exploding with contempt.

"Maybe. But Tara was in your heart, James. You wanted her, and you missed her. I felt that. And I told you, even though I didn't understand it then. You said I was crazy."

Danielle folded her arms. "Let's not do this with Annie standing here. It's done, James. Now we have to live with it."

"I washed you, I fetched and carried." Getting loud. "Don't you fucking pretend I didn't. Don't pretend I neglected you. That's a fucking lie and you know it."

"Fine, it's a lie. But there's no lie about," she moved closer to whisper to him, "there's no lie that you locked your child out of the house so you could dick some bitch. But I suppose that's not neglectful. That's being a real, prize-winning dad."

She turned away. A second or two later, Danielle had the sensation that she couldn't breathe. As if her diaphragm had suddenly been paralyzed. Her first flash was that James must have punched her in the stomach. But when she turned to look, her husband hadn't moved. Now she felt the need to hunch over. She was hot, and aware that she might blush.

James was waving to Annie, saying something in a soft voice, and moving away. His face, she noticed, was red. Her feeling was changing to…disgust. A need to escape, leave her body. A desire—she was amazed at the strength—to kill herself.

But the feeling diminished as James walked away.

The next day, when Danielle arrived home from work, no one was there. She drove back down Silvertip Lane, past the post office and gas station, to the highway. Looking straight ahead, the banks of Fish Camp's tiny lake were empty. Danielle turned right, parked in front of the deli, and went inside. The plump checkout clerk, who'd just had her third child by as many men, said she'd seen James and Annie walking north along 41.

Danielle felt a rush of relief, inquired about the woman's six-year-old, who sometimes played with Annie, and got back in the Jeep. Just before the bridge where 41 crosses Big Creek, Danielle spotted James. He was bending over some rocks along the bank; Annie was squatting below him, reaching down to something in the shallows.

Danielle pulled into a wide spot next to the creek. Dust billowed for a moment as her brakes locked and the Jeep skidded to a halt. James didn't look up. In fact, he was sitting now—on a low boulder—shoulders hunched forward, forearms resting on his knees. Annie could be seen skittering over the rocks, apparently chasing something.

Danielle felt her body slump against the wheel. She noticed the beginning of a headache. And now came a physical heaviness, as if she had put on chain mail. She glanced up again at James; he was pressing his fingers into his forehead. Rubbing slightly. She felt…sadness. Residing in her abdomen. Like a fist punching her from the inside. Now she had the impulse to hide her face, to shrink away and not be seen.

She took a breath. Annie was lifting something to show James. He looked up briefly, but returned to massaging his forehead.

"You've got to break this spell," Danielle said out loud. But she felt crushed. With an effort, Danielle attempted to sit up straight. Then she called out to James. Father and daughter turned at the same time. There was a blast of anger—as McAllister lobbed a rock in

Danielle's general direction. And pure joy—as a grinning Annie held a frog high above her by one leg.

That weekend, James and Danielle stayed away from each other. But on Monday, I learned from Danielle, they would meet again where she least expected it.

The hotel was closed now, with a skeleton crew of maids and maintenance workers locking things down for the winter. They stripped the beds, stored away the sheets and blankets, and gave the rooms one last going-over. Maintenance guys carried long, wooden toolboxes along the verandahs as they fixed plumbing, windows, hinges, and the like.

Danielle was working in Room 1 at the east end of Washburn Cottage, a two-story building with a peaked roof, dormers, and a wide porch that circled the first floor. She was folding blankets. Afternoon sunlight streamed through tall windows, casting bright oblongs across the floor. Dust drifted in the light, pushed by tiny currents from the blankets as Danielle shook them out.

The door opened behind her. Without turning she asked, "What?"

"I'm bleeding, Dani."

"What?" She snapped her head around to see James standing in a T-shirt and jeans, arms outstretched. Blood oozed from shallow cuts across his biceps and forearms.

"How much do I have to bleed before I've paid…" He was slurring. ". . . enough to satisfy you?"

She saw that he had a thin-bladed hunting knife in his right hand. He pulled up his shirt and delicately placed the honed edge against his stomach.

"Don't." Danielle reached toward him, but James backed unsteadily toward the door.

"How much do you want, Dani? More? Shall I give you more?"

He drew the knife along his abdomen. She could see the flesh open, and the thin, red line begin to swell and drip toward his belt.

She stood frozen. James touched two fingers to his stomach, smearing the blood, and wiped them on his pants leg.

"Do you want more, Dani?" Swaying slightly, he looked at her, then down at his arms and stomach. "I'm fucked up, aren't I, Dani? Aren't I?"

"James, you need a doctor. Put the knife down. Over on that chest of drawers. Then I'll get some towels so we can put pressure on those cuts."

James raised the knife to eye level and inspected it. "You want more, baby girl? You want it all? I'll give it all to you." He touched the blade to the side of his throat and gave her a thin smile. "Tell me and I'll do it, Dani."

"No." She felt him falling. Sick, weightless. Nothing to stop it. "Put the knife down. Then we'll talk."

"About us?" It sounded like "bou ushe."

"Yeah."

"Tell me," he said. "Tell me what's gonna happen to us."

Silence. "James, I...You're with Tara."

"I don't care about Tara." He pushed the blade down his left forearm, pressing the blood in front of it like it was a squeegee. "What about us?"

"I don't know. Please." She took half a step toward him. "Drop the knife. Just—"

"You fucking know, Dani. You know." He raised the knife above his head, slowly waving it, taking aim. Like a blade thrower at a carnival. Then he tossed it, just wide of Danielle. The knife landed handle first against the wall, and clattered to the floor.

"You know," he repeated, turning toward the door. "Gotta go lie down, baby girl."

He stepped out into the sunlight. Heavy footsteps on the porch, silence as he weaved across the lawn. He waved once, to no one in particular, and headed toward the stand of trees bordering the highway.

CHAPTER 16

*T*he rangers picked James up about a half-mile east of Wawona, trying to hitchhike back to Fish Camp. They treated his cuts, and after getting the story from Danielle, kept him in the drunk tank overnight.

It was his first of several encounters with the authorities.

Two days after the hunting-knife incident, James borrowed Bill Fagan's pickup. I'm not sure what he'd originally intended, but when I saw him, a front wheel of the pickup was dangling off a low bridge spanning one of the golf course water hazards.

McAllister was popping the clutch in reverse, trying to drag the truck—now sitting on its tie bars—off the bridge. No luck.

I walked over from where I'd been rolling the eighth green, and asked if he needed help.

McAllister looked at me like I'd caught him masturbating. Alarm, then anger danced across his face.

"What are you doing here, Harper?"

"I work here. But I guess I could ask you the same question."

He didn't like that, and jerked open the door of the truck. "It's my business what I'm doing."

He stepped down gingerly on the extreme edge of the bridge,

holding the door to steady himself.

"It's my fucking business." Mumbling. And starting to sway, yanking the door back and forth as he fought to keep his balance.

"Fuck!" He fell in the creek.

And now he was fit to be tied, screaming "fuck" about fifty more times as he pulled himself through bull rushes and nettle bushes to get up the bank. Finally he stood in front of me—dripping, unbuttoning his shirt, glaring in different directions as if he suspected someone had pushed him in.

"Listen, guy," I told him, "if you want my help, you'd better get friendly in a hurry. Otherwise I'm gone."

McAllister looked at me for a moment, lips pressed into a thin line, the seams of his face darkening.

"OK, what would you suggest? Levitation?"

"The tractor," I said. "I can pull you off the bridge."

McAllister spread his legs, and I noticed he was working rather hard at staying upright. For the first time it dawned on me that he was drunk.

"OK, fine." He started patting his mustache. "That'd be nice of you." He shook both his arms, as if trying to fling the water off.

Thirty minutes later, I attached the tractor to the pickup's bumper with a chain. As I began to pull the truck, the tie bar made a god-awful scraping noise on the wooden decking of the bridge. McAllister was screaming something, but I was gunning the tractor and couldn't make it out. When the truck was finally back on the road, I cut the engine and could hear James.

"You fucking idiot. Didn't you hear me shouting for you to stop?" He bent to inspect the truck's front wheel. "You broke the fucking pin on the tie bar. Now the fucking thing won't even drive; you can't steer it."

He stood up straight, and began kicking the wheel. Violently.

"You fucking broke the truck. Thanks a fucking lot for all the help. You helped me like Hitler helped the Jews, you stupid fuck."

His voice was carrying all the way across the road, and I could see people in the parking lot next to Wawona Store turning to look.

The fusillade made me angry, but I didn't say anything. The guy was so crazy, I thought he might hit me. I just got off the tractor and began to detach the chain from the pickup's bumper. Meanwhile, James was rummaging in the truck's cab, making the whole thing shake while he bounced around in there.

I was wrapping the chain around the tractor seat when McAllister hit the ground again. He was carrying a plaid coat, a white plastic trash bag, and a pair of binoculars.

"Doing some birdwatching?" I said mildly.

"What did you say? What...the fuck...did you say?" He ran unsteadily toward me while I backed around the other side of the tractor. James started to climb on the running board, to get to me, but he slipped and barked his shins. Which set him off on another rant. Five long minutes later, a park ranger pulled onto the bridge and stopped in front of Fagan's truck. His conversation with James went like this:

"What's going on here, Mr. McAllister?"

"Nothing."

"You seem upset."

"I'm fine."

"Good. Glad to hear it. What brought you out here, Mr. McAllister? On this private access road to the golf course?"

"I had a problem with my truck." He touched the fender of the pickup, gently steadying himself. "This man," he waved in my direction, "was trying to help, but he ended up really screwing it up."

"OK, but I asked what brought you out here. This isn't a public road."

"I was just keeping an eye on a few things." He raised the binoculars as if that clarified the explanation.

"What things, Mr. McAllister?"

"Just things...that I wanted to check on."

"Again, I'm asking you, what things?"

Silence. I realized then that James had come to spy on Danielle. Using binoculars, he'd have a good view of the hotel from the golf course.

"What's in the bag, Mr. McAllister? Could you show it to me?"

"No."

"I'm going to ask you to pick up the bag, Mr. McAllister, and bring it here so I can examine it."

The ranger, who was a middle-aged, florid-faced man, let his right hand begin to hover near his holster. Once brown hair was graying at the temples, and I could see a bead of sweat make its way along the edge of one ear down to well-nourished jowls.

James picked up the bag, one hand on top, one grasping the bottom. He seemed to be moving in slow motion. He dropped the mouth of the bag and, holding it from the bottom, flung it in a wide arc. Ground leaves flew out and settled in the weeds and bushes at the creek's edge. Some landed on the water, beginning a short trek to the south fork of the Merced.

The ranger reached for his cuffs. "Thank you for your cooperation," he said. "If you don't mind, Mr. McAllister, I'll be giving you a lift."

Dusk holds the mountains. The trees, black ghosts pushing into the twilight, guard the edge of the wilderness. Now begins the work of raccoon and field mouse. Of the screech owl. Now begins the time of blindness, when men lose dominion. When we feel unsafe. I walk up the old carriage drive, past the two stone pillars with their lamps, to the green French doors. A piano is playing inside.

CHAPTER 17

*M*y father died at St. Mary's Hospital in San Francisco on Sunday, November 16. I had not expected it so soon. He didn't call to say he was in St. Mary's, please come. My mother—divorced and living in Boca Raton—didn't call. My sister—just finishing med school in Pennsylvania, who hadn't spoken to my father in five years—naturally did not call.

And I am ashamed to say, though I knew my father was mortally ill, I had only called him once since his visit to Wawona. We spoke of the cedar waxwing. And Willie McCovey winning the MVP.

The night after the funeral I had strange dreams. I don't remember them now. But there was a feeling of isolation. And I recall listening to the children play in the school yard next to the church, while a priest intoned the words of the Introit, the Kyrie, the Gloria inside the walls. So I had the odd feeling of being cut off while still in the middle of everything. Imprisoned in the memories and damage left from my father's life—while smiling, shaking hands, and waving to the handful of mourners who had bothered to show up.

The next day, rising from my father's couch, I sat at his chrome and Formica dining table. In the faint illumination of a kitchen light well, a poem called "Island" wrote itself:

The chain drops through transparent bursts of tide;
his anchor rests between the inlets at a full cafe;
only thin trees come down to violets on a window ledge.

The hull he leaves for foreigners, partly burned
and shining in the depths. Downstairs
he entertains the sand with stories of his father

who liked birds and tattooed a lark on his arm.
The island is his own, men
who never loved circle his fire.

He opens his hands and the lark is dead.
The sound of clapping shuts off; only
wind comes up the inlet,

whipping the flame,
finding holes in the forest,
blowing fine drifts over his legs.

I got back to Wawona on Thursday, November 20. It had snowed heavily in my absence. The golf course was under several feet, and the white buildings of the hotel blended, chameleon-like, with the snow-covered lawns.

A lot had changed in the past month. For one thing, my duties were now entirely different. Instead of greens keeper, I was night watchman at Wawona. I carried a clock suspended from a leather strap around my neck. And I walked from station to station, inserting the old brass keys I'd find there in my clock, marking the progress in my rounds. All night I worked a circuit through each building on the property.

With the recent snow, Danielle also had a new job. At the ski lodge at Badger Pass, seventeen miles from Wawona. Badger, as I recall, had five or six second-rate ski runs, a slightly decrepit snack shop, and a slow, dreamy feel. Danielle worked as a food preparer in the Snowflake Room—a place where you could have anything you wanted, as long as you wanted potato chips and ground beef.

James, who'd escaped jail because the cops never found enough marijuana to charge him with a felony, worked at the ski rental desk. It was a dark, low-ceilinged room crowned with water pipes and dim fluorescent fixtures. Since his arrest, James had stayed away from the ever-excellent Red Mountain wine, veering instead towards copious amounts of homegrown weed. He and Fagan could occasionally be seen in the camper on Bill's pickup, hot-boxing till they were high as kites, and finally leaving in a cloud of smoke so thick that one tourist mistook it for a forest fire.

James's relationship to Danielle had sustained further damage from the cutting incident. Her anger was now laced with fear that he was dangerously impulsive. And it was only his solemn promise not to drink that persuaded her to let James take care of Annie again.

My trip back from San Francisco had taken all day. First, I'd boarded a bus to Oakland, then the train to Merced, then another bus to the Valley. I'd had to hitchhike the final thirty miles to Wawona. No plowing had been done at the hotel, so I climbed over some pretty fair drifts to get to my building, and then up an ice-crusted stairway to the second floor and my room.

I was surprised, when I got there, to find a note pinned to my door. "Heard about your father," it read. "I'm truly sorry. I remember how you felt during his visit, how lonely it was. This must be very hard. I hope you're OK." It was signed Danielle, with her phone number.

I called her that night, and she told me she'd drop by the next day on her way home from work. My first reaction was anxiety. My tiny bedroom felt like the wrong place to visit with Danielle. And I worried that I'd find nothing to talk about that would make her trip worthwhile.

Much of Friday I felt an odd sort of agitation. As if I was standing at some great height, no barrier to protect me. Around five o'clock I built a fire in one of the parlors—a room with walnut wainscoting and a slight Edwardian air. I placed two Windsor chairs next to the hearth. Driven snow had covered the verandah on the room's south side, and was piled two-thirds of the way up the French doors. Through a high window I could see the dusk-gray snowfield covering the lawns and golf course. An occasional car slid into view along the ribbon of blacktop; as it passed, the taillights burned against the frozen ground.

Danielle arrived at six-thirty. As the Jeep's narrow-set headlights turned into the carriage drive, I ran outside to greet her. She parked against a snowbank and quickly got out. But, once on the ground, she hesitated, appearing to inspect the canvas top of the Jeep. Then Danielle stepped back, extended her arms, and leaned against the roll bar—like someone stretching before a run. She lowered her head and held the position. The twin lamps marking the distant entrance to the hotel touched her with a faint light. I'd been high-stepping across the snowdrifted lawn, but I slowed down, watching her. No movement—just the frost from her breath. Finally I snapped a twig or something, and she looked up.

"Harper, hi. I didn't see you coming."

I waved. Danielle walked toward me. She was wearing jeans, a dark-colored down jacket, and pink, little-girl mittens. Her dark hair was tied back.

One of the mittens reached out briefly to touch my arm, then Danielle pushed both hands into her coat pockets. Our visible breaths merged in the space between us.

"How are you doing?" she said.

I shrugged. "It's nice of you to visit." I pointed toward the long, two-story building known as the Annex. "Got a fire going in the parlor. Come up and get warm."

I led the way, eventually passing the dark clubhouse on the bottom floor of the Annex, and up a narrow flight of stairs to the parlor. By now the fire was roaring, and I gestured toward the chairs I'd set out. Danielle took off her coat; she was wearing a pretty burgundy sweater.

The case of nerves I'd had all day seemed to get worse when I sat down, and somehow I couldn't think of a way to start the conversation. Danielle gave her funny, downturned smile and just looked at me. She pulled her sweater sleeves and adjusted her ponytail.

"Are you embarrassed?" she asked after a while.

"Yes. Probably so."

"Why?" She was still smiling, head slightly cocked, a look of curiosity.

"I don't know. I'm not sure what to say. And...I'm not sure why you came. I mean, I'm glad you're here, but I guess I'm not—"

"Why wouldn't I come?" she interrupted. "I think of us as friends. You were there for me once when I needed it. After I heard your father died, I just wanted to see how you were. See if there was anything I could do."

She crossed her arms—not a good sign, I thought.

"I have to admit I've been very nervous about seeing you." I pushed my palms toward the fire. Turning them, rubbing them. "I don't know why. I wanted you to come. Maybe almost too much."

Silence. I was instantly filled with shame.

She uncrossed her arms and leaned toward me. "I know you feel very alone, Harper. You don't have to hide that. I don't see how you stand this night-watchman thing, walking around an empty, dark hotel."

Her words made me feel a little lighter, more comfortable.

"And suddenly your father's gone. I know you weren't close, but nothing can ever be done to repair that now. It's a sad thing."

"His funeral was like his life," I jumped in. "A few handshakes, nothing much said. I don't know what to think about it."

"You're cut up," she said, "I can feel it. Was anyone there—at the funeral—who could comfort you?"

The word *comfort* had a strange effect. It was as if I'd never heard it before. Or considered its meaning. But now, the idea of it, quite suddenly and unaccountably, filled me with longing.

"No, my mother sent her regrets and stayed home with her new 'gentleman' in Florida. My sister hasn't spoken to my dad since she moved in with her boyfriend and he told her she had 'round heels' and was going to hell. She said she'll visit in June, after she gets her MD."

"That doesn't do you a lot of good now."

I shrugged. Danielle got up to prod the fire, setting off an explosion of sparks. I watched her hips, the lovely curve of her buttocks as she bent toward the flames. But as soon as she put down the poker, I averted my eyes.

Danielle was smiling when she got back to her chair. "You lookin' at me, Harper?" she asked softly. "You lookin' at something?"

"Yes." I was mortified.

"Is that what you want?"

"What?"

"To see me undressed?"

I stared at her. We hadn't been talking ten minutes, and I was already in over my head.

"To me you are very beautiful," I said. "I can't help—"

"It's OK." She spread her hands as if to calm me.

"Wait. I want you to understand."

"I think I already do." She had a sardonic smile.

"Well, let me say it anyway." I paused, searching for words. Believing that everything was at stake, everything depended on saying the right thing. "I can't help seeing...how lovely you are. I try not to focus on it. To tell you the truth, it feels wrong. You're married, and everything. You have Annie. So I..." She slouched down in her chair, legs slightly spread, looking at me with half-closed lids. "I try to be the way I was on the day of the accident. Just there for you. That's all. If you want to talk, if you need me for anything, I'm there."

Danielle angled her feet closer to the fire. "But the other feelings, the sexual feelings. You just—"

"I have them," I interrupted. "But basically, you know, I don't go very far with that."

God, I was uncomfortable. The room, which was still rather chilly, seemed unbearably warm. I moved my chair a foot or so farther from the fire.

"Like I said, it's OK." She sat up and put her hands on her knees. For a moment rubbing the denim, and then pinching it, as if she was testing the thickness of the cloth. "Tell me more about your dad. Wait. Start with the funeral. What was that like?"

I had a copy of my poem folded up in a back pocket—kept there in the hope she might ask such a question. I took it out and handed it to her.

"Oh," she said when she'd finished. Her eyes scanned down the lines again. "What emptiness." She looked up at me. "'The hull he leaves for foreigners'—that's your life growing up? Your history?"

"Yes."

"And it carried you to the island, this place of absolute...aloneness?"

I nodded. The feelings of anxiety and shame were giving way to something else. Some ferment I didn't have a name for. But it was that sense of being seen. Being known. As if she were raising parts of me from a depth where light had never penetrated. And as she held them and looked at them, I, too, could see them for the first time.

"'Only wind comes up the inlet.' That's where it turns, where it gets helpless." She was shaking her head and pulling at her jeans again. "That's where you give up."

"Yes," was all I could say. And after I waited, and she didn't add anything, I made another try at keeping the conversation going. "I think that's right. But it's over. He's gone."

"It's not over, Harper. You're lying there on the beach—with your ghosts. Don't you see? And it's killing you." She put her hand to her throat. "I can feel it like a constriction. Like choking."

Silence. I began rubbing a little—under one eye and then the other—to make sure no emotion was visible.

"How's Annie?" I asked. I think I was wondering when she had to get home.

"Annie's with James—in the caboose. Hopefully, he can manage to take care of his daughter for one night without toking himself to the moon." Her voice was bitter.

I got up and added a log to the fire. Out of the corner of my eye I could see Danielle shaking her head, then looking around like she was restless to go. But as soon as I sat back down, she leaned forward, hands cupping her knees, and resumed asking questions.

"Tell me about your father. Stories from when you were growing up."

"Why?"

"Because I think you need someone to tell them to. That's how people grieve, anyway. They tell stories. And every story is like a strand broken—of the connection. So they can let go." She was smiling. "So tell me, Harper. Stop fucking around."

I sat maybe thirty seconds, and then I just started talking. The first thing that came to mind. Which turned out to be the day my mother left.

"I was fourteen. When I came home from school, she was sitting at the kitchen table, smoking. I remember she'd gotten her hair done, and she looked different. Prettier. My mother didn't fool around. She said, 'I'm going to Florida, and you're welcome to come if you want.' I knew she was talking about a one-way trip.

"But all I could think about was that my father wouldn't survive without her. My sister was away at college, and my mother brought all the life to the house. It's funny, looking back, I didn't even think about myself. About my loss. I just felt how crushed he'd be. That maybe he'd be suicidal.

"She drove off in her yellow Fairlane. I watched from the window. She was saving herself—I knew that. And I knew—"

"Yeah. You had to save your father. 'Cause he was going down, and you would have hated yourself in Florida if you'd left him to sink alone."

Danielle hooked one arm over the back of the chair and crossed her legs. "Got anything to drink? Anything warm?"

"I'm sorry. I didn't think of that. I've got a hot plate in my room, I should have brought it down."

Danielle was nodding distractedly. I felt like an idiot.

"Harper, don't worry about it. What happened when your father got home?"

"I told him she was gone. He just nodded and got his binoculars out. Absorbed himself watching a towhee in the front yard. Then he carried a trash barrel into his bedroom and started throwing out the things she'd left behind. Very methodical. Humming. Later he made himself some tea. Then he did his soapbox thing— lecturing how John XXIII was destroying the Church. I let him talk; I didn't care about the Church. When he'd finished his tea, he went to bed."

As I talked, I felt detached from all emotion. I was just reporting facts.

"What was that like?" she asked. "That silence? He never spoke of her?"

"A few times. With contempt. Sometimes she'd call me and he answered the phone. Then he'd say in a loud voice, 'A woman claiming to be your mother is on the line.'

"I got used to it. The house was so quiet you could hear the clock ticking, the refrigerator clicking on and off. He'd be reading

Audubon magazines, or shit about the Church. Books by theologians arguing the nuances of free will. Paul Tillich, guys like that.

"He'd read during dinner and encourage me to do the same. He used to—"

"What did it *feel* like in that house? You're telling me what he did. When you got home, when you walked in the door, what was that like?"

"There was this stale, old-smoke smell. That was the first thing when you walked in. Then a feeling of pressure—like the walls, the silence, the smell were squeezing you. Like you couldn't breathe. Then you'd wander from room to room, looking for something interesting. But there was nothing. Then you turned on the television and maybe watched the Three Stooges.

"The furniture was all mahogany, very dark. The light was fading through the Venetian blinds. All you had was the voices on the TV—the screen flickering, reflecting on the wooden chairs and end tables.

"Then he'd come home and tell me to turn it off, and then there was silence. Nothing. And it was night. He'd only use these dinky forty-watt bulbs, so the lamps just gave this little halo of light. Islands in the dark house. We'd live near our respective lamps." I felt a tightening in my throat. "I used to wait for my mother to call—thinking each night the phone would ring. And sometimes she did call. But I got tired of it, waiting. I got tired of it."

Danielle leaned forward. "In a moment I'm going to do something. I'm going to pull my chair closer, and I'm going to take your hand. I'm going to hold it. And when I do, something's going to happen inside you. You won't have to hold back anymore. You won't have to keep everything closed up. You'll just let it happen, whatever needs to happen. OK? Whatever you feel, whatever you *need* to feel, OK?"

The fire was starting to burn down, and a chill was rising in the room. Her chair made a scraping sound.

My left hand was resting on my thigh, feeling paralyzed. Her fingers—oddly warm—brushed the tendons on the back of my hand. With the slightest pressure. Then my knuckles, tracing each ridge. Then she pushed her fingers under my palm and lifted up my hand.

Holding it, caressing it with her thumb.

I felt a wave rising in me. A tightness. Beginning in my stomach and climbing to my chest.

"It's OK," she said. "Let it happen. It's good. I'll be right here with you. Yes, Harper. I'll be here, I'll comfort you."

Those last words did it. I could feel the tears starting to spill. And my face twist up. And this high keening sound that I remember being amazed was coming from me. Then a convulsion, the air rushing from my lungs. And another. I started to lean, in slow motion, till my head rested on our joined hands. And then she was kneeling next to me, her arm across my shoulder, holding me.

"It's OK," she kept chanting. "That's good, Harper. You can let go now." She kept repeating the words, but I barely heard them.

Then she said something I will never forget. "If you want to be alive, Harper, you have to feel this."

I tried to say something back, but I couldn't talk. And she just went on with her chant.

I don't know how long the whole thing lasted, but she stayed right there. And when the crying was finished, she still held me a while longer. Then she gently kissed the top of my head.

"The fire's about out, Harper. You're OK now, I can tell."

She stood up. I felt an admixture of exhilaration and fatigue; for some reason I couldn't look at her.

"You're a sweet, sweet man," she said. "Thank you."

"For what, Danielle?"

"I think...for showing me so much."

She touched me once more, a brushing caress on my cheek, and she was gone.

CHAPTER 18

The night watchman makes his rounds
in winter, in the silent mountain hotels
he opens the box and slowly the chain
falls, dangles, the key shines
in moonlight. He holds it, blows
the frost from it, turns it in the clock.

For some reason I remember those lines—from a longer poem now lost. That was my existence. I can still see how the watch stations were lit, each sending a thin beacon of light, guiding me from one to the next. Like the syllables of a chant that together pull one deeper and deeper into the emptiness.

Every night was the same. The same rutted snow paths. The same cold. The familiar shapes of the trees pressing from the edge of the light.

It was a week or more before I saw Danielle again. She arrived unannounced, on a night James had surprisingly kept Annie for a sleepover in the caboose. I was sipping a glass of port and listening to KFRC, a San Francisco rock station you could only hear at night. The knock came around nine. Danielle had on the same basic outfit she'd worn the week before—including the pink gloves. But her hair was down this time, falling in thick tangles on her shoulders.

"Are you working tonight?" were her first words.

I said I'd have to start my rounds in an hour.

"Good, I want to walk them with you. See what it's like, keep you company."

"Why?"

She was already past the door, and I gestured her toward the overstuffed chair. I sat on the unmade bed.

"I don't know." She was smiling. "Nice." She pointed to a Brueghel reproduction.

"It's *The Fall of Icarus*," I said. "I like it because the farmer's plowing his field, completely unconcerned, sweating in the sun. But look out to sea. At the splash. That's Icarus drowning while the world goes on—oblivious."

Danielle nodded. "It works like that, doesn't it? Private disasters that no one notices." She waved a finger toward my glass. "What are you drinking?"

"Port. It's sweet."

"Can I have some?"

"Sure, if you don't mind it in a water glass."

I'd been leaning, picking up some clothes and books that were scattered across the floor. I stood and poured her wine.

"You're uncomfortable. I've come in like an avalanche." She raised her glass, a downturned smile. "But I…last week I could feel the bleakness here. How winter changes this place. I don't know what it is. The quiet. The rows of closed doors. So I," she shrugged, "wanted to walk your rounds with you. Once. So you'd have a memory of being with someone—when you did it alone again."

"That's very nice."

"I don't think you mean that."

That stung me. "I feel weird, I guess, for you to see my room. How dirty it is. All the chaos." I swept my hand in the direction of the chiffonier and bed table—clotted with books and papers, dirty plates and port bottles, junk from my pockets.

Danielle picked an empty key ring off the floor; it had an embossed picture of Half Dome. "Because I'd think you were just a boy," she said, "with no style? No idea how to make something out of a room?"

"Yes."

"You're right, I do think that." She held up a finger like a lecturing school teacher. "But I see other things in you, OK? Like kindness, like honesty. Things that mean something to me—especially now."

I looked down.

"All right, Harper, I'll stop embarrassing you. But let me walk with you a little while tonight, OK?"

We sipped our port in silence. Danielle looked at the pink and purple afghan on my bed. Something my mother had made during a period of Florida-inspired excess.

Danielle's eyes drifted to the Brueghel again. "I think maybe all of us are the farmer—and we're Icarus, too," she said. "Ignoring everyone else's pain, lost in our own."

It would turn out she was more right than she could know.

The first station of my rounds was on the back porch of the main building—near the bathrooms. A single bulb above the watchman's box illuminated glossy white siding. We stepped gingerly across the ice crusting the gray floorboards. Danielle started to slip, but I caught her—grabbing her around the waist, holding her against me for a moment till she was steady.

When the key and chain were back in their box, we turned to climb the stairs to Moore Cottage. They looked treacherous in the beam of my flashlight. Snow over ice, without a rail. We took them slowly, our bodies oddly separated. Avoiding, perhaps, any possibility that we again might touch.

"This is where I work," Danielle said. "I clean these rooms all summer. It looks so different now—like some outpost in Siberia."

"How did you end up here, Danielle? In Yosemite?"

She waved a hand and looked away. There was a long pause. "I grew up in McMinnville, Oregon. Never went anywhere—my father didn't care much for travel. He had a hardware store. My mother sold the housewares on one side of the aisle; my father had the tools and building supplies on the other. The back room was a honeycomb of floor-to-ceiling shelves, full of every nut and screw and washer known to man."

Danielle opened one of the station boxes. "Let me put the key in. I want to see how it works." She slid her fingers between my chest and the dangling watchman's clock, lifting it slightly.

"Anyway, the whole scene was boring as a typing class. They took care of me and my sister; they fed us, they taught us to say, 'Yes sir, yes ma'am.' They talked a lot about the store: how the Pyrex was selling, the cheap Japanese wrench sets.

"When I was eighteen, I went to Linfield College—right there in town. I still lived at home, still did the dishes on my nights. The only thing that changed was my dad gave me his old Studebaker. But, in return, I had to ferry my little sister all over town."

We were heading down the path to the Sequoia, a squat, brown-shingled building used for employee housing. In the twenties, it had been the Washburns' version of Motel 6, offering tiny, plain furnished rooms to penny-pinching travelers. The path was steep. Danielle reached for my hand as she crunched unsteadily into my old footprints. The grip was strong; I could feel the warmth of her fingers through the mittens.

The watch station was at the back of the Sequoia, not far from where a disgruntled Curry Company employee would set it ablaze in 1977. Danielle again wanted to insert the key into my clock.

"You still haven't told me how you got here. In the last chapter we had you at Linfield College."

"It just sort of happened. I was looking for a summer job at the end of my sophomore year. The placement office at school had posted a flier from the Curry Company, inviting college students to apply for seasonal jobs in Yosemite. I signed up, I worked the snack shop at Happy Isles that summer, and then I just stayed.

"In the autumn, I worked a few months for the Park Service doing trail maintenance, and after the first snows I got a job at Badger Pass. For the last eleven years I've been migrating with the seasons—to Badger, to Wawona, to Badger. And never went home, never finished college."

We were on a flat snowfield now—what in warm weather was a

parking lot. To the left was Hill's Studio, a gray, three-room gallery once used by the great landscape painter.

"John Washburn," I told Danielle, "built this place in 1886 because he was in love with Thomas Hill's daughter. Estella. A little payoff to the old man."

"Did it work out? John and Estella?"

"Yeah. Except he was forty-seven, and she was twenty. And she ended up being a widow for thirty-three years."

"You're enjoying this," Danielle said. "Leading me around. The history lesson."

Once again, I was embarrassed.

"Is that OK?" I was opening the box on the front porch of the studio. Danielle was still on the path, five or six steps below.

"Yeah, Harper." She looked up, making sure she had my eyes. "It's OK. You can go all professor on me anytime."

A minute or two later, we were struggling through the drifts toward the tennis court, and down the stone steps toward Wawona Store. Danielle and I held hands as we descended, then let go. After hitting the watch station at the store, we crossed the covered bridge that spans the south fork of the Merced.

"Henry Washburn built this in 1875," I announced. "It's patterned on the ones he grew up with in Vermont. It's the only covered bridge in a national park."

"You're so smart," she mocked.

On the north side of the bridge were the stables and a circle of buildings called Pioneer Village. This was a collection of nineteenth-century log structures, moved here from sites all over the park. The beam of the flashlight revealed watch stations at the old schoolhouse, the Wells Fargo building, the jail, the blacksmith's shop. We said little, just concentrated on following the path I'd made through the snow on previous nights. Danielle was rubbing her arms and I started to worry that she might be getting too cold to continue. I was also kicking myself for not keeping up much of a conversation.

We recrossed the bridge, our footsteps echoing against the rough-hewn beams. We crunched uphill, through snow-heavy pines, toward the carriage path and the Annex building beyond.

"This is lovely," she said. "I had a picture in my head that it would be very lonely out here. But I like the quiet—hearing your boots break the ice, and nothing else."

I knew she was reassuring me. Talking directly to the voice inside that kept whispering doubt. But I couldn't thank her. Instead, I tried to get Danielle talking about her family again. What, I wondered, would she have wanted to change about them?

"That's simple. They were all over my business. My mother went through my homework every night—to make sure I hadn't lied about finishing. She had to know everything I did after school; she'd call wherever I was supposed to be to make sure I'd gotten there. She read my diaries, she searched my drawers. She checked my purse and pockets. She made me keep all my money in a little box—then we'd go and count it to see what I was spending."

"That had to have driven you nuts. I can't even imagine it."

"It was just the way things were. It was regular life."

We were walking past her Jeep now. I was relieved she didn't stop. The sky, which had been starless, started to open above a moon-silvered bank of cumulus in the east.

Danielle pointed. "Pretty soon it's going to light up the meadow. The snow gets like porcelain."

We paused by the now buried putting green, next to the clubhouse. The Annex rose above us, its white railings beginning to catch the faint moonlight.

"Didn't it piss you off, all that intrusion?"

Danielle shrugged. "I didn't really have much to hide—in terms of anything she'd find in my pockets and drawers."

Something in Danielle's voice alerted me. A sudden flatness. I wasn't sure how to ask about it.

"Was there something…she couldn't find?"

I was clocking in at the station next to the clubhouse. My fingers were so cold, the key slipped and dangled for a moment on its chain. I think Danielle was looking away toward the meadow. I heard her grunt. Like the start of a bitter laugh that doesn't go anywhere. She traced a gloved finger along the bridge of her nose.

"Well, there was nothing tangible. I knew she was looking. I planted things in my diary about how much I loved her and my father. Stuff about what great parents they were—because I knew she'd find it.

"Sure, that makes—"

"So there it is. Blah, blah, blah. The story of my first twenty years." She was rubbing her mittens together.

The message seemed to be: Don't ask any more questions. We'd now climbed to the first floor, near the parlor where we'd talked the previous week.

"That was nice." Danielle pointed toward the dark room. "I liked that."

On the second floor, we passed the rooms rented by Colonel Hall each summer—facing west toward the golf course and Chowchilla Mountain. I pointed them out to Danielle.

"I wonder what it's like," she said, "to live a life focused only on your own pleasure."

"Not great, by the looks of him. If the word bummer were in the dictionary, there'd be a picture of the colonel next to it."

"My parents distrusted pleasure. If you did something solely for the joy of it, they saw that as indulgent. Wrong."

We were walking on the side of the building that was protected from the driving snows. The meadow and golf course now shone in a ghost light. Snow-burdened trees cast shadows on the white.

"How did that affect you? Their disapproval of pleasure?"

Silence. She kicked for a while at an ice patch.

Finally: "When I was a little girl of…seven. I know I was seven because it happened the day after the Normandy Invasion. I was straddling the footboard of my bed, kind of riding it. But really I was masturbating. Just enjoying the feeling, the pressure on my crotch. And my mother came in. I didn't see her behind me. She was watching me, watching my face. I think I had that kind of expression where you're concentrating on something that feels intensely good—in your body."

We'd gone back downstairs to the first floor, found the watchman's box, and were laboring up a rutted snow path to the manager's cottage. As we arrived, Danielle moved away from me, holding the stair rail with both hands.

"What happened?" I spoke softly.

"Oh, my mother said I was nasty. That people weren't supposed to do that with their privates. Then she slapped the back of my head. Later, she told me it wasn't healthy, and that it made you lose track of the important things in life—your values and goals.

"I was humiliated. I wanted the whole thing to be over, never spoken of again. But, for some reason, she got very worried about it. She was always popping into my room, checking to see if I might be 'doing something.' She'd look to see where my hands were under the covers. If they were near my crotch, she'd have me fold them on my chest 'like a prayer.' And she'd get all cold and upset.

"She also took the trouble to notice how long I was in the bathroom, and remark about it. I guess she thought I was doing something in there too.

"Which I was." Danielle tried to peek in the window of the manager's cottage, but it was ink black. She borrowed my flashlight, playing it on the twelve-foot-high walls of what appeared to be a sitting room.

"The more she tried to catch me doing something, the more I was interested. It wasn't anything intense; I was a little girl. It was just a nice feeling. It was kind of soothing. When she caught me, or thought she had, I was totally embarrassed. And then, somehow, that became part of it. The embarrassment—actually the fear of it—was exciting. It kind of added to the whole thing. Worrying she'd barge in and be disgusted."

The fenced-in manager's garden had deep drifts. We walked its perimeter, stepping high across the loose powder. Danielle seemed engrossed in the act of walking. She watched her boots crushing the unmarked snow.

"What happened? Did she loosen up after a while?"

"No, it just went on. For years. Until I was old enough to insist on sleeping with my door closed. But by then…"

We were negotiating steps to Clark Cottage now, a one-story building with wide verandahs and a high-peaked roof. I clocked in at a watchman's box.

"But by then what?" It was clear there was more, and she wasn't certain she wanted to tell it.

"I don't know if I should get into this, Harper."

"Look." It suddenly felt urgent to me that she tell the rest of the story. "You can see through me, I know that. But I don't have that...gift. I can't see you the same way. You have to show me."

The flashlight caught her mittens as they tightened into fists.

"You want the rest of the story. OK, Harper." Her voice had metal in it. "You can have it. But afterwards it will bother you." She leaned against the porch rail.

"When I was fourteen, McMinnville had this big explosion. A plant that made chemicals blew up. All over town you could feel the concussion; a lot of windows broke. I was in my bedroom dressing when it happened. I freaked, and ran to look out. I was at the window trying to see something, and I didn't notice that this neighbor kid was staring up at me. I caught sight of him—finally—and a split second later realized I was in my underwear."

Danielle pushed herself upright, beginning a slow, loose-jointed walk to the far end of the verandah. From there we crunched eastward through the snow to Washburn Cottage.

"This is where James went crazy," she said. "Where he cut himself. Room 1, down on the end."

"Go on with the story, Danielle—the neighbor kid was looking up at you."

Silence. I was pulling out another key. In the light of the station's single bulb, I could see a gray fox out on the snow. Motionless. Waiting to pounce on a mouse hole.

"OK, Harper," with a warning tone. She gathered a handful of powder and threw a snowball at the fox. "As soon as I realized what was going on, I ducked back into the shadows of my bedroom. I was totally embarrassed to be seen like that. But, at the same time, I felt excited. Like when I was doing something and worried that my mother would catch me.

"It was weird. I didn't know what to make of it. From time to time after that, I saw the neighbor—Billy—in his backyard. Looking up at my window. And the sight of him reminded me of that feeling. I just looked back at him, and I was totally uncomfortable.

"One day, months later, my mother and I had a fight. She was screaming about some chore I was supposed to do. Really lighting into me. I ran upstairs and closed my door. She came up after me and started twisting the knob, trying to wrench the door open. I felt this incredible urgency to keep her out of my room, to protect my territory. I don't know where it came from, but it seemed almost life and death at that moment.

"After a couple of minutes, my mother went away, but I was sure she'd be back. It occurred to me that if I took a bath, I'd be in a room I could lock. So I pulled my drapes, undressed to my underwear, and put on a robe. Then, for some reason, I opened the drapes again and looked out. Billy was down there doing something—watering or mowing. I don't know what. Maybe I'd heard him and that's why I looked out. Anyway, he stared up and I just let my robe fall open. I stood there and let him see me. And, after a minute, I closed the drape and padded down the hall to take my bath."

We'd walked the circumference of Washburn by now; the beam of my flashlight played faintly on the main hotel. In a few minutes we'd be back where we started.

"Was that something you did because you were angry at your mother?" I wanted to know.

"No. I did it for the feeling."

"The excitement?"

"Yeah. And also the embarrassment. The sensation that I was doing something wrong."

Danielle put her gloved hands in her pockets, shrugged and looked up at me. Her shoulders seemed dense, self-protective. Her lips tightened in a hard line. I looked back at her and tried out several responses in my head; none of them made sense.

"You want me to go on? Of course, you do." An odd bitterness. "I kept on doing it. Now and then. When I saw him out there and I...wanted his eyes on me. But I wouldn't stand at the window more than a minute. After each time I'd resist it for a while, feel disgusted for what I'd done. But then I'd start to feel a hunger for it. I'd want him to see me again. It was wrong, but that desire was such a pressure in me.

"My father caught me at it finally. Saw Billy staring up at my window, and walked into his yard to see what was so fascinating. Then he came right up to my room and he took a big, open-hand swing at my face. So hard it snapped my head and I stumbled. He'd never done that before."

We were on the back porch of the main building now. Our faces gray in the thin light from the watch station. "He'd never hit me before," she repeated. "That night they made me switch bedrooms with my sister. And from then on, my mother took a lot of interest in when I was dressing and undressing. I never did that thing at the window again."

Silence.

"You don't know what to do with that, do you?" she said.

"No."

"It's OK. James knew what to do with it. But that's another story."

I should have been grateful for what she had just given. But I felt deflated. Who did this make her? What variant of human damage had she just described to me? I had an image of her at the window. The curtain drawn aside; it was gaily colored, with a child's print of some kind. I could see Danielle's young legs rising to the white V of her underpants, and I could feel the desire to be Billy, joined with her in that intimate moment of exposure. It was as if I, too, was a voyeur. Excited. Repulsed.

A new feeling coursed through me. A fear that Danielle knew my reactions; heard them like an overdub in a Truffaut film. She would sense my distress. She would be angry at me.

We were scraping the snow from our boots on the edge of the stair. Danielle touched my arm. I thought at first it was to steady herself, but saw she was looking at me with a sweet, lopsided smile.

"You wanted so much to hear that story, but it's disturbed you. Whatever you feel, it's OK. Perhaps I shouldn't have told it. I don't know. But, Harper." She peered through one of the windows into the dark lobby. At the bulking shadows of sofas and writing desks. Her mitten brushed distractedly at the window frame. "I won't hold what you feel against you. OK?"

I couldn't speak.

"OK?"

I nodded.

"Good, good. I got to go."

She reached up, and for the briefest moment her lips brushed my cheek.

CHAPTER 19

*T*his part of the story comes from Tara, from some long conversations we had afterwards. The bed James was building for her was a simple design: a plywood platform mounted on short four-by-fours, with brass L-braces to stabilize the legs. Tara had already bought the foam mattress down in Oakhurst, and it was leaning against the wall of her one-room cottage, still wrapped in plastic.

"I think it's gonna be wobbly," Tara said in a compressed voice. "Those braces aren't gonna be strong enough when you get people on top of it. Two people, plus the wood, is gonna be heavy as hell."

"Don't you worry, baby, when I'm done this bed could hold up the Taj Mahal."

James grunted with effort as he sunk each screw. His shoulder-length hair fell across his eyes, and he was obliged to stop periodically and hook it over his ears.

"Ta da!" James spread his hands like a magician who'd just performed a mind-boggling trick. "Ready for testing."

He pulled the zipper on Tara's jeans. She leaned toward him, holding her arms out, letting him work her pants over her round buttocks.

"Let me get some sheets."

"Forget the sheets, Tara." He pushed her, and she fell back onto the raw foam. The bed wobbled. James knelt on either side of Tara's legs, letting himself topple forward on his hands. The bed wobbled again.

"I told you," she said.

"Baby, people will be fucking on this bed a hundred years from now." His voice had grit in it. "Flip and pull your panties down. I want to do you from the back."

On the third thrust, the bed collapsed.

On the way to the lumber store in Oakhurst, James kept a dangerous silence.

"Those braces were thin," he finally said. "They make 'em cheap these days. Cheap shit from Korea or somewhere. You can't design for that."

"Maybe not." Tara had her elbow leaning against the window of her VW bus. She was resting her head on her hand.

"I'm not kidding you. You can't plan for shit like that. A few braces should make that bed solid as Gibraltar."

"All I know is the thing went down faster 'n Sonny Liston." She laughed at her own joke.

James suddenly became very concerned about Tara's driving. "Did you notice it's starting to snow? We're not racing at Le Mans, baby. I'd like to live through the next turn."

Then he complained that her ashtray was full.

"You're the one who smokes," Tara came back at him. "Maybe you ought to clean it out."

"If you own a car, you've got to keep it up. That's all I'm sayin', baby."

Five minutes later, he was fretting that she didn't have a rack on the VW.

"We went through this with the plywood, Tara. You got to have a place to carry shit. Where are we gonna put the two-by-fours?"

"They'll fit inside."

"You don't know what you're talkin' about, baby."

"Yes, I do."

"Well, I want a twelve-footer. That's how much we need. This van ain't no twelve feet. I'll eat shit if it is." James's voice was getting a thin, belligerent edge.

It's early, the air chilled. Four horses stand together mutely. A trace of frost thrusting from the nostrils. Their eyes are immobile. Numb. I am sitting on a fallen log. Writing slowly, hands turned thick and careless in the cold. The first jay of the morning watches from a fragile patch of light. No sound.

They got—at Tara's suggestion—two eight-footers that fit in the bus very nicely. This seemed to further deteriorate James's mood.

"So tell me," Tara was smiling, "what does shit taste like, James?"

"Fuck you!" The words erupted like a well fire. "Do you want a bed? Do you want me to make you a bed, baby? Or do you want to shoot your mouth off? 'Cause you can sleep on the fuckin' floor if you keep talkin'. You follow me? Do…you…follow…me? Tell me, or you can just drop me off at the Sugar Pine."

"I want you to finish the bed." In a sullen voice.

When they got back to Tara's cabin, she sat outside on a rotting wooden chair. James went to work reconstructing the bed platform. The new plan called for bracing the legs diagonally with the two-by-fours. James had to make a little jig for cutting the boards on a forty-five-degree angle, which he was rather proud of. He asked Tara several times to come in to see it, but she was pouting and refused.

An hour later, when the new bracing had been nailed into place, Tara consented to inspect the bed. James had put the mattress back on, and had even gone to the trouble of fitting it with a sheet.

"Genghis fucking Khan, and his whole army, could fuck on this bed and it wouldn't fall down. I'm telling you, baby. What do you think now?"

Tara walked around all four sides. She leaned against the wall and looked at it some more. She started combing her long, black hair with her fingers.

"Well?"

Silence.

"What do you think?"

"Look, I'm afraid to tell you. You'll get all bent up." She was twisting strands of her hair, biting them.

"For fuck sake, say it. What's wrong with it?" He kicked it. "This fucking thing is strong. You could survive a nuclear blast if you got under this thing." He lifted and dropped it. "This thing will still be around when you're dust, baby."

"It looks...kind of heavy. I mean, all the wood on the sides. It's massive. I thought maybe the braces would be smaller—little triangles right at the top of the leg. But these go halfway down."

"Get on the bed." Very flat voice.

"I don't want to."

"Get on the fucking bed."

"No."

"OK, then I will."

James stood on top of the foam. Motionless for a minute, looking out one of the windows. Then he jumped—maybe a foot up— landing heavily on the bed. He sprang again, higher this time, coiling his legs as he came down.

"Does...this...bed...look...strong?" Jumping between each word. Violently crashing back; the wood creaking, hammering the floor. Then he abruptly stopped. Jumped down. "Can't have it both ways." *Sotto voce.* "Can't be strong and be some delicate, artistic thing at the same time. Can't..." His voice trailed off.

For the next three hours, James sat on Tara's sofa. Watching night fall. Listening to a Procol Harum record over and over.

"You're right," he finally said. "I don't know what the fuck I was thinking."

"You were trying to do a nice thing."

"It's a stupid-looking piece of shit."

"It's OK, James. I'll get used to it. And I feel safer with it—in case there's a nuclear attack." She was trying to kid him out of it.

Now came a fifteen-minute silence—while James tore up the lumber receipt into microscopic pieces.

"Do you want a beer?" she asked.

"Yeah, but I can't. Danielle won't let me see Annie if I drink."

"She won't know."

"Not this time. But if I start, I'll keep at it. Sooner or later, she'll see me fucked up."

More silence.

"It's shit." He got up and shoved the bed against the wall. "We'll leave it there tonight."

"What do you mean, tonight?"

He didn't answer.

The next day, James borrowed Tara's bus and drove to Oakhurst. She was off working at her winter job, a place near Bass Lake that rented snow mobiles. James bought a brass-dipped iron bed at a used-furniture store in town. He got it home and all set up before Tara returned from work. As she approached the cabin that evening, she heard furious hammering. Through a window she could see James smashing the legs, the braces of the bed he'd built. His eyes held a thick, comfortless rage.

CHAPTER 20

*T*he seventh of December was a day I easily recall. The sharply angled light, the sudden, scratching sounds of climbing squirrels. The snow surrendering to thaw, dropping in a wind-like rush from random boughs.

What is it, I wonder, that makes memory at times so crystalline, so acute? Perhaps it's the presence of emotion—fear, love, loss. And, depending on the emotion, we remember, "Yes, this feels good, do this again." Or "No, never again, the pain is too great."

So I retain images with near perfect fidelity—the seventh, a day with Danielle, her birthday.

I'd learned Danielle was going to be alone—James had taken Annie to see his mother in San Francisco—so I asked if she'd like to celebrate via dinner at the Ahwahnee Hotel. All our previous meetings had been initiated by Danielle; I wasn't sure she'd say yes. But, to my surprise and delight, she suggested spending the afternoon together in the Valley. Hiking, then dinner. She'd pick me up at one.

From the moment I got in the Jeep, it was clear the conversational focus would be on me. Danielle showed no interest in returning to the subject of her childhood, or events with young Billy next door. The first thing she asked about was what I most enjoyed doing with my mother.

That was easy. "My mother used to hire this college kid to drive us down to San Mateo Park—as an escape from the perennial fog in San Francisco. He'd go off then, to kick around on his own, while we picnicked and talked. And then she watched me climb the twisty slide, or took me on this little train that sputtered around a big oval."

"What made that the best?"

"I had her all to myself. She was looking at me; she was paying attention. I'd just go on and on, telling her one infinitesimal thing after another."

"What happened after you got home?"

"Regular life. She was a real-estate agent. In those days she didn't drive, so there was always a taxi waiting for her. Always a ringing phone, always houses needing to be shown. And when she was around, she was usually distracted. I'd ask a question a dozen times before she'd finally tune in and say, 'What's that, darlin'?'"

"So, yeah, San Mateo Park. And this one other time. When we spent a few weeks—she and I—up at the Russian River. A place called Murphy's Ranch. My sister had gone to summer camp or something. I don't remember. And my father had to work. So we were alone up there. We had this little cabin on a hill, looking out over a cornfield. Full of redwings and swallow-tailed butterflies. She read a lot to me. Pooh stories, stuff like that. I'd memorize the plots and tell them back to her the next day."

"That was lovely." She slowed as we came to Chinquapin, where the road branches right to Badger Pass. We bore left, beginning the long descent into the Valley.

"It was an island in time, that's all."

"Like the lamps," she said, "making islands of light in your father's house."

"Yeah, but it's stupid to idealize it. The thing only stands out because all the rest of the time she spent buttering up an endless cavalcade of home-buyers. I'm talking lunches, drinks, little gifts—anything to make the dupes like her and fork it over for one of her listings. And after she learned to drive and bought that Fairlane, it supercharged the whole frenetic scene. When I think of my mother, I think two things: that she's someone who loves to talk, and someone who lives to herd folks toward the signature line."

Danielle gave a harsh, grunting laugh. "Jesus." A few miles later, she said, "You're not going near it, are you?"

"What?"

"The pain."

We were entering the blasted granite tunnel just west of Inspiration Point. Neither of us spoke while the orange-lit shards of rock streaked by.

"Thinking about your dad much?" she finally asked.

"I don't know. I guess I'm staying away from that too."

"That's OK." She touched my arm. "It takes time."

Above us, Bridal Veil was full, its long, falling strands glinting in the windless afternoon.

Danielle decided to lighten things and changed the subject. "There's a lot of water up there," she said. "It's been incredibly warm this week. Must be a big melt and runoff."

The thaw Danielle referred to turned out to be quite fortunate for our hike. While El Capitan Meadow, nestling in a wide turn on the Merced, was still covered with snow, areas near or under the trees showed bare ground, or only thin patches of ice. We chose a trail that hugs the north rock face under Washington Column, and turns into Tenaya Canyon on its way to Mirror Lake. Danielle parked the Jeep in the lot at the Ahwahnee Hotel, and we set out on that oddly warm December afternoon.

There was smoke in the air, blending with pine scent. We walked toward the Merced, crossed it twice, and headed into a ragged forest, littered with talus broken from the cliffs above.

After half a mile or so, Danielle took off her down jacket and tied it around her waist. She was wearing a red, checkerboard flannel shirt. I remember wanting to touch it, wanting to innocently brush her arm before pointing to a squirrel or rock formation. But I never did. We just pushed on; the sound of the river receded as we passed Indian Cave.

"A guy named Savage," I told Danielle, "led the first party of white men into Yosemite. The Mariposa Battalion. They were chasing Indians who'd been raiding ranches in the foothills. A lookout finally noticed a spiral of smoke rising in the distance, and Savage sent men running all over the Valley, searching for the village it came from. In the end, all they found was an old woman sitting in this cave,

MATTHEW 100 MCKAY

waiting to die, poking the embers of her fire. So they discovered one of the most incredible places on earth, but Savage was bummed 'cause the only Indian he could locate was this old woman."

"He didn't see this beauty? He should have been awestruck."

"Right. One of his men said later that if they'd known the Valley would become so famous, they would have looked at it."

Danielle released one of her grunting laughs. The path was threading among jagged boulders. Some two stories high, moss covered on the north side. It was colder here. Silent, except for the claws of an occasional frightened squirrel. Above us, Half Dome's gray face cut into a Prussian-blue sky. Ahead, the trail began to climb the steep gorge named after the Miwok chief—Tenaya.

Danielle grabbed my arm. "Let's climb that." She was pointing to a twenty-foot-high piece of talus, with a series of smaller boulders leading like stairs to the top. "I think we can see Tenaya Creek from there. It'll be a nice spot."

She scampered up, easily navigating the sharp, moss-crusted rocks. Late afternoon sun painted a circle of light on the boulder's crest, catching her there. When I finally reached Danielle, she gave me her hand, pulling me the last few feet. Looking back now, I remember how much I liked that. Her leading me. The strength of her grasp, the sense that she knew exactly the right thing to do. I was flooded with a sudden, deep trust, a letting go to whatever she might decide.

From the top of that great rock we could see the naked branches of sycamore and black oak. We could see the creek, carrying its cold waters from the high granite bowl of Tenaya Lake.

I began to tell Danielle stories about Chief Tenaya. About his leading the flight of the Ahwahneeches into the high country, and through the passes to join the Mono Indians. "The white man took the valley then, and gave new names to everything—even though it already had a perfectly good Indian name. When the chief was told that Lake Tenaya had been named for him, he said it had a name—*Pywéach*—Lake of Shining Rocks. The honor was completely lost on him."

Danielle nodded; she didn't say anything. I became aware of our hips touching. Of the warmth of her body. I felt aroused, and I realized that all the Tenaya stuff was a thin screen. A way to hide my feelings from her—and myself. And I remembered, looking back to the night she joined me on my watchman's rounds, how I did the same thing then. Spouting desultory histories.

Danielle turned to look at me, making a study of my mouth and eyes. "It's OK," she said.

"Everything?"

"Everything."

I dropped my eyes, then looked up. Half Dome was turning a faint rose color in the dusk light.

"What do you want to do right now?" she asked.

"Hold your hand."

She hesitated, then gave it to me.

During daylight, the great windows of the Ahwahnee dining room look out on a wildflower meadow—and behind it the 3,000-foot cliff supporting Glacier Point. But it was late now, and the three-story casements admitted only winter dark. The room was beautiful and vast, walls filled with baskets and blankets of classic Indian design. Yet taken as a whole—rows of tables beneath night-muted glass—the Ahwahnee dining room purveyed a sweet loneliness.

Over dinner, Danielle asked more questions about my mother. Which I answered. Then I worked up the courage to ask what happened after the discovery of the scene with Billy.

"What you'd expect, I guess." Long pause. I think she was hoping I'd move on to another subject. "Like I told you, they put me in my sister's room. But, worse than that, I was stuck with all her little-girl furniture. And these pink and blue stenciled ducks that ran around the top of the room. She, on the other hand, got my beautiful cannonball bed that had come down from my grandmother. Plus my desk and this very ornate floor lamp that I liked. I was totally humiliated by my new room—and I stopped inviting friends over.

"Then they enrolled me in a Bible class run by two seventy-year-old widows. It was all about sin and retribution. With sin defined as basically anything that felt good. My mother started taking walks each evening—I suspect to see if I was up to anything at my window."

MATTHEW 102 MCKAY

She was delicately picking at the coq au vin. Then twisting her wedding ring. The waiter fussed around us—pouring water, inquiring about our meal. When he'd retreated, Danielle began to carefully line up her silverware.

"But I think I did more to myself than any of the shit my parents cooked up. I developed this fear I might somehow display myself again. Without knowing it. That I'd forget and end up at the window—like that first time after the explosion. So I always had to be on guard, always watching myself. I kept the shade down. My room was perpetually dark. And I always wore pajamas under my robe—just in case. I can't explain it now, but I was *really* afraid. My room was this alien place, and I only went up there to sleep."

"What a nightmare. That went on till you left?"

"It got somewhat better, but yes. I couldn't trust myself. That was the heart of it."

I wanted to take her hand, like I had on the big rock. Instead, I ran my fingers along the starched tablecloth. Then pulled wax from the wrought-iron candleholder, my hand throwing shadows.

Danielle's face seemed pale, tired in the room's cautious light. She shook her head, looked up for a moment at the high-peaked ceiling. "I don't know what I'm doing, showing you where all the bodies are buried."

"I'm glad you are."

"Why, Harper?"

I had no answer.

"What's gonna come of it? If we know all of each other's secrets, what then?"

"We'll be friends. I know you're married and everything, I know—"

"My marriage is over." She made a quick, cutting gesture. "But I'm asking where this goes, this thing we're doing. How can we live in glass rooms, totally visible? How do friends survive that?"

For a long time, I didn't know what to say. We sipped our wine. The waiter cleared the dishes and made a big display of scraping crumbs from the table.

Finally there was something that seemed clear to me. "There's nothing you can do, Danielle. You'll *see* whoever's close to you. But you have to decide one thing: Will you live in a glass room too?"

She nodded, the slight, downturned smile. "Yeah. I guess that's the question."

Silence. I worried I might have offended her. The check came, and I paid it with cash. We drained our glasses, stood, and made our way between the tables to the front of the great hall. Night pressed against the windows. Hiding what the glaciers carved when they came grinding down from Mt. Lyle.

Somewhere in the lobby Danielle took my arm. "Thank you for a lovely birthday," she said. "I guess, all these years with James, I was used to being understood but not seen."

I didn't quite get that, but I let it go. We strolled past the bar and through the front doors. On the way to the Jeep, we paused in front of a little pond. Danielle bent to touch the veneer of ice.

"It's getting cold again," she said.

She rose, facing me, our mingled breath illumined by a street lamp. I may have moved toward her, but have no memory of it.

"I know," she said.

Then I felt her kiss. Soft, the briefest pressure on my lips.

CHAPTER 21

Here then is love, entering
the disused garden, the arranged, familiar
wicker chairs.

It doesn't change. I come in
expecting death and am afraid.
I come in mute or talking just to talk.

The shadows stretch across me in the chair.
Cool and lengthening. It doesn't change,
and this is the only place I can enter love.

Pound's friend, the bank teller, said
we are consumed by either fire or fire.
We are consumed by love or its absence,

by the absence of desire or desire.
It's funny, but in a dream
I'm taking a shower.

She's undressing and for the first time
I will see her. I have only to turn
to see her. I can't do it.

I look down. Because it is so much
what I desire.
It never changes. Years gather.

The face grows quiet or more anxious
in the glass. At intervals we know.
We know then it never changes.

*D*anielle put it down—her face pensive—and looked up the hill toward Moore Cottage. We were on the porch in front of my room, on another of those unseasonably warm days. In the silence, I felt a surge of anxiety that the poem said too much. And that Danielle would see clearly both the enormity of my hunger, and the dense pessimism that had long protected me.

Looking back, I wonder what might have happened if I'd never written that poem, or if Danielle had never seen it. At least one event, three weeks later, would likely have been different. And a long chain of cause and effect, the subject of this journal, might have been altered.

But quite obviously I did write it. Mostly because that moment by the pond—when Danielle had kissed me—kept running through my head like an endless-loop tape. And I found myself imagining dozens of possible lives—each starting with a single genesis. That brief touching of our lips.

Now, as the silence lengthened and Danielle seemed to study the delicate scroll work on Moore Cottage, I felt something shift between us. I felt her withdrawing.

"Who's the bank teller in the poem?" she asked finally.

"T. S. Eliot."

"Why didn't you just say Eliot? Why disguise it like that?"

"I don't know. I didn't want simply to quote him, make it sound like an English paper. I hoped a little mystery would make it more interesting."

"I think being indirect like that gives it a kind of fake literary quality. Like it's only for people in the know."

I looked up at the sky, toward the east where wisps of cirrus hung above the pine-clad ridges. Trying to keep the sudden tears from spilling.

"You're probably right." I discretely pressed under each of my eyes, like I was checking for swelling. "But other than that you love it." I forced a thin laugh.

"I'm sorry, Harper." She waved a hand. "I don't know." Now she shrugged and turned her head away.

"Nothing to be sorry about—that's your opinion."

"It's true—I don't like that part." She was staring at the shadows on the far end of the verandah. "But the poem scares me. You're talking about love, about wanting something with me. I don't think I can be what you're looking for."

My chest felt stiff. I tried to breathe, but the air had become viscous. I was flooded with all the false hopes I'd held about women. Starting with my mother.

"I already know that," I said. I touched Danielle's arm and she turned back to me. "I know it can't work. That's what the poem is about. Desire and emptiness are sides of a coin. Sometimes you feel one, sometimes the other, but they both burn you. Everything ends in the same place."

"Like the Greek myth? The whole time you're rolling the rock up the hill, you know it's going to fall back again?"

I nodded.

"So it's—"

"Yeah." I bent to pick up some dried mud and tossed it over the rail. "But you do it anyway."

"And I'm supposed to just watch this? You getting all fucked up because whatever we are, it's not really what you want? It's not enough?"

I didn't know what to say.

"I'm sorry," she repeated. "I can feel everything I say hurting you. I don't want that. You're the last person…" Danielle was rubbing her neck, making a nice red blotch. She slumped a little in the chair.

"Don't worry about it, Danielle."

"Really? Don't worry? I don't think that's possible, Harper. I don't think I can stand," she got up, "how much I'm disappointing you."

"What are you doing?"

"Going home. To see Annie. We're in the middle of a project:

sewing a new puppet."

The light was starting to fade, the air becoming thin, serrated. I stood up.

"What do we do now?"

"Maybe we wait," she said. "Take some time. See how we feel."

Three weeks later, I still hadn't heard from her.

CHAPTER 22

*S*ugar Pine locomotive No. 10 had labored continuously since 1928—first for the Pickering and later the West Side Lumber Company. Now, at the venerable age of forty-one, it needed a flue job. Which was a big deal—expensive and time consuming. It involved replacement of several hundred steel tubes that run the length of the boiler, from the firebox near the cab to the smoke box in front.

James had been pressed into service for the project, and was now working weekends in the Sugar Pine engine house. It was a cramped, two-stall structure—thick with the trainman's perfume of creosote and engine oil. On this particular Saturday, according to Tara, the job was more than halfway finished. The old flues had been removed, and all the new ones cut, turned, and beaded. James was inside the firebox with an acetylene torch aimed at the rear flue sheet—an inch-thick steel plate with hundreds of holes where the new flues would be welded.

From what I've heard, working in a firebox is less than pleasant. It's a tight six feet from the floor to the crown sheet, the walls are coated with carbon, and it gets hot as the planet Mercury when you're using a torch.

James was welding at the bottom of the flue sheet. He knelt on the hard steel, bending awkwardly to watch the blowtorch circumnavigate each hole. After a while, when his back started to ache, James leaned a forearm against the flue sheet—which was a mistake. In less than five seconds the referred heat had seared the soft tissue from his wrist to his elbow. James screamed and dropped the torch. It went on burning against the firebox floor while he cradled the injured arm. He was swearing, the words ricocheting off the steel walls at an ear-shattering volume.

The machinist, a bald-headed man with a drooping, white mustache, popped his shoulders through the open fire door.

"What happened?"

"I burned my arm. I fucking cooked it."

"Turn off the torch and get out of there."

James was waving his arm back and forth, trying to fan the pain away.

"Come out. We'll take a look at the thing and dress it."

James didn't move. "It's turning white—it's turning fucking white." Voice high pitched, laced with panic.

The machinist, who wore a knotted kerchief over his head, removed it to dip in a tin of white grease. He again leaned through the fire door.

"Here, put this on the burn. And for Christ's sake, turn off that torch."

James looked down at the jetting flame. Then he stood and turned—sleepwalker style—in the direction of the fire door.

"James, shut off the damn torch. Now. Before it fucks up a stay bolt or something."

Which is what happened. The torch burned long enough to damage one of the bolts that holds the firebox to the frame.

A half hour later, James was kneeling in the snow just outside the engine house. His arm was thrust, elbow deep, in a heavy drift. The machinist was standing a few feet away, talking to James's back.

"You have any idea of the work it's going to take to fix that stay bolt? You really set us back in there."

"All I care about right now is I fried myself, OK? I don't care about the fucking stay bolt. I just want to stop this pain. Maybe you don't understand that, but I don't give a shit what you understand."

"You're a piece of work, McAllister. Go home, get out of here." The machinist had been carrying James's work gloves, and he threw them in the snow. "We'll talk about this later."

James was lying in the iron bed he'd bought for Tara, arm wrapped in a plastic bag of ice. A frail afternoon light drifted down through the pines, washing the dresser and floor with a sallow luster. Tara was sitting at a battered oak table, working her way through a magazine. She glanced over at James just as he was opening his eyes.

"It's good you got a little sleep. Want a sandwich or something?"

He didn't answer right away; his eyes scanned across the room, catching on random objects. "I had weird dreams on that codeine pill you gave me."

Tara turned to the window, hearing a rush of falling snow in the branches of a nearby pine. "Yeah? What kind of dreams?" She didn't sound interested.

"I was hiking in the high country. With Danielle." Tara tossed her magazine on the table. "Things seemed OK. None of the bad shit had happened. We must have been above the timberline because the trail—everything—was granite. Very beautiful, very desolate."

Tara got up to fetch a beer from the refrigerator.

"After a while, we were on some switchbacks. Very steep with a pretty good drop-off on one side. But I was afraid to be on the outside edge. Like maybe Danielle would push me or something. So I kept changing sides so I'd always be away from the edge. Isn't that weird?"

There was more to the dream than James was telling, a part he didn't think Tara wanted to hear.

Tara sipped her beer. "It makes sense to *me*. I think you're pretty afraid of her."

Silence.

James pulled his arm out of the bag, touching it gingerly. "Numb as a motherfucker. Like it belongs to somebody else." He sat up. "You'd be afraid of her too, if she had the power to take your kid away."

James stood and joined Tara at the table. She was flicking a bottle cap around like a hockey puck, making a game of trying to hit the beer bottle. With supreme carefulness, James was pressing the blisters on his damaged forearm.

"I can't believe how stupid this was." He held the arm up as if offering a courtroom exhibit.

"At least you didn't burn your hand."

"Only because I had a glove on. Otherwise, I'm sure I would have scorched that too."

"We'd better get some gauze on it, James. Why didn't you let them dress it there? You said they offered."

"I was too pissed. Fenton—the bald-headed asshole—kept hassling me about why I didn't turn off the torch."

"What'd you tell him?"

"I told him to shove it. I didn't give a shit about the torch right then. I was watching my arm blister up." Getting loud. "I had bigger problems. I couldn't believe how fucking much it hurt."

She pointed to his arm. "Let's get that covered."

Tara, who'd bought gauze and adhesive tape while James slept, applied the bandages.

"I'm not going back," James said.

"That's right, take tomorrow off."

"No. I mean I'm not going back at all. I've got my job up at Badger. So why bother?"

"You're kidding."

"I look like a fucking idiot, OK? I don't want to hear any more about the stay bolt, and all the fucking work to fix it. I don't want them looking at my taped-up arm," he dropped it to the table, his knuckles banging the oak, "and thinking I'm incompetent. I can do without shit like that. I can do without the Sugar Pine."

"But you love being a fireman."

"That's in the summer. I'll be their fireman when the train's running. But fuck boiler repair." He swept the bottle cap she'd been playing with off the table.

Tara flinched, cocked her head to one side, and widened her eyes. A look of concern. "Is the stay bolt that big a problem?"

"Big enough. It's gonna take time to fix. I can't be around for that, everyone going, 'What happened to you, James?' and shit like that."

"But it's not your fault."

"Sure it's my fault. I'm the nitwit who burned himself; I dropped the torch. There was no one in that firebox but me."

"But I thought you said you were in too much pain to think about—"

"I screwed up. From beginning to fucking end, OK? OK?" Voice rising. "Can we stop talking about it? Would that be all right with you?"

Much later, when Tara described this scene to me, I was again struck by the weave of shame and rage. How the shame would abruptly surface, only to dip below the running thread of anger again.

In less than an hour James had returned to bed, his arm resting delicately on the ice bag. Tara was just finishing her second beer. The radio was on.

"Fuck," James murmured, apropos of some internal conversation.

On signal, Tara came over and lay down next to him, propping her head with one hand, staring at his face. After a minute or two, James reached for her hand and placed it on his crotch. He closed his eyes. Tara started to pull his zipper, but he stopped her.

"No, I can't."

"Can't what? I'm going to do everything."

"No. Just keep your hand there. That's all."

"OK. And not move it?" She sounded unsure.

"I just want to feel your hand. It would just be nice…if you did that."

The grass is new mown. Scented with the broken leaves. Shadows of cedar pierce the field. A road, with a hundred footprints shaping its dust, cuts into a thin stand of trees.

CHAPTER 23

Dear Dani:
1/2/70

I had a dream about you, baby girl. We were walking on those high switchbacks, I think near Vogelsang, where we went during that first summer instead of visiting your folks in McMinnville. Remember how weird it was when we got above the trees? All that granite, with the wind whistling around the crevices.

I had the same feeling in the dream I had when we were there. Of the awesome beauty, but also the barrenness. Yet we were together, and the granite was just something that surrounded us. We were the most important thing, Dani, the only color and life.

In the dream nothing bad had happened. No accident. No Tara. We were like always: laughing, my hand on your ass.

When I woke up I missed you. It felt like I'd been left up on that trail without you, and with just the sky and the cliffs.

You seem so angry at me, I'm afraid to write this. But I think what's happened has been a mistake. I think it's a mistake to lose each other.

I knew, while we were together, that everything would be all right. And nothing is right now. All I want is to be back up on that mountain with you.

Love,
James

I have that letter here, in my hand. The creases are sharp, unwilling to fully open; the paper oddly thick, heavy. Slightly yellow at the edges. Toward the end, words are scrawled—as if James was in a hurry.

I turn it over, as if the blank side might offer something further, some deeper explanation of his pain. Nothing, except a thin green stain. Perhaps a leaf or flower he enclosed.

I know for a fact the letter was never answered.

CHAPTER 24

*M*aybe a few days later—Tara was never very exact about the time—James had Annie for an overnight in his caboose. It was cozier by then, the broken window boarded up and a bright flame in the new heater. A checkerboard oilcloth covered what had once been the conductor's desk, and two lanterns washed the gray enameled walls with amber. Most of the concrete floor was hidden by throw rugs Tara had scrounged.

James was cooking spaghetti on a Coleman stove while Annie watched. He was telling her about dark stars, how the red giants implode to form a sphere of pure iron, no more than a few miles in diameter.

"Do you know how dense that iron is, baby girl?"

"You call Mama that."

"Every girl I love I call that."

"You don't call me baby girl," Tara said.

James ignored her. "The iron is so dense that a teaspoonful would weigh millions and millions of pounds. Isn't that crazy?"

Annie had her arms crossed; she didn't say anything.

James gave an elaborate display of tasting the sauce, and making appreciative moaning sounds. He smiled over at Annie. "Want a taste?"

"No." Her pitch rising slightly on the vowel, suggesting he'd been an idiot to ask.

"It's good."

"I don't like spaghetti anymore."

"You used to, I know you did." Sounding hurt.

"A long time ago."

"Don't worry, I'll eat it," Tara said. "Just leaves more for me." She held the opinion that Annie was spoiled, and refused on principle to "play into her shit."

James pointed to Annie. "Could you put some water in the big pot? It's time to boil up the noodles."

"That thing is hard. I can't do it." She was referring to the five-gallon water jugs James had bought in Oakhurst. He'd recently made a plywood mount for them so it was easy to use the spigot.

"Come on, Annie, give me a little help here."

"I can't."

"You're being really grumpy. How come?"

Nothing.

"You in a bad mood, baby girl?"

"Why do you live here? It's always freezing when we come in. The paint's falling off." She climbed to the cupola and plopped herself in one of the leather seats. "I don't like it when I'm here."

"I thought you said this was cool, that you didn't know *anybody* who lived in a caboose."

"Wrong again," Tara chimed in. "You can't do anything she'll like today, James. Stop trying."

"Mama said you live here 'cause you don't have any money."

"That's because most of my money goes to taking care of you, baby girl."

"Why?"

"Because little girls are fucking expensive, OK?" Voice sharp as a punji stick.

"She's trying to bait you, James. Don't play into it, don't get yourself all upset."

When it was time for dinner, Annie refused to come down from the cupola. They tried several inducements, including cookies and the promise of playing Monopoly after dinner. Finally James got Annie down by saying he'd help her build a miniature bed for her puppets.

But, with the spaghetti steaming on their plates, Annie's persona remained caustic, resistant. She flicked at the petals of some early-blooming poppies Tara had found in the foothills.

"What?" James spread his hands, cocking his head to look directly at his daughter.

Annie said nothing. She laid a small index finger on the oilcloth, pointed at Tara.

Ten o'clock. Annie was finally in her sleeping bag, eyes closed. Tara sipped a beer she'd chilled in a snowdrift; James smoked. The oil lantern burned at the far end of the table, casting their shadows against ceiling and wall. The silhouette shifted as James took each drag of his cigarette. Outside, a powdery snow fell, the near flakes glinting in the lantern light.

"So how come you don't call me baby girl?" Tara was smiling, but her tone could cut steel.

"I don't know, you just get into certain habits."

"I'm serious, James. You said you used that name for all the women you love."

"Oh, for fuck sake, Tara."

"No. Don't blow me off. I saw you through a lot of shit. Going back to last summer, when you told me your wife was brain dead. Remember? I'm entitled to a straight fucking answer about how you feel about me."

"You're beautiful, Tara. How do you think I feel?" James was stubbing out his cigarette with a violent, twisting movement.

"All that tells me is I make your dick feel good. I want to know what I am to you, what we're doing here. I don't mind playing house for little Miss Pinch Mouth in there as long as there's some point to it."

"Don't call her that. Christ, why did you call her that?"

"Because that's what she is. She's pissed because her family blew up. But she's no boo-hoo girl. She's gonna torture you instead. So fuck that, answer my question."

"What fucking question?"

"How you feel about me."

"Right now, I don't know."

"After seven months? There's blocks of wood that know more than you do. You know, but you don't want to say."

James put on his coat. Tara's eyes burned him.

"Nice, now you're running away."

"Like from a fucking hurricane, ba-by." He said both syllables distinctly, to make it clear he was leaving off the word "girl." James stepped out the door and down the platform stairs. By the side of the car he paused. Then, with an effort, he stretched up, smashing his fist against Tara's window.

CHAPTER 25

The first thing I noticed was voices. Loud and angry. And then the address—1190 Silvertip Lane. Danielle's house. I stood on the street for a moment, irresolute.

The place was a fair-sized log cabin, with a narrow front porch and a chimney of mortared river rock. I'd hitchhiked there from Wawona. On a bread truck making its daily return run from Badger Pass. The voices—a man and woman—continued to argue, but I still hesitated. Snow fell steadily from a white sky, dusting my hair and woolen coat.

I had come without invitation, driven by anxiety after hearing no word from Danielle for three weeks. When I called, the phone just rang. Twice I'd seen Danielle's Jeep streaking by Wawona, on her way to work at the ski lodge. But her old habit—visiting when Annie was staying with her dad—seemed to have ended.

I approached the cabin, my boots soundless in the new powder. The voices slapped against each other, high and low, words becoming more distinct as I got closer.

Male voice: "All these years and you're going to throw it away? Like it was a fucking waste of time?"

Inaudible female voice.

Male voice: "You used to like it fine. You used to come if I rubbed you through your pants."

Inaudible female voice.

Male voice: "Did you read the letter?"

I was at the front door now. Solid wood with a tarnished brass knocker shaped like a fish. For the first time, I recognized Danielle's voice.

"Of course I read it," she said. "Many times." There was a pause. "I have it right here. But it's not enough, James. Too much has happened. You can't just tell a sad little dream and say you miss me—as if that was supposed to change everything."

"Are you talking about Tara? That was a mistake; I've been trying to tell you that."

"It's not Tara, it's *you*. Your selfishness. How everything is for and about you. And if it's not, you're angry. How you always try to make yourself look good. And if anybody criticizes, what a surprise: you're angry. But mostly it's just when I look inside you, I see emptiness. With a lot of disguises." She paused. Her voice got softer. "There it is. Do you feel it? That's what I'm talking about. There's a river of shit in you. Right now. That's what I'm talking about."

I heard a crashing sound.

"You think you know all about it?" James's voice, high pitched. "You think you know about the shit? You don't know—because you wouldn't be fucking with me if you did. You wouldn't be standing here like a stupid bitch and—"

I knocked on the door.

"And ripping me open. We could have been good together, but you fucked it. You *fucked* it."

There was a dull thud, and then a screech. I started to bang on the door with my fist, shouting at him to open up. I was filled with the same fear and urgency I'd known when I pulled Danielle out of the crash. The same desperation to protect her.

I could hear Danielle shouting, "No," in a high, frightened voice.

"Is this what you were talking about, Dani? Is this the shit?" Another thud. It sounded like he was kicking her. "Do you think you're gonna destroy everything and I'm gonna just go down like a lamb?"

I was slamming my body against the door, trying to break the latch. Suddenly it opened and James stood staring at me. Beyond him, I could see Danielle lying across a splintered coffee table.

"What are you doing here?" He looked momentarily confused. "Oh, I see. I see, Dani. You got something going with the water boy here. You like the water boy? Is that why we've gone to shit, Dani?"

"No, James." She was propping herself on her hands, trying to get up. "I don't know what he's doing here."

James smiled and grabbed the lapels of my coat, pulling me close to him. I noticed the big bandage on his arm. I could see the broken capillaries in his cheeks, the beginnings of crow's feet. His breath was sharp with nicotine.

"Get Annie," I said to Danielle. "You have to leave."

"She's OK. She's with Cherie." Danielle was standing now. I could see her over James's shoulder. But her face was rigid with pain. And a moment later she bent to rub her leg.

"There's no time. Get out of here—now." My hope was to keep James occupied while Danielle fled to the Jeep.

"Shut up, water boy." James still held my lapels. In one motion, he pulled and butted me—smashing his forehead into my nose. I was stunned, gushing blood. I started to raise my hands defensively, but he did it again.

"Time to say good-night, water boy."

I knew that meant a haymaker punch was coming. Before he could set himself, I raised my right arm and crossed it above his wrists. Then I crouched, twisting to my left, and whipped my arm down on James's hands. His hold broke.

That trick I'd learned in junior high. But the next one had come later, in a bar in Durango. I stood quickly, still turned to my left, and pumped my elbow full force into the big man's jaw. James staggered back, his hands reaching behind till he steadied himself against the door.

"That's enough," I said. "Just let Danielle by. Let her get out of here." I wiped at the blood coursing over my upper lip.

James stood up straight and took a step toward me. He appeared to stagger. But it was a boxer's feint. As he dropped to his right, he planted and threw a roundhouse punch at my eye. It landed square on the socket, with a twisting motion that split open my eyebrow and knocked me off my feet. I fell at the edge of the porch, momentum rolling me down the steps to the snow-covered path.

"Go home, water boy. Go beat off or something; you're not getting any here."

Blood completely blinded the eye he'd punched. I got to my knees, but I was dizzy and having trouble keeping my balance.

"What are you waiting for? Want me to beat you like a drum? Want to spend time in the hospital?" He started down the steps. "Sure you do."

At that moment Danielle appeared behind her husband, holding his shoulder. "Don't, James. He's a friend, nothing more."

I was on my feet, but bent over, hands on knees. I watched my blood dripping in the snow. Melting shallow holes with its heat.

James stood on the first step. "You like this little shit?" he asked Danielle.

I could tell from the teasing tone he was ready to do something else. I lunged up, thrusting a sharp blow at his gut. It caught him loose, unprotected. Air made a rushing sound from his throat. He started to jackknife. As he toppled in slow motion toward me, I cocked my hands in a double fist and swung in a short, hard arc at his face.

There was a dull thud, like a cracking melon, and James's head snapped back. His knees buckled and he went down, crashing against the steps. Danielle did a quick side jump to avoid his falling weight, and a moment later was standing over him.

She started to scream. Over and over shouting for him to get out, that he was crazy, that he couldn't take Annie.

James's head lolled against the edge of the porch. He tried to raise himself up, but fell back to the hard wood. His mouth was bleeding; his right arm waved vaguely, as if he was shooing flies.

"This is fucked," he finally slurred.

"No, you're fucked." Danielle had what seemed to be a folded paper in her hand. She threw it at his chest.

James said nothing more. I sat on one of the steps, wiping blood with my sleeve, and just watched the man. Eventually he sat up, cautiously propping himself, then stood with an unsteady list. The rage was gone. He seemed collapsed, shrunken.

Danielle was standing, arms folded. A mottled light from the pines touched her face. "Good-bye, James," she said, as he shambled towards Fagan's pickup. The word "good-bye" said slowly with biting emphasis.

After the truck rumbled away, there was silence. Danielle kept staring at the curve on Silvertip Lane where James had disappeared from sight. She was bent slightly, arms crossed to the point where she seemed to be hugging herself. Her pants were wet, but she appeared not to notice.

I continued to bleed. My nose, I began to suspect, was broken.

After a long time, Danielle said two words that I can hear as clearly now as then. "Come in." She turned toward the door.

I picked up the folded paper—James's letter, the letter I've kept all these years—and followed her.

CHAPTER 26

*T*he body speaks a language of hope, of invitation. But the body also listens. Like small animals listen, in the dangerous open, to the pouring warmth of the sun. I could feel it then—my body waiting to receive the touch that I had always longed for. A touch that would tell me I was good. That I was known. A touch that would become an armor, and would always—long after it was gone—protect.

As I followed Danielle through the cabin door, I watched her body move. Her gait seemed stiff, cautious. As if she were preparing for another attack.

"Bring that in the kitchen," she said. Danielle pointed to a dun-colored armchair that belonged more in a school principal's office. "Sit down."

She wasn't looking at me, and seemed to be fussing with something at the sink. The pipes banged as she adjusted the water.

"Maybe I should go." I was feeling something dense and impassable between us.

"You're just saying that. You don't really want to." Danielle was looking out the window, a washcloth poised in her hand.

"No." I realized she could read exactly how much I needed her to touch me.

"What you want is to be taken care of."

"Yes." I felt sick. I felt like I had no clothes on.

"You want me to hold you—like that night when you cried about your dad."

"Yes."

Danielle turned, took a few steps toward my chair, and slowly knelt. She leaned for a moment on the wooden arm, and looked at the damage to my face. Her eyes tightened. An ephemeral sadness arrived in the lines around her mouth.

"I know it makes you uncomfortable," I said. "How I feel. I'm sorry."

She shook her head; made a gentle shishing sound. Then she raised the cloth to where the blood still seeped above my eye. Danielle pressed the wound, and with exquisite carefulness wiped at the stream of drying blood on my cheek and jaw. "Shish," she said again, and began washing my lip, my nostrils. I was reminded of the accident, when I had tried to clean the blood from *her* face—not knowing if she was alive or dead.

Danielle went to the sink to rinse out the cloth. When she returned, it was deliciously cool. She knelt and continued her work, very tenderly. Touching—almost caressing—the cuts and bruises with one hand, cleansing them with the other.

I hardly breathed. Danielle's dark hair fell across my fingers. For a moment, her lips moved with some unvoiced feeling. But then her face went still again. In time, she rose slightly and kissed my eye, the one that had been hurt. Then her fingers brushed my cheek, and she kissed that too.

"Thank you," she said, "for protecting me. I can feel," she kissed me again—lightly on the lips, "I can feel how much you want to keep me safe."

A moment later, she opened her mouth and covered my lips with her own. Sweetly. Slowly.

As the kiss ended, Danielle pulled back. Then reached up to hold my face in her hands. "And I realize," she said, "what a rare and lovely thing that is."

I didn't know what to do. It seemed like the moment I'd wished for had come. Yet I was afraid to touch her. She was wearing a flannel cowboy shirt, and I yearned to caress her arms. To feel their slender strength. I wanted to spread my hands over the smooth cotton on her back, feeling her shoulders, the archipelago of her spine. I wanted to press the thick denim where her hips swelled.

For some reason I stood up. Perhaps I hoped Danielle would decide again—unmistakably—whether we would touch. She rose to stand directly before me. Her body had a faint lilac smell—mixed with fear and sweat. After a moment, she leaned against me; I could feel the pressure of her breasts and her arms pushing up my back. I held her, taking into me the geography of her shoulders, the hard thoracic muscles on her back, the simultaneous strength and frailty where her ribs curved beneath her arms.

I felt the surging power of our physical warmth. I felt my need for her, and gave in to it. And when I thought it would end, Danielle continued to hold me.

Even after all these years, that embrace is a fulcrum. A balancing place in my life. It is the way I answer the question of whether I have been loved. It is the way I know I have given love.

While it went on, I felt an incredible desire to know Danielle's most intimate places. I wanted to touch her belly, the place between her breasts, the forbidden cleavage below her hips. Yet I couldn't do it. It seemed a violation of her gratitude. A turning of that sweet moment into a demand that she give me her physical self.

I kissed her lips again, and then her cheek. For a moment I held her head in my hands; our foreheads touched. I breathed in her fragrance, her own warm breath.

Then we let go. Together. As if we had seen the precipice at once. In no more than fifteen minutes, Danielle had bandaged the wound above my eyebrow and sent me home.

CHAPTER 27

*H*ow do we decide things? How do we choose directions when the distant consequences lie hidden from us? I think we choose what appears to nourish us, keep us safe, hold us blameless. We choose a convenient version of the good. And usually ignore the whispering catastrophe, the dark forest swallowing the road ahead.

I made a decision in late January that I would pay dearly to have back.

The relief night watchman—who did my job twice a week, and the rest of the time worked through a list of repair projects at the hotel—was a twenty-year-old black kid named Frank Riles. Riles was smart, taciturn, and took no shit from anybody. He was also sinewy and strong, with the fluid grace of a natural athlete. His main interests were drinking and baseball. During the summer, I'd see him, most nights, practicing his pitching. Throwing fastball after fastball at an old tire he had rigged up behind the Sequoia. I liked him. Sometimes we'd talk about the state of baseball—he'd tried out for a couple of single-A teams—or the idiocies of the Curry Company.

At around eight or eight-thirty, on one of the nights Riles was watchman, he noticed a shape crouching behind the rail of Moore

Cottage. He was taking a six-pack up to his room—about three doors from my own—when the light from the watch station up at Moore caught some definite movement.

Riles got his flashlight and headed up the long, snow-covered stairway to investigate. He kept the beam off most of the way, and only when he was a few steps from the top snapped it on. The light hit James, binoculars in hand, as he tried to back away.

"What you doin', man?" Riles followed James with the beam as he jumped the side rail, landed in a snowbank, and retreated toward a thin stand of trees behind Moore.

Silence. Then the sound of snow rushing off the branches of a nearby pine.

"Hey, man. Talk to me. What are you doing back here?"

Nothing. Riles walked up to check the porch where James had been crouching. There were footprints in the light powder by the rail, and a binocular case lost during James's hasty egress. Now Riles crunched along the porch toward the back of the cottage; he played the light across the line of trees.

"I guess he's gone," Riles said quite audibly, and cut the light.

But, halfway down the steps heading to the main building, Riles stepped off into the drifts. He moved quietly, staying downhill of the cottage until he reached the snow-covered road in back of the Sequoia. Once across the road, he took cover in the trees, working cautiously through the branches so he could circle behind the intruder.

Riles had just achieved the top of a small incline when a shadow rose, maybe fifteen feet in front of him. It was James, scanning with his binoculars to see if it was safe to make a run for the road. Riles took a few stalking steps, then accelerated cheetah-like, tackling James just as he turned toward the sound.

A second later James was on the ground, Riles shining the flashlight in his face.

"Once again, man, what you doin' here? Don't fuck with me, you understand what I'm saying?" Riles emphasized his point by shaking the flashlight back and forth.

James pushed his body backward through the snow, trying to buy some distance from his assailant. "I'm just watching. There's somebody I know who lives here."

Riles kicked James's foot. "What kind of shit you playin'?"

"Nothing." James was struggling to sit up, propping himself on one arm.

Another foot kick. "I told you not to fuck with me. What's your shit? Who you watchin'?"

"Guy named Harper." James had rolled over to his knees and was starting to get up. "He lives here, I'm not sure where. I just want to talk to him."

Riles gave James a two-finger shove, knocking him off balance and forcing him to take quick, compensating steps backward. "What kind of conversation were you gonna have hidin' up here in the dark? Maybe I'll call the rangers and you can explain to them."

Getting in trouble again with the rangers held little appeal for McAllister.

"Look, I just gotta ask him something."

"Why?"

"It's personal."

Riles started tapping the flashlight against his hand like a billy club. "He's not here now. It's his day off; he's down in the Valley. So get the fuck out."

"What's his room number? I want to leave him a note."

"I'm not telling you his number." Riles laughed contemptuously. "Why would I give some asshole who's sneakin' around and spyin' anybody's fucking room number?"

"Maybe I could make it worthwhile for you." James reached into his coat pocket and extracted a rolled-up baggie. "That's some primo weed. Yours for the room number."

Riles took the bag and shook it. He opened it, pinched a little of the contents in his fingers, and smelled it.

"So what's the room number?"

Riles handed the bag back. "Fuck you—that's the room number. Whatever shit you're playin', I'm not helping you with it."

"I got to ask him something, that's all. I'm not lying, that's all it is."

"Fine, ask him sometime when it's light out. Or send him a letter—general delivery, Wawona Post Office. Now get out of here."

"OK, wait." James was rummaging in his pocket again. "Could

you just give him a note for me? Please? This is serious shit, just give him a note."

He got out a small paper bag that contained a couple of oil lantern wicks. The wicks went back in his pocket; the bag he ripped open. James produced a stubby pencil like the ones you keep score with in golf.

This is the note he wrote:

Harper:

Don't fuck me out of my family. I'm asking you as one man to another. Leave it alone.

Now she won't even let me see Annie. My girl needs a father. Please tell that to Danielle.

The letter was unsigned.

When Riles gave me the note, he rolled his eyes. "You know some crazy fuckers, man. Guy's way out to sea in a rowboat. You understand what I'm saying? He ain't never makin' it back to shore."

But when I read James's words, they seemed sad. Not angry. They carried—and his letter to Danielle was the same—an emptying sense of loss. They were an echo from every barren surface inside the man.

I found myself wanting to help James. Not because I liked him, but because I could feel where the nails had been driven into him. And I felt very strongly the importance of keeping his child, perhaps because of the unhealed ache from losing my own mother.

Yet there was something else. And this is the place where the corruption starts. I wanted to be with Danielle. And unless Annie were allowed to stay with her father, there'd be no time for us. Danielle would be a full-time parent with a full-time job. And I'd be waiting for her—looking for something that would never happen.

So I decided to intervene. I called Danielle. On a frigid night, from the pay phone on the back porch of the hotel, I told her about James's paper-bag note. And about a feeling I had that both Annie and James might be damaged if they were kept apart.

I remember huddling in my coat, kicking at a patch of ice by the phone. I remember a thin thread of a moon riding above the roof of Washburn Cottage. I remember the static on the line as Danielle thought about what I'd said.

"When Annie was born," more line noise while she searched for a way to finish the sentence, "and James carried her for the first time into our house, he held her up so she could look at everything. 'You're home, little girl,' he said. 'You're with the people who love you.'

"I knew that was true. I knew he loved her. I knew he loved me. But now, I try to erase that. Because of everything."

Silence.

Then I heard her voice again, soft, distant. "Maybe that's wrong. Maybe you shouldn't forget…"

I had a feeling there might be more, but she didn't finish. If I could go back, I'd never make that call.

I am watching the old stone fountain. Its spray, caught in a slicing wind, scatters across the lily pads. Hand in hand, a man and his daughter walk the edge of the pond. He is looking down at his girl. I can see the shining weave of all the threads that hold them.

CHAPTER 28

I'd no contact with Danielle for a few days. When it came, it was another of her late-night visitations. She arrived shortly before ten, wearing a compressed yet luminous energy. Like a bottle of fireflies. We didn't embrace, but she squeezed my hand for a moment with her gloved fingers. I felt oddly surrounded by that touch. As if strong arms were holding me.

The first thing Danielle said was that she wanted to walk my rounds again. The second was that she'd taken my advice; she was letting Annie have overnights with her father. I remember how her cheeks were rouged with the cold, and that her lips, in that characteristic downturned smile, also held some kind of irony. Or mischief.

I collected my flashlight and clock, and we made our way downstairs to the watch station on the back porch. As she had in the past, Danielle wanted to turn the key in the clock. She lifted it from my chest, and in that moment I could feel her weight shift. Very slightly she leaned against me.

A half minute later, when the key and chain were back in their box, Danielle turned toward the long stairway heading to Moore Cottage. In the faint illumination from the watch station, her dark hair fell across her cheek.

"Come," she said, brushing it back. "I shouldn't delay you." Her voice had a light, teasing quality I wasn't used to.

She reached to take my hand; her grip was firm, certain.

"Yes, I know." She smiled, her brown eyes holding me. "You're afraid to trust it—maybe it will all disappear in a second. Maybe I'll be like your mother." She shrugged. "I know."

I had no words. She was already saying what I felt. As we carefully planted our feet on each icy step, it seemed like she was always a little ahead. As if, very slightly, she was pulling me. And it occurred to me how Danielle was reversing roles from the young woman she had been with James. That she had always been led, controlled; their world was filled with James's music, James's humor, James's love of the high country. With me, Danielle made the decisions; Danielle saw the path and led me to its end.

At the top of the stairs I noticed something peculiar about Moore Cottage: there seemed to be a lucency on one side, touching the railing and the snow. It wasn't the light from the watch station, but instead something filtered. A faint glowing. My first reaction was to wonder if James had returned, perhaps trying to observe my visit with Danielle.

As we drew closer, I could see a light through one of the curtains. I told Danielle to stay back. She didn't listen, instead following me to the door next to the illuminated window.

The lock turned easily with my passkey. I pushed the door wide; the room was lit by a single globe dangling from a twelve-foot Victorian ceiling. An electric heater glowed by the far wall. Instead of a bare mattress, the bed carried two fluffy pillows over a lovely patchwork quilt.

"My mother made it," Danielle said. "She lent it to me when I came to work in Yosemite that first summer. Never got around to giving it back."

She pushed me gently into the room, closing the door behind us. "Let's not lose the heat."

"How did you do this?" I was stunned.

"I work here, remember? I have my own passkey." She laced her fingers and looked at the floor. Her forehead wrinkled—a look of regret or embarrassment.

Silence. I finally thought to click off my flashlight.

"It's warm enough; we can take off our coats." Danielle

unzipped her gray down jacket. I did the same and hung them over a chair.

I felt a sudden, dark fear that I would do something wrong. Or worse, that my anxiety would be apparent to Danielle, and somehow might offend her.

"It's OK," she said in a husky voice, touching my chest. "I'm nervous too. We can be nervous together." She took each of my hands in hers, studying them for a moment, and finally placing them around her waist. "We can be slow, we can be uncertain, it's OK."

We kissed. Her lips were soft and open. I could smell the lilac. She leaned against me, her hips pressing into mine. I was aroused and for a moment pulled back, afraid, I think, for her to feel it.

But she reached around and pulled me to her. "That's OK, too," she said softly.

She kissed me again. I could hear the wet sounds of our mouths, the slight rush of air as our lips parted. Now I could feel her fingers beneath my throat, starting to unbutton me, working down the length of my shirt, letting it fall open. She caressed my shoulders; she kissed my cheek.

I was holding each side of her chest, just below her arms. I moved my hand so I could feel the beginning swell of her breast.

"Not yet," she whispered as she took off my shirt.

She laid her cheek against my chest, and for a moment just held me like that. I could feel her breath on my skin, the coolness of her hair feathering down my abdomen. Then she undid my buckle and let my pants fall.

For a brief moment Danielle looked at me, before bending— touching and pressing the muscles of my legs—on her way to help me step from my puddled clothes.

I wasn't sure what to do. I reached toward her shirt to see if I should undress her—but Danielle pulled back.

"I need to do it," she said. "At least this time. It has to be different."

I understood what she meant. "What should I do?"

"Nothing. It would be good if you didn't help me. Didn't even touch me."

She folded her arms around her stomach, and stared at the

floor. "It's because he made me do things. Not bad things. But things he liked. Things exactly the way he liked. I'm afraid if you touched me right now, it would be the same. I'd let go of myself. I'd be whatever you wanted."

I nodded, silent for a moment. Then I spoke slowly: "What would make me happiest is to know—to be certain—that you've done only what you wanted to do tonight."

Her eyes worked around my face; she let out a sigh. "You want things. I can tell you want me to get undressed." A grunting laugh. "But there's something else, something above that." She began to unbutton her shirt. Efficiently. Like she was undressing alone.

Now appeared a white T-shirt that said "San Francisco" and had a faded silk screen of Coit Tower. Danielle unbuckled her belt. As her jeans opened I could see light blue underpants.

For a moment I looked away. That old reflex—to protect her from my desire—pushing my eyes to the floor.

"You can look," she said simply.

She bent to pull off each leg of her jeans, tossing them toward the ornately carved oak dresser. Her thighs were strongly muscled, yet very pale. Danielle stood still, legs tightly together, eyes focused somewhere behind me. In a single motion, she pulled her T-shirt over her head.

"Here I am," she said, looking down. Shy.

"Can I hold you now?"

She nodded.

I drew her to me, feeling her lovely breasts touch my chest. The warmth of our joined bodies, after all the deference and waiting, after all the hunger and moments of lost hope, sent through me a shiver of intense pleasure.

She lifted to kiss me. Deeply. Taking each of my lips into her mouth.

"Can I touch you?"

"Yes."

I held her hips, feeling the smooth nylon of her underpants. I touched her buttocks, reading the shape of her intimate places. Danielle's breath changed. She leaned into me. She kissed my cheek, my neck. She was whispering something I couldn't hear. Instead I was listening to the texture of her skin—telling me about her soft-ness, vulnerability. Telling me about sinew and bone, and hidden strength.

She kissed me again, exploring my mouth, tasting me. Danielle tightened her arms, crushing herself against me. For a moment it felt like she was preparing to leave. I had an image of lovers reluctant to part, standing at the dock. But then Danielle spoke again, *sotto voce*, and I had to lean down to hear her.

"I wanted to do this. . .before. Starting that night in the parlor. When you cried. I wanted to do this when I kissed you by the pond. And while I cleaned the wounds you got protecting me. But I always thought it was wrong. That you were a sweet and beautiful boy who could be destroyed if I was selfish and took comfort in you."

I started to speak.

"Shish." Very softly. "Harper, listen. I didn't want to take your love for me and twist it up. Use it to soothe myself. There is some-thing pure about you. Something clear and lovely. And I felt I'd rather disappoint you, keep my distance, than betray that thing." She hesitated; I could feel the faint movement of her breath across my chest. "That thing I loved.

"This morning, when I woke up, I knew I would come here. And do this. The idea came all at once. Whether it was right or wrong I knew I'd do it. I made up reasons: I owe you for protect-ing me. I need one good night. I'm starting to love you." Another grunting laugh. "The reasons don't matter. I knew I'd come here."

Silence. Her hold loosened and she looked up at me.

"What do we do now?" I asked.

"I think lie down next to each other."

Danielle took my hand and led me to the bed. On the way, she punched off the overhead light. A red glow from the heater shone on her legs as she pulled open the covers. She crawled in, the shad-ow of her dark hair falling across her face as she gestured for me to follow.

Under her mother's quilt we touched again. Slowly. Without urgency. In time I found the soft flesh of her stomach, with its slight roundness from bearing a child. And I held the place where her breasts swelled from the ribs—thinking of that day in the ambulance when I was afraid to look at her. Finally she brought my hand between her legs, opening them, letting me feel where the cloth covered the musky warmth of her pubis.

"I'm ready," Danielle whispered, slipping off her underpants, and then mine. "I can't believe we're here, doing this." Her breath was deep and rapid, with little stutters.

"When you're inside, could you just hold me for a moment? I need that."

I nodded. And for a moment I traced the lovely arch of her cheek, rose colored in the electric fire. As I entered Danielle, we were still on our sides. My legs between hers, curled up against her buttocks. My feeling was that I had been let into a place of exquisite specialness. And I knew a gratitude I had never felt. As if I'd been given what I was always afraid to ask for, yet most wanted.

For the longest moment I just held Danielle. Not moving. Deep in her warmth. Our lips touching with the slightest pressure, breath entering each other's mouths.

Two hours later, Danielle sent me out to finish my rounds. It felt like I was leaving a bountiful oasis for a journey to the Arctic steppe. Danielle was curled in a fetal position, watching me as I knelt to kiss her.

"Go," she said. "Come back to me soon."

When I returned around three-thirty, she was sleeping. Her mouth was slightly open, and I stood there for a time, held by the sweet privilege of watching her unguarded breath. Then I undressed and pulled up the covers to slip in beside her.

But I felt it immediately. While she slept, Danielle had wet the bed. Cautiously, without waking her, I rolled to the edge. Then I stood and put on my pants. For a moment, I watched her again, face held in the heater's thin, dusk-colored light.

Without much thinking, I moved the electric grate to the bathroom and closed the door. I slipped outside to the utility closet, intending to ignite the water heater. To my surprise, the big tank was already hot; Danielle had thought of that too. Tiptoeing back inside, I turned on the hot water for the tub—letting it get steaming before I tried to wake Danielle.

She was hard to rouse. But when consciousness finally came, Danielle looked startled.

"What?" She stared at me in the dark, rubbed her fingers across her eyes.

"Your bath is ready," I told her.

"Now?"

"Yeah. It's all toasty in the bathroom. Come on." I held out my hand.

Danielle started to get up, and then said, "Oh." She was feeling the sheets.

"Come on, the water'll feel good."

She threw the quilt back and shoved herself to the edge of the mattress. When she stood, I could see the long, milk-white lines of her legs. And the dark triangle where they met.

Danielle was looking at me intently. "Did you. . ." she started. She nodded and looked away. "It happens sometimes—since the accident. But much less now."

She shrugged. The muffled roar of the bathtub spigot surrounded us.

"It's OK. Come with me."

I led Danielle into the bathroom and closed the door behind us. Steam rose from the water. I kissed her, helping her step over the high rim of the claw-foot tub.

"Oh God." She settled back. "You coming in?"

"No. It's for you."

I turned off the light and knelt next to Danielle. Her eyes were closed, face softened by the steam and warmth. I rubbed the soap in my hands till I had a lather.

"I'm going to wash you now."

I began with her shoulders, my hands gliding over the skin. Stopping again and again to get a lather, returning to gently rub her neck and clavicle, and under her arms. Now, with just my fingers, I soaped her forehead and round high cheeks, and along her jaw and chin.

Danielle rose to kneel in the tub. I washed her back. Then, tenderly, her breasts and belly; her pubis and lovely, full hips. She sank back into the water, and with a washcloth I rinsed the soap from her face.

We said nothing. From time to time I turned on the hot water to warm the tub. She lifted one leg at a time while I soaped them, my fingers rubbing down to the calluses of her feet and the individual toes.

When I was finished, Danielle didn't move. Her eyes remained closed, breath deep and steady. After a few moments she opened her legs.

"Could you touch me?" she whispered.

I kissed her very softly, holding and caressing her face. Watching it tighten with pleasure. Her breath catching, slipping to a shallow staccato. Then feeling her legs close. Twisting. A small, clenched sound.

As I write this, I am there again. Feeling the privilege of knowing her face without defense. Without mask or adornment. No words, no carefulness, no concealment. I am there again as she opens her eyes. As she touches my cheek, as she releases a breath and slips deeper into the water.

CHAPTER 29

"*L*ook how the water drops," Tara told Annie. "Straight into the ice cone."

Months later, I heard this story from Tara. Starting with a cold walk to the base of Yosemite Falls. James was to their right, on the wooden bridge spanning the creek. The falls gave off a muffled thunder, water exploding against the rocks inside the ice.

"All through the winter the cone grows," Tara said. "Like the turret of an ice castle."

Annie seemed to be hanging back. "It's cold. It's blowing."

"Yeah, all that rushing water. It's like we're in this little storm of spray and wind chill."

"Come over here," James called to Annie. "Look at it from the bridge. You can really feel the power of that water."

"No, I don't want to. It's too cold."

"Come on, Annie, please. This is the spot where you can really understand a waterfall. How awesome it is. You can feel it vibrating the bridge."

"No. Can we go back now?"

James reluctantly returned to stand next to his daughter. "I wanted you to see this. How beautiful and scary it is." He shrugged.

"I see it, Daddy."

"OK then, I guess you did."

The trio started down the path toward the parking lot. James walked with a loose-limbed gait, seeming to throw his legs out in front of him as he descended each step. Then he stopped suddenly, holding Annie's shoulder.

"You know what, Annie? I'm thinking of a girl that you remind me of. She lived back in the eighteen hundreds. She's buried right over there, on the other side of Yosemite Creek." He pointed vaguely.

"Are you getting all Boris Karloff on us?" Tara was smiling.

"No, there's nothing creepy about it." He picked Annie up, supporting her against his side while he kept walking. "She was an incredible girl. Tameless. Her name was Floy."

"How is she like me?" He had Annie's interest.

"Even when she was six, she did her own thing. She wouldn't listen to anybody. Her parents were hotel-keepers here in the Valley. They tried to raise her to wear pretty dresses and read poetry—like other little girls in those days. But she was wild. She'd walk off and be gone for days, camping by herself, studying different plants. When she was a little older, she rode bareback all over the high country with just a scarlet braid for a bridle—exploring, climbing mountains alone."

"I'm like her?"

"Yeah, 'cause you're so independent. A lot of the time you like to be alone—up in the tree house or with your puppets. You want to do things your own way. Nobody can tell you how to dress. Or how to act. You're not into plants like Floy, but you love animals—finding and learning about them."

They were treading down the last slope, the trail beginning to widen as the afternoon sunlight withered on the granite. Tara was helping Annie navigate a patch of ice, and she looked at James.

"How do you know about Floy?"

"When Danielle and I first met, we used to go to all these ranger talks. It was something to do on a date. One of them got to telling about Floy because Mount Florence is named after her."

Tara wasn't happy to have Danielle's name mentioned. Her footsteps took her a little distance from James.

"Daddy?"

MATTHEW **142** MCKAY

"Yeah, baby girl?"

"What happened to Floy?"

"She became a guide up here. In the early days. She'd take people out on the trails and teach them about the mountains. How ice rivers carved everything.

"One day, a lady she was guiding asked her to pick a wildflower. Way up in this crevasse that was hard to reach. But while Floy was up there getting the flower, a rock slide came down on her. That's how she died—doing somebody a favor. She was seventeen."

They were in the parking lot now. James was noticing Tara had withdrawn.

"Hey, baby, want to have an early dinner in the Mountain Room? On me?"

She brightened immediately.

"Did Floy look like I do?" Annie asked.

"No, I've seen pictures. She had raven-black hair that used to flow behind her when she rode. And her skin was darker, probably from always being in the sun." He sounded sad. "I can't imagine what her father felt when they brought his beautiful daughter back, all broken by the rock fall. I can't imagine what that man must have felt. To lose such a wild and special girl."

Annie said nothing. At that moment they were crossing the road, walking toward Yosemite Lodge. And, also at that moment, I was sitting in a VW Bug, waiting at that crossing, watching them walk in front of me. I remember thinking that it looked like a happy family tableau. The dad carrying his daughter. Annie's arms clutching his neck, surveying the world from her high, safe place. Tara with her fingers hooked in James's back pocket.

In the restaurant, an hour later, James was still talking about Floy, and how much he admired her individuality.

"When they made this place a national park, her father lost his hotel. And the family lived in San Francisco for a while. Floy hated it there. Especially school. Even though she read constantly, she hated being told what to read. She hated sitting in a chair instead of roaming free in the high-country meadows."

Tara interrupted him: "Careful what you hold up as an example, James. Annie might become exactly that."

"I'd be proud if she was."

"Look where it got Floy."

That put a damper on things, and they sat for a while looking up at the sheer rock face next to the falls.

When the conversation resumed, it was James again: "Losing your kid is the worst thing in the world. And it can happen a lotta ways."

Silence.

"How can it happen, Daddy?"

"Do you really want to get into this?" Tara's eyebrows were halfway up her forehead. High disapproval.

"My daughter asked me a question." Self-righteous tone. A lot of emphasis on the word "daughter."

"How, Daddy?" Annie was enjoying that she appeared to be winning out over Tara.

"Well, you could lose a child like what happened to Floy. Something unexpected, something you just get hit with. Or you can lose a child because she's angry at you, doesn't want to see you anymore. Maybe you were too hard on her, or someone poisoned her mind against you. Of course, some parents and kids just drift apart—time and the river. Who knows why?

"But what scares me most is having my child taken away from me—by her mother. If I don't do everything just right."

"James, don't. Don't pull her into this. She doesn't need to…" Tara made a zipping motion across her lips.

"Well, I worry about it. When Danielle wouldn't let me see her, I—" He abruptly stopped talking.

Annie was landing forks on a runway made of mashed potatoes. She wasn't looking at her father, but her body leaned in his direction.

"When I couldn't see my baby girl, it felt like I didn't have enough air. You know? It was like I'm not going to make it."

"What are you talking about? It wasn't more than a few days." Tara's face looked pinched, irritated. She shoved her plate away. "Nice meal. I'm not so sure about the conversation."

"I'm just saying it was a bad feeling. Before Annie came along,

I never had any great need to have kids." He pointed at the child with his fork. "But afterwards, it was completely different. I could never be without her now. I have to have her; I have to see her."

"You do see me, Daddy." A wrinkle had appeared between Annie's brows.

"I know, baby girl, but there was a period your mama wouldn't let me. That's what I'm talking about. And I was kinda going out of my mind thinking I might lose you. Different from how Floy's daddy lost her, but just as real."

"Oh, for God's sake." Tara flounced off toward the bathroom.

CHAPTER 30

*A*fter I saw James and company pass in front of me at the crosswalk, my ride took me another mile or so to Yosemite Village, where I picked up my paycheck. With check in hand, I started to walk across Stoneman Bridge. I was planning to watch Half Dome do its twilight transformation from rock to fire. But I found myself retracing my steps, standing instead on the snow-covered bank of the Merced. The light had turned mean, seeping through dark trees to brush the water with a pale phosphorescence.

It fit my mood. I'd seen Danielle only once in the previous week. And that had been an exceedingly brief walk on a thawed edge of the golf course—with Annie in tow. Danielle was taking her daughter for a ski lesson at Badger, and the child was not pleased to suffer a delay.

"I've missed you," I told Danielle, while Annie ran circles chanting, "Bye-bye."

"Yeah. James seems to want to do more things with Annie during the day. But less overnights."

"I hate the caboose," Annie chimed in. "It's too cold."

"What does that mean?" I felt a ripple of panic. "That we can't—"

Danielle made a quick, two-handed gesture that resembled an

umpire's "safe" sign—which told me to drop it.

"Mama says we're not going to be here long," Annie informed me. "I've got a lesson and we can't be late." Long pause. "Why are we walking around out here?"

"'Cause it's kind of pretty." I bent toward her, smiling.

"I don't think so," Annie said decisively.

Silence. I touched Danielle's shoulder.

"Does Tara want James to herself? At night? Is that what's happening?"

Danielle shook her head, looking pointedly at Annie, and wouldn't answer me.

About ten minutes into the walk, Annie said, "I think we're going to be late."

"We still have a little more time, sweetie. Let's enjoy the walk. You know Harper was very kind to me when I had the accident. He helped me after we were hit, and then he visited me in the hospital."

"I remember him." Annie's face tightened.

"He's a friend, Annie. As a favor to me, could you be nice?"

She shrugged.

We labored uphill towards the first green. There were so many questions I wanted to ask Danielle. About how she felt about our night. About whether she'd missed me, yearned to see me—as I had her. About the distance evident between us.

Annie pulled her mother's coat, looking at me sideways like I was something that belonged in formaldehyde. "Why'd you say I could have a lesson if we're going to be here?"

Danielle sighed, hunched slightly. "I guess we'd better go."

We turned, heading back toward the bridge and the hotel. Annie, to my surprise, became engaging.

"You rolled my window down." She was referring to the accident. "It was stuck, and you opened it. Mama was in a coma." She said "coma" with a kind of reverence, like it was something both mysterious and frightening.

"It was scary, not being able to get out of there," I said.

Annie looked away. "I like those shoes," she ventured, "with the rings." She was referring to my Mexican boots.

I thanked her.

"We're going now," she said. "Good-bye. We'll be back if we ever want to play golf."

Danielle laughed. "I, for one, will be back before that." She looked uncomfortable, eyes sliding. "I'm sorry, Harper. I'm not sure exactly when, though."

That hit me. I picked up a fallen branch and threw it. I twisted away to look at some ash-colored clouds building in the east.

"Don't be upset. I wish I could call you, but you haven't got a phone."

"I could wait by the pay phone at a certain time; we could arrange it."

"I never know for sure when Annie is finally getting to bed. I do want to; I can tell you feel—"

She never finished because Annie was pulling her hand. "Bye," the child waved cheerfully to me.

Danielle gave a helpless shrug. "As soon as there's another overnight, I'll try..." She didn't finish that either.

The visit left me depressed. My night with Danielle had opened a searing hunger in me. Yet the uncertainty of when I would see her—or whether she even wanted to—added a feeling of emptiness to my yearning.

So I stood on the bank of the Merced, the sacred waters of the Ahwahneeches, replaying the visit with Danielle and Annie in my mind, trying to find a reason to believe we could somehow be together. Yet as I watched the water rub along the ice and sand, I began to feel that I'd never have her. And a quixotic idea took shape, that for years I would go on seeking Danielle, trying to draw her closer, trying to overcome a fate bent on sending us to our separate lives.

It was getting cold. The light was starting to fade. The moon came out. I tried to imagine where I would go from here. As darkness mounted the gray cliffs, I wrote a poem—which I include as a document of my mood.

The Fording Place

The water's still and cold.
Rocks shine
in the white, ungiving moon.

Somewhere, in a warmer season,
a trellis breaks
in the labyrinth of one rose.

But here the water glitters,
a river of shards.
Again I see that fording place

where some have tried to cross
above the deep cascade.
Someday when the ice

grows thin,
the visit is long overdue,
I will step in.

The stones are slippery
but the chance
becomes everything there is.

I never showed it to Danielle.

CHAPTER 31

*F*agan's pickup rattled along the trolley tracks descending Taraval Street. A slate-colored ocean rose above a canyon of storefronts lining the road. Crushed in the cab were James, Tara, Annie, and Bill himself. They were heading to Fleishhacker Zoo—at 48th, three blocks south of Taraval.

At that moment, the quartet was in the middle of an argument about Mark Twain's famous quote: "The coldest winter I ever spent was a summer in San Francisco." Tara had worked for a summer in Barrows, on the shore of the Arctic Ocean, and took the position that Twain was an idiot and had never been to Alaska.

"The coldest summer I ever spent was in fooking Dublin." Fagan was leaning against the wheel, looking over at Tara on the far side of the cab. "I worked at a farmer's market—starting five a.m. So cold you could feel nothing with yer fingers; they were like cylinders of lead. The whole city is a fooking refrigerator."

"My tree house is cold," Annie said.

"Why is that, baby girl?"

"Because it's in a tree. Trees are cold."

"Why?"

"Because they live outside. And when they get snowed on, they never get warm again."

Everyone was amused and agreed heartily—except Tara, who

wanted Annie to know that trees didn't have nervous systems and, therefore, couldn't feel cold.

This bit of science didn't go over well.

After Fagan parked the truck near the entrance to the zoo, he was oddly reluctant to leave the cab. The man seemed nervous, twisting his neck to look up and down the street. Tara and Annie were already on the sidewalk; James walked around to stand at the driver's window. He and Fagan were discussing something in low tones. After a minute or two, Fagan pointed down the block—toward the corner of Sloat and 48th.

Now he was all action, popping out of the truck and instructing Tara to take Annie through the gate. "James and I will catch up with you at the hippos—say half an hour. We've got a little something to attend to."

Tara walked to the entrance, but she didn't go in as instructed. Instead she watched James and Fagan walk cautiously toward a rust bucket VW van. As they approached, the sliding door opened. And a cloud of smoke wafted out to join the stiff breeze blowing toward Lake Merced.

What she was watching, Tara learned later, was a drug deal. The men in the van—long-haired and sporting tie-dyed thermal undershirts—had suggested this meeting place to discuss a bulk purchase of Bill and James's mountain-grown dope.

The conversation was thick with gestures and finger-pointing. Fagan glanced up and down the street. Then, oddly, he surveyed the sky—which had high clouds with dark cumulus piling to the west.

Tara felt Annie pulling her sleeve, trying to urge her through the gate. But Tara waited until the boys climbed into the back of the van and the sliding door shut them out of sight.

Once inside the zoo, Annie became a font of excitement. She dragged Tara to see the gorillas, the gibbons, and some of the exotic birds. While they waited for her father at the hippo house, Annie wanted to know about gorillas.

"Do they have to be careful with their children because they're so strong? Could they hug them to death?"

"I suppose so. But that's not special to gorillas. A man could do that. Believe me, men are strong. When they're angry, they can do a lot of damage…to a child. Believe me."

"How do you know?"

"I'm not going to tell you, OK? But I know, believe me."

When Fagan and James finally showed up, they were dark and irritable.

"What was all that about?" Tara asked them. Her voice could do surgery.

James shrugged. "Business."

"If it's the kind of business I think it is, you shouldn't be doing it with" and she nodded toward Annie. "You don't know what's going to happen, what she could be exposed to."

"Don't go pouring Coke in the gas tank, Tara. It's just some hippies hoping to score a few lids."

Annie was standing in front of a peanut vendor, gesturing that she wanted to buy some.

"OK, baby girl," James shouted. "Let's see if any of those fat old elephants can catch a peanut. Shall we? You ever seen that? An elephant pull a peanut out of the air with his trunk?"

James's burst of good cheer wasn't doing much for Fagan, who walked with his hands in his pockets, eyes drifting randomly from cage to cage.

"Come on, Bill." James took his friend's arm. "We'll deal with it tomorrow. Right now we're gonna feed the elephants and forget it."

The shorter Fagan pushed up to get his lips near the big man's ear. Then talked so loud Tara heard him anyway. "Why couldn't they have just done it now, instead of waiting? Huh, you understand that?"

James whispered his answer. But, a few minutes later, he was talking about going to some of the used-car lots in Daly City and looking for a Malibu.

My guess is there was a good deal more money involved than James was telling Tara. If he was expecting a big chunk of change, maybe the hippies had been forced to go away and raise more capital.

They remained at the zoo another few hours, during which James and Annie got deep into a discussion about safaris and poachers, how they destroyed much of the African wildlife. Annie was horrified.

"There aren't many tigers left?"

"No."

"And there aren't many elephants?"

"No."

"What about monkeys?"

"They don't hunt monkeys much."

"Do they still have a lot of them?"

"I think so."

Annie brightened. "Good. They're my favorite."

As they walked, Tara drifted away by herself; Fagan continued to brood. Above them, somber clouds from the west had begun to gather, knitting into a huge bank that threatened rain.

The last stop was Monkey Island.

"There're sure a lot of them," Annie said. "But there's a lot more of them in Africa?"

"Yes, baby girl."

"And they don't hunt them? They're safe?"

"Yes, sweetie."

"I heard they hunt the gorillas," Tara said.

"No, they don't, not much." James gave his girlfriend a hard look. "Isn't that right, Tara? Now that you think about it?"

Tara shrugged. "Nobody cares much about monkeys. They don't have tusks, they don't have much meat. So hunters leave them alone, I guess."

"Right," James said. "So the monkeys are safe, baby girl." He lifted Annie and brought her face next to his. He kissed her, making a loud smacking sound. "It's all good, and tonight we're at Grandma's. And you can help her make oatmeal cookies."

"I don't like raisins."

"Then they won't have any stinking raisins."

I don't know if they made cookies when they visited James's mother. Or anything much about it. Tara was vague on this subject. But I know her opinion of the old lady. "Battle-ax with a heart of shrapnel," she once described her.

The next morning—which was a Sunday—Fagan drove every-one to the archery range in Golden Gate Park. It was beginning to drizzle, but he had rejected all suggestions that the group wait to see if things dried up. Fagan said he was going to show Annie and Tara how to shoot a crossbow.

The range consisted of a wide grass field, with a row of haystacks propped up at one end. Fagan unfolded a target, and pressed big nails into the haystack to attach it. Cocking the crossbow, he handed the weapon to Annie. Which she immediately dropped because it was too heavy. Fagan tried again. Same result.

"I'll hold it for her and she can press the trigger," James said.

"No, I can hold it."

"Annie, it weighs a ton. Let me do it."

The child was trying to pull it out of her father's hands. He let go and she dropped it—but not before firing an arrow into the grass, causing the crossbow to buck and knock her over.

"OK, Annie, it's time to be careful." Fagan pulled the arrow out of the ground.

"I don't like arrow things. I don't want to do it." Annie was on her feet, backing away from the weapon.

"Then I'll try," Tara said, picking up the bow and handing it to Fagan. "Set it up so I can shoot."

For the next half hour, Fagan gave Tara a lesson. Standing behind her, touching her arms and shoulders to get the stance right. Arrows went to ground all over the hillside behind the haystack. Meanwhile, James and Annie took a walk in a eucalyptus grove near the range, foraging for the long strips of bark shed by the trees. They decided to cut these into thin, weavable ribbons to make a rug for Annie's puppets.

At around ten-thirty, a rust-stained VW chugged into the park-ing lot. Fagan recognized it, and gave a loud call to James, who short-ly emerged with Annie from the forest. The two hippies met them halfway up the range, today sporting sweatshirts with different ver-sions of the Grateful Dead skull-and-roses logo.

The conversation had the same look as the day before—a lot of arm movement, a lot of emotional heat. Then one of the hippies, whose hair was tied in a blond ponytail, produced a plastic bag. Tara heard the word "ludes" rising from their murmurings. The other hippie—with flowing brown hair and beard, looking like a holy card of Jesus—slid a second plastic bag from the pocket of his sweatshirt.

At the sight of this, Fagan went into a rage. He slapped the bag to the ground, spilling dark-colored capsules. Tara could hear him say, "I want money; I don't want that shite. I won't take it. I won't be a fooking peddler of shite." He and James walked away, back to where Tara and Annie were standing.

But the hippies followed them. "Don't fuck this up, this is a good deal," ponytail said.

Jesus had a different agenda. He was pointing at Fagan. "You're gonna pay for that shit—however much we lost. You're gonna stay here till we count how much we lost. Then you're gonna pay for it with the weed."

By now, Fagan had reached Tara. He plucked the crossbow out of her hands and turned to face the hippies.

"Which one of you pillheads wants an arrow in his gut? Just say the word and you can have one. A gift from me to you."

"Whoa, man. You don't want to get all freaky about this. We can be brothers about this, man. We can work this out." Jesus looked like he was about ready to speak in tongues. Or soil himself.

"I don't fooking care about working anything out. And for fooking sure I don't want to be your brother. Just leave."

The men backed away, arms half-raised. "Can we pick up our shit?"

"Get the bag, but forget whatever spilled."

Ponytail bent to retrieve the pills. "This is fucked up, man. It's fucking bad business."

"Keep going." Fagan gestured with the crossbow in the direction of the van. "You know what's bad business? Not bringing all the money. If you make a deal, fooking keep it."

Fagan fired an arrow into the ground near Jesus' feet. Reloaded.

"Fuck, you're crazy, man." They sprinted for the VW.

Fagan walked to the edge of the road, listening to the motor catch and gun. The gears started to grind, the engine making its characteristic chirping sound as the van pulled away. Fagan lifted his bow and pulled the trigger. The van's back window exploded. Beads of safety glass blew across the asphalt like rolling diamonds. The van hesitated; Fagan started to reload. Then the driver hit the gas and the old VW lurched around a copse of scrawny pines and out of sight.

Fagan stood in the road and looked after it, eyes flaming. At that moment, a Chrysler drove by him, heading in the same direction as the van.

"What'd you do that for?" James was enraged. "What the fuck, man?"

"Keep your shirt on. It's no biggie."

But that's where Fagan was wrong. In the first place, Annie ran off into the trees, and it took Tara twenty minutes to find her. There was also the little problem that someone in the Chrysler hadn't liked Bill's idea of target practice, and apparently called the police.

A cop showed up while James was still ranting at Fagan, blaming him for Annie's disappearance. The patrolman, young and pink, and looking like a Hitler youth, immediately relieved Fagan of his crossbow. Then got down to the task of checking IDs.

"Mr. Fagan, we had a report that someone shot out the window of a passing car. With a bow and arrow. Would you know anything about that?"

"News to me."

"I see a lot of shattered glass here, Mr. Fagan. Know anything about that?"

"Not a thing, Officer."

The patrolman led Fagan to where his arrow lay buried in the lawn, halfway to the target.

"Did you shoot this?"

"I may have. I'm not very good. I'm learning."

"It's thirty yards from the nearest target," the patrolman observed dryly.

Fagan nodded. "The thing slipped. I'm thinking of taking up a different sport."

"I wouldn't recommend guns," the cop said.

"Peashooters maybe." Fagan laughed, trying to get on the officer's good side.

"Did you know," the cop said, "that someone who shot an arrow into a car would be guilty of reckless endangerment, possibly even attempted murder? Were you aware of that, Mr. Fagan?"

Tara listened to this conversation from the edge of the eucalyptus grove. She had Annie's hand, and they were hiding behind a fallen tree. "Stay quiet," she whispered. "The cop might arrest them, and we don't want to get taken too."

Annie, who'd already been crying, started to sob. Tara put a hand over the girl's mouth, and crouched down to look at her.

"Don't! He'll hear you. Then we might end up in jail."

Annie's eyes were filled with fear. "Are they going to take Daddy to jail?"

"I don't know. Just be quiet and watch."

What they saw was the patrolman pointing to Fagan's pickup. There was a discussion about whether the cop had a right to search it.

"I believe there's Miranda laws," Fagan declared.

"That has to do with confessions—not relevant here."

"Well, I mean search and seizure. You can't just do that. The Supreme Court says you have to have cause." Fagan was talking at a machine-gun clip.

"Probable cause. That's right. We have to have probable cause that a crime has been committed. Which we do, Mr. Fagan. With the shooting at the vehicle." The cop hooked his thumbs in his holster belt.

"I know nothing about that."

"The description we got of the shooter matches you, Mr. Fagan. You see what I'm getting at? That's probable cause."

The cop pointed to the ground, and demanded James and Fagan sit on the spot. He went to his cruiser to make a call.

Five or six minutes later, another squad car pulled up. Tara watched while the new cop began a search of the pickup. He was fat, with a nose that looked like the inside of a pomegranate.

The first patrolman continued his questioning of Fagan: "Were you having any disagreements with anyone while you were here at the archery range?"

"We were just teaching—"

"He was teaching me," James interrupted Fagan. "I asked him

to give me some pointers, but neither of us were enjoying it. The blind-leading-the-blind sort of thing."

The cop surveyed the scattered arrows and nodded. The fat patrolman began wiggling backwards out of the camper shell.

"What's this?" he said with a drawl, holding up a cardboard box. "Lots of plastic bags in here with some kind of ground-up leaves in 'em. You bo-ez aren't chefs, are you? Carrying a lifetime supply of thyme and oregano?" He laughed.

He opened and sniffed one of the bags. "Uh oh. I don't think you bo-ez cook with this, do you?"

Five minutes later, James and Bill had been cuffed and pushed into the back of a squad car.

"You bo-ez watch your heads now, getting in the car. 'Cause you don't got anything to help with the pain." He laughed again, revealing a big gap in his front teeth.

As soon as the squad cars departed, Tara pulled Annie to her feet. "We got to go now, honey. I know where Bill hides his spare key in the truck. We got to get out of here before the cops find out we were with them."

"What would they do?" Annie was standing like she'd been nailed to the ground.

"I'd probably end up in jail. And you'd spend a few nights in juvie, guest of Child Protective Services."

Annie started to cry again. A thin, keening sound. She tried to pull away.

Tara yanked the girl's arm. "No, we've got to go."

Annie held back. "What's juvie?"

"I'm not going into it, OK? But, believe me, I know what it is. And you're gonna end up there if I don't get you home to your mama."

Annie still kept herself planted. "What is it?"

"It's where you go if your parents aren't fit to take care of you. Like right now with your father going to jail. Come on!"

Annie stumbled and fell, but Tara jerked her up by one arm, and pulled her on a dead run to Fagan's pickup.

CHAPTER 32

he wall sconces are faded. On each is printed the same fire-hollowed sequoia. Light shines around the tree. Like the radiance at the edge of clouds. The floor slants beneath me, tables and chairs leaning together. The diners leaning. For a hundred years there have been voices here, the click of plates and glasses, a sudden, high-pitched laughter. Across the lawn, they have watched the pines consume light, the light consume years. I see my silverware press slightly on the thick tablecloth.

Danielle left a note on my door. It was a Friday, two weeks after our night together in Moore Cottage. Annie was going with her dad to San Francisco for the weekend. Would I like to get picked up on Saturday, noon?

I talked Frank Riles into taking my shift, and called Danielle to confirm. She said she had some shopping to do in Oakhurst, and would I mind coming along? Needless to say, I didn't mind. We chatted; I told her nothing about my angst the previous week.

I hadn't been in her Jeep ten minutes when she started to open me like a letter.

"You've been upset," she said. "It's not this minute, but I can feel it. It's something to do with me."

Nowhere to hide.

"I missed you," I said. Long pause. "I was...afraid. That something made you want to pull back."

"What?"

"I don't know." We were going through the park gates now. The ranger waved, seeing Danielle's familiar face. "Maybe there was something wrong with—"

"You mean when we went to bed?"

I nodded.

"No, there was nothing wrong, Harper."

"Is there something else?"

"No, the only thing wrong is how scared and little boy you are about this."

I felt struck down. Silenced. The road twisted in front of us. We pushed through Fish Camp, the lake just below Danielle's house. Then passed the turnoff to the Sugar Pine Railroad.

"I've hurt you. I'm sorry," she said. "Look, what happened was good. But you're so scared it wasn't, that I feel like you're collapsing on me, caving in. I feel like I've got to carry you."

I went down again. For the count. The world was a relentless white, full of canyons and rivers where nothing spoke, nothing was human. I imagined walking up a trail till the cold made me sleepy, and then just lying down.

"Stop it, Harper. This is what it's like. Being with me. This is what you signed up for. If we're going to do this, it has to be without walls. You asked for this. Remember? The glass houses? There's no other way."

"OK." I looked for clarifying words. There weren't any. Finally I said, "You're right. It makes me weak. Being afraid of you."

Danielle nodded. The snowbanks rose above us, turning the road into a white canyon. "It's OK." She touched my arm. "We'll deal with it."

In Oakhurst, Danielle parked next to an old-fashioned toy store. I say old-fashioned because you didn't see brands like Mattel and Hasbro. There was no Barbie, no Hot Wheels or GI Joe. Instead there were exquisite wooden trucks, trains, hobby horses, dollhouses. The owner's father made many of the toys—from templates handed down from the nineteenth century.

Danielle was getting a house for Annie's puppets. Something she'd commissioned and paid for in layaway installments. The old man came out of the back to greet her. He had a full head of white hair and matching mustache, a thin aquiline nose, and green eyes that shifted constantly between Danielle and me. He shook our hands. His Pendleton shirt—with worn leather patches on the sleeves—smelled of Ben Gay.

"I enjoyed this puppet house," he said, the word "puppet" lilting up, the "Ps" exploding. "To make such big rooms—much bigger than for dolls. I had to make a new pattern, yes?"

I realized the accent was German.

"My daughter says, 'Why? Why work so hard on one house?' And I say why not?" He smiled, the wrinkles deepening on his face. A radiance. "It's so big, but I couldn't make it heavy. So the roof is tin instead of wood. And some of it is braced with balsa—strong but light. It was an interesting problem to solve, yes? But I will show you."

He brought it from the back. I was amazed at how beautifully it was crafted. Doors and windows that opened, the rooms painted cheery colors, a staircase with railing to the second floor. We both exclaimed over it.

"Yes, it is lovely. I say so myself. Here is the chair you gave me for the scale." He handed Danielle a rough-made plywood seat. "So big. Seven rooms—plus attic." He shook his head. "The puppets will live very happily in this house. I will wrap it, yes? I have the butcher paper."

While the old fellow cut sheets from a big roll of paper, Danielle drifted to the front of the store to a counter that sold jewelry. Mostly suitable for little girls. She seemed to examine several items shown by the toymaker's daughter, but I hardly noticed. My eyes were still mostly filled with the puppet house.

When we'd loaded the big package into the Jeep, Danielle seemed very pleased with herself. "It took me six months to pay for it. He told me it wouldn't be done for Christmas, but I didn't care. It's so special. I think I wanted to see Annie completely surprised. Expecting nothing. Just an ordinary day, and there it is."

Danielle had the key in the ignition, but didn't turn it. She was looking at a bank of dirty snow next to an old brick warehouse.

"What's so interesting over there?"

"Nothing. It's just that I bought something. You might think it's silly."

"Show me."

She got out a small cardboard box. Inside was a pair of stud earrings, with small round stones, ruby colored. Danielle put one in her ear. The other she attached to the lapel of my flannel shirt.

"It's for us," she said. "Whenever you feel scared about how I feel or what's happening," she ran her hand back and forth between us, "look at it. Touch it. And know that I'm wearing the other one."

I couldn't help it. Tears started to well in my eyes.

"Yeah," she said, and kissed my cheek where the glistening path had started to form.

Danielle's house on Silver Tip Lane looked smaller than I remembered from my first visit. Only one window faced the street. The logs were dark, charred looking, and the paint on the honey-colored shutters was starting to peel. The porch where James and I had fought had a few cracked boards, and the brown paint was mostly missing.

Inside the house was cold, and Danielle lit the fire in a granite hearth big enough to sit in. I wandered through the rooms while she watched the flame catch in the kindling. On the right side of the house was a combination living room/dining room filled with old comfortable furniture and a big mahogany table scarred by a plethora of knicks and scratches. On the left side was the kitchen and two small bedrooms. The patchwork quilt from our night in Wawona was on a double bed in the back bedroom. Its window had white, polka-dot curtains and a view of Fish Camp's pea-sized lake. An old-fashioned cherry dresser supported an ornate, possibly hand-carved mirror frame. On the wall opposite the window was a cedar hope chest, with lovely, stylized roses edging three sides of the lid.

"It was my grandmother's." Danielle had come up behind me. "I went back and got it. Just basically walked in and said I'm taking this. All the other things—my bed, my lamp that I got from her—I left behind. But I had to have her chest—where she put the linens and the blankets she made before she got married."

"It's beautiful," I said, touching the narrow cushion that had been designed to expose the carved rosebuds. "Do you sit on it?"

"Yeah. It's solid as a block of granite. Besides, the room doesn't have space for a chair, so this is it."

After a moment more of examining her room, Danielle asked me to get the puppet house out of the Jeep and put it on Annie's bed. Then we stood together in front of the fire.

I felt intense hunger to touch her. Danielle bent with a fire iron to adjust the logs. Her hips, the long curve of her back, her dark hair parting over the white line of her neck were so beautiful to me that I felt it as a physical pressure. Pushing, permeating me.

When she stood up, she wiped the soot from her hands on her jeans. She looked at me, slowly rolling up the sleeves of her cowboy shirt.

"It's getting warm in here," she said.

Silence.

"You want to touch me." It was a statement.

I nodded.

"But you don't want to be a boy who can't wait. Who can't think of anything else." She was smiling.

I nodded again.

"Do you want to touch this?" She put her hand on her buttocks. "It's OK," she whispered.

I felt its lovely curve, the strength of the underlying muscle.

"Do you want to touch me here?" The tone was slightly teasing, but I could hear Danielle's breathing change. Her fingers pressed for a moment against her pubis.

Then I touched her in that place, feeling her body open, leaning against me. We kissed.

Again Danielle wanted to undress herself. She suggested we do it together, watching each other. When our clothes were on the floor, she took me into her bedroom. In the curtains' filtered light, her skin was moon colored, her hair raven black and cascading against her shoulders and breasts.

She knelt at the foot of the bed, sitting back on her haunches. She pointed to the far end. "You go there," she said. "I want to just look at you. And you can look at me."

I knelt by the pillows. Shrugged.

"I know," she said, "you're not sure what to do. Let's just feel this, what it's like before we do anything. Feel how turned on we are, how much we want each other. OK?"

I smiled, nodded. In her eyes was a dense emotion I couldn't read. I tried to tell her, without words, that I loved her. That she was the only thing important to me.

Danielle lowered her eyes. "Yes," she said. She put her hands flat on the quilt. "Can you tell what I'm feeling?"

I shook my head.

"I love you too, Harper. I don't know how this happened, but I know for sure now." She hesitated, looking hard at me. "I know for sure."

For a little while, we continued to kneel at our ends of the bed.

Then she said, "I'm ready. Inside I'm ready for you." She laughed. "And I can see you're ready for me."

Danielle looked for a fleeting moment at her grandmother's chest. I didn't know what it meant, but her eyes were soft when they returned to me.

"Pull the covers and lie back," she said.

When I had done it, she crawled forward, arms and legs on either side of my body. She kissed me, very sweetly, and lowered herself until her belly touched mine. The warmth of her skin flooded me.

"You want me this way," she said. "I can feel what your body wants."

She kissed me again, letting her mouth open as she moved so I could enter her.

The next morning we slept in. When we awoke, Danielle made me pancakes. Then she had chores—laundry and cleaning—which I helped with as best I could. Danielle found a ribbon to wrap around Annie's present.

"I can't wait till she sees it," she said. "I've looked forward a long time to this."

I felt a sudden jealousy—about this moment in her life I wouldn't be part of.

Outside it started to snow, random flakes drifting in a wind that kept changing direction. The fire was dying, and cold was seeping into the house. Danielle got it roaring again. We dragged her mattress into the living room and lay down, covering ourselves with her mother's quilt.

It felt heavy. Safe. We kissed and talked. Danielle asked again about my father, how I felt at that moment about the loss.

"I feel him receding; he isn't around, he isn't watching me. All I wish is that I'd said good-bye to him. I let him die without that. It was wrong. He raised me. He kept me when my mother left. He deserved better."

Danielle pulled me closer. "It's sad. It's like he was totally shut down, and all he had was religion and books. There was nothing he could give you. And when he needed something, when he was dying, it came back around. And you had nothing for him."

That did me in.

After a long while, I pulled back to look at her. "What's going to happen with Annie and us?"

Danielle took a breath and let the air out with a hissing noise. "I don't know. I'm not ready to tell her yet, Harper. I think she'd resist you. And do everything she could to push you out of our lives." Danielle put her hand on my chest. "I don't think I could stand being torn like that."

We were quiet for a while. Listening to a pulsing wind, to the sap crackling in the burning logs. And a branch somewhere at the back of the house scratching against a window.

"I don't want to scare her again—that there might be some big change. She had more than enough of that when I had the accident."

I understood. It meant I would have to live with the long intervals between visits. I would have to accept it with grace, or force a choice on Danielle that could destroy us.

"Is that going to be OK?" she asked.

I was quiet for a moment. Then I said: "It's OK. I have my ruby pin."

We made love then. And afterward we slept.

At around three-thirty, the clapper on the front door began to bang. Danielle sat up in alarm. Then she heard Annie's voice.

"Mama. Open up, Mama. Daddy's with the police."

Danielle stood naked and threw my clothes at me.

"Harper, you have to go. Out the bedroom window. OK? She can't see you." Voice sharp with urgency. "Go. I'll see you as soon as I can."

To Annie she shouted, "Coming, sweetie. I was napping. I've got to get my robe on."

Outside the back window, I felt the crush of the cold. The snow was driving now—from the north. Like a soft, frigid wave. I buttoned my old wool coat. The last thing I heard was Tara saying: "They're fucked. They're gonna do time in County."

CHAPTER 33

I once asked Danielle what she felt when she "knew" things, when she read someone's emotions. I wondered if she heard actual words, or perhaps sensed people with impressionist images.

"It's more like I lose my skin," she said. "Like my edges dissolve. And there's nothing separating me from the other person. Whatever they feel, that's going to be my feeling too. For a long time I couldn't tell whose emotion it was—it was like being a radio receiver and I didn't know what station I was listening to."

"OK, but what does it *feel* like?"

"I feel it in my chest—almost like a pressure, a force that penetrates me. It's weird, I might be going along feeling calm. And suddenly I'm not. I'm sad, I'm hurt, I'm scared. I feel literally hit by the feeling.

"But it's not just emotions. It's attitudes, intentions, desires. I feel them in people like I feel my own. When you're scared of me, and trying to hide, *I* feel fear. I feel like crawling into some safe place and covering myself."

"So if I'm imagining something—a mental picture—you couldn't see it?"

"Not unless there was a really big emotion to go with it. What I think happens then is I create a picture in my head that comes from the emotion. Like when I could see what James wanted sexually. It started with feeling this incredible brutality, this desire to humiliate. Then I saw these fragments, a flash of what he wanted to do. But those were *my* pictures, not his."

So that was how it worked. Danielle, the empath, could read the moment with astounding clarity. But she was no clairvoyant. For all her awareness in the present, Danielle's future remained as dark and hidden as it was for the rest of us.

"We're going down," James said. "I know it."

"Why'd you say that?" Fagan hit James with his manacled wrist. "You going fruitcake like your wife? Gonna be a fooking seer?"

"I can tell, that's all." James shifted in the creaking chair, leaning away from his friend. "I can feel it coming."

"For fook sake, hold yer water."

They were bedecked in orange jumpsuits, with cuffs and leg chains, waiting for arraignment in a courtroom at the San Francisco Hall of Justice. Tara was with them. The holding cell smelled of vomit and antiseptic. The walls were institutional beige, with more scuff marks than a barroom dance floor. One of the fluorescent tubes above them flickered.

"I called Danielle," James said.

Tara looked at him sharply. "That was a waste."

Silence. James was pinching little creases along the pant leg of his jumpsuit.

"I wanted to know if Annie was all right."

"That kid's made of steel. She's fine."

Fagan pointed to Tara. "I'm glad you got the truck. And they didn't impound it."

"I knew where the key was. I kept Annie hidden in the trees till the cops left. Then we hightailed it back to Fish Camp."

"So one thing went right anyway. The cops probably think the truck was stolen." Fagan gave a mirthless laugh. He tried to hook one arm over the back of the chair, but the chain at his waist prevented him. "This shite'll drive you loony. You can't fooking move. No wonder there's so much violence in prison. When they finally take yer chains off, all you want to do is hit somebody."

"Danielle isn't going to let me see Annie anymore." James spoke in a soft voice.

"No? She say that?" Tara didn't sound interested.

"Yeah." Almost a whisper now. "She was cold as the grave. She said she wasn't going to let me put Annie in danger again."

James was creasing both pant legs. Then smoothing them out and starting over. A guard came in—sixtyish, heavyset, with sunken eyes and a fringe of salt-and-pepper hair.

"Stand up, they'll be calling you next," he said. "The judge don't want to wait. Gotta be smooth as an assembly line." He turned to Tara. "Visit's over."

Bill and James stood, with the requisite shuffling and chain rattling. The taller man bent slightly, touching his friend's arm. "I don't think I'm going to be able to take this."

"You mean jail?" Fagan asked.

"No. What's gonna happen with Annie."

"She'll be fine, for Christ's sake. She's got her noot-case mother fawning over her. Let's worry about us, for a change. We've got some shite we've got to get through here."

"It's not Annie, it's me. I don't think I can take not seeing her." James's eyes darted around the holding cell. His hands patted his chest. "You know what I mean?"

Tara, on her way out, spoke from the door. "Danielle relented before. If you make bail, you might see Annie this weekend."

"No, I won't see her. Danielle's gone hard now, she won't let my girl near me. I know it."

"Don't drive yourself noots about it, OK?" Fagan was chewing a fingernail with some relish; he spit it out in the direction of the guard.

The door to the courtroom opened, and they were signaled to walk through. "OK, gentlemen," the guard said, "time for your thirty seconds in court. Don't blink or you might miss it."

The guard escorted them to a table, chains tinkling as they shuffled forward. Their lawyer was already seated—pink cheeks, center-parted hair brushed in two big loops across his forehead, a near invisible mustache. The man looked about fifteen.

"Your Honor." The lawyer rose. "I haven't yet had a chance to confer with my clients, but—"

"What do you plead?" Loud, stentorian voice, blasting across the courtroom.

"Not guilty, Your Honor."

"What a surprise." The judge looked at the defendants and coughed. "Seems that no one's ever guilty in this courtroom."

The bailiff suppressed a giggle.

"In the matter of bail?" the lawyer asked uncertainly.

The judge again regarded the accused. He had a Roman nose on a thick, pasty face that might never have been touched by the sun. One hand gently pressed his comb-over; a polka-dot bow tie peeked above his robes.

"The defen-dants," the syllables enunciated like a battering ram, "live in Mari-posa County, and may there-fore be a flight risk."

"He's greased us up," Fagan whispered. So loud Tara could hear in the audience. "Now watch him fook us."

CHAPTER 34

Dear Dani:

It's crazy here. A lot of protesters got arrested on the weekend and the jail's filled up. All night they're chanting, "No more war" and "Fuck Nixon." They're singing "We Shall Overcome" in their cells.

We're trying to make bail. Bill's having Tara sell his truck so we can pay this bloodsucking bail bondsman. Hope to be home for the weekend.

Dani, I'm asking you to please reconsider about me not seeing Annie. I have to see my girl. Above all else, she's what matters to me. I don't know how to say this so you'll understand.

I think of Annie. I imagine her. How her face gets all these expressions when she's talking for her puppets. How she pretends all these different moods for them. Sometimes I think about how she looks when she's concentrating, how her forehead gets that little wrinkle. How she gets all popeyed, with that funny lopsided smile when she finds a frog.

Then I think about never seeing those things again. I can't stand that. Can you understand me, Dani, when I say I can't stand that? Can you imagine what you'd feel like, never seeing Annie again?

I know my life is fucked. I don't care about it. I'm numb. Maybe you're going to hold it against me that I'm feeling like this. It wouldn't surprise me. But I'm asking you, let me see my girl when I get home.

James

The letter was sent from jail, the same day as the arraignment. I know Danielle read it because she showed it to me three weeks later.

CHAPTER 35

*S*now was dusting the tables and railings of the deck at Badger Pass. The air was still, cutting. A plume of smoke rose from the stack above the fry kitchen of the Snowflake Room. On the slopes, a straggling group of late-afternoon skiers pressed through the flurries.

Danielle, her dark locks imprisoned in a hairnet, was flipping hamburgers. She stood hand on hip, one foot stepping on the other. In the back of the kitchen, a college-age girl wore a paper cap over a halo of blonde wisps. She worked an assembly line of maybe twenty plates, dropping onto each a bag of chips, a bun, tomato, pickle, and a shred of deceased lettuce.

Periodically, Danielle dumped a cooked burger on a plate, and hit the bell to signal the arrival of another Curry Company meal. At around four o'clock, according to her journal, a tall man stationed himself near the window where the servers picked up orders. When Danielle saw him, she froze.

"Hi, James."

He waved stiffly, fingers splayed. "Hey, Dani."

"I can't talk, I'm working."

"I just got off. Not enough people skiing so they told us to go home."

Danielle shrugged, turned back to the grill.

"I'll wait till you're done."

"No. I'm glad you made bail. That was good. But—"

"I gotta talk to you."

"No, James. I already said all I had to say." She was pressing the patties with her spatula, watching the fat sizzle.

"I'll wait."

"Don't, James. Please."

Silence.

"There's no point in this." She made a wiping motion across one cheek. "I've decided; there's nothing to talk about."

"I'll wait."

Danielle concentrated on the black expanse of griddle. She scraped it with the edge of the spatula. Grease and pieces of charred meat fell into the trough. She laid out a half-dozen patties. Adding cheese to some; watching it darken and melt.

When Danielle looked up, James was still there. Her stomach clutched. She felt the first shards of sadness. Cutting. Filling her with blood. She got the image of a street, Annie walking on the other side with someone. With her! But the sun was obscured. And the street impassable—a canyon that could never be crossed. She could see it in flashes—mother and child were still strolling the far sidewalk. With someone watching, someone left out: James. James lost on the other side.

It was too painful. Danielle looked away from him.

The waitress brought a new order, clipping it to the revolving wheel that hung above the serving window. When Danielle turned and yanked it down, she saw that James was rooted in place. Arms crossed. Legs spread in a wide stance. An almost violent forbearance.

Danielle leaned into the window. "Good-bye, James." Her voice was thick. Holding back anger.

No response. James's only movement was to shift his gaze to the floor.

"You think you're Mahatma Gandhi or something?" She threw a piece of lettuce in his direction.

James held his station until five o'clock, when the kitchen closed. The windows lining the south side of the dining room were nearly black. The snow was heavier now, shining with reflected light as it dropped across the panes.

Danielle threw her apron in a hamper. She removed her hairnet, shaking out the long tresses and combing them with her fingers. As she emerged from the kitchen, James spread his arms. A gesture that might have been beseeching. Or a blockade.

"James, I'm going home. I've got to pick up Annie." Danielle tried to slide by to the right, between his body and a table. She felt the brush of his hand as she turned away. Lightly across the shoulders. Almost a caress.

Danielle now sensed in James a great tenderness, a yearning for the past. All they had been together—all the years of a man showing a girl how to live—was slipping away. His eyes glittered with moisture.

Yet, when James spoke, none of the softness reached his voice. "You can't keep a man from his daughter. It isn't right."

Danielle looked back while she kept walking. "A man's job is to protect his child," she told him over her shoulder. "You don't know how to do that."

"It isn't right, Dani." His voice was louder, to cross the growing space between them.

She was moving fast, weaving between the tables. When Danielle reached the stairs, she paused. "I wish it could be different," she said before she disappeared.

It was a small gift. Not enough. A dozen people were still eating. They all looked at James.

The tall man bowed. "Thank you for watching," he said to the dining room. He turned and walked into the deserted kitchen.

By the thin light trickling through the serving window, James made his way to the sink. It was a deep basin, stainless steel. Carefully, he placed both hands on the edge, leaning slightly. And didn't move. James later told Tara he felt an unexpected calmness. As if he were a fighter who had dropped his arms. Who was stretched on the canvas, not even feeling the last blow. Delicately, with almost no sound, he threw up.

Fifteen minutes later, the manager of the snack shop flipped the lights. The hard neon caught James in a chair, a plastic tub of potato salad between his legs. While the manager stood there, McAllister took a scoop with a big mixing spoon, gently inserting the tip in his mouth.

"Good," he said. "Quite tasty. I'm surprised."

CHAPTER 36

*T*wo things happened on February 21 that had no effect on anything—yet I remember them because each had a distinct quality of pain. And each, in its own way, bespoke the kind of blindness Danielle and I were drifting toward.

The first event was a letter from my sister. I remember it imperfectly. She was suggesting a visit; I think during her Easter break from med school. The letter started out in a newsy style. Brook was getting married in the summer—she had picked out a church, the invitations would soon be sent. She was sixth in her class, had secured an internship at Johns Hopkins.

But then, as I recall, the letter took a turn. Brook talked about our father's death, how the three months since he was buried had changed some of her feelings. She had always been disgusted by his religiosity. He was too busy reading theology, she said, to pay attention to his kids. "He could pass judgment, but he couldn't ask about our day at school."

Now she regretted skipping the funeral. She wished she hadn't left me alone with it. She wished she could have seen our father in the casket; maybe she would have forgiven him, let go of the man. Or of her anger.

She signed off asking how I was. And, unnecessarily, providing her phone number.

But I didn't call. I didn't even go to the wedding. I may have written, but I don't think so. I was angry because Brook had left me. Long ago when she went to college. And then when she had the falling out with my father. The very last time I would need her was already three months past. I had someone now. I was on my way to Danielle's house. In an hour I could hold her. I dropped the letter into the trash.

But now, sitting where the lawn gets ragged, morphing into thistles and tall grass, I would give so much to hear Brook's voice. And if the years would let me, I would retrieve her letter.

Before me, a cabbage butterfly seeks nectar deep in the petals of Indian paint-brush. White wings fluttering against the raging red. Brook's marriage didn't last. She joined Doctors Without Borders, and moved to Africa. Where she died in the Beechcraft that flew her from village to village.

A horse trail cuts across the field that slopes downward toward the gas station. Flattened manure sings with flies.

On February 20, Danielle left me a note saying that Annie was spending the next day at a friend's house in Oakhurst. Could I hitch over to her place around ten?

There was an arctic chill in Yosemite the next morning. A storm was about to sweep in from the north, but at the moment there was a numbing stillness. No birdsong. No sound of traffic. Just ice—the gingerbread atop Moore Cottage glittered with it.

When I got to the road it was gone. Beneath a white patina cut with twin tracks from an early-morning car. The cold chilled my lungs, then beat its way through my old woolen coat. Nothing came. A gray fox dashed across the road.

By the time I got a lift from a restaurant-supply truck, it was already ten o'clock and my body was screaming with the cold. The driver gave me a shot from his whiskey flask. But I still shivered.

When I got to Danielle's, she wasn't home. I paced outside, beating my arms or doing jumping jacks. A razor wind was starting to blow. Danielle's Jeep pulled up as the first snow began to drive diagonally from the north. She hugged me, apologized for being late, and let me inside.

The house offered little more warmth than the gathering storm. Danielle stood for a moment, contemplating the ashes in the fireplace. Our breath sent long trails of frost into the room. I was shivering again, rubbing my gloves over my arms as the wind began to thrum across the eaves.

"I can't stand this," Danielle said. "It's too cold to wait for a fire." She was moving toward the back of the house. "Let's get warm under the quilt."

In the bedroom, Danielle kicked off her shoes and pulled the sleeves of her coat. She slipped beneath the covers with her clothes on. "Come on," she said.

I was feeling, I suspected, the first leaden sensations of hypothermia as I prepared to crawl into bed. We embraced under the quilt. Rubbed each other's backs and legs. As the warmth of our pressed bodies took hold, our movements quieted. We lay encircled by each other's arms.

The wind was lashing the front of the house, and sending snow in a long plume off the crest of the roof. We could see it from the back window—the white spray fanning into the pines.

I brushed Danielle's lips with the barest kiss. She gave me her lovely, lopsided smile. It was the kind of moment that makes you utter the obvious:

"It's cold," I said. "And I'm so glad to be here."

Danielle made a grunting laugh. After a while she said: "Everything's so out of control, Harper. And crazy. The storm's perfect—it's exactly what the world seems like now."

"What's going on?"

Danielle filled me in on the drug deal, the arrest, Annie running away into the woods. And McAllister's statue act in the restaurant the previous day.

"He's crazy, stupid, or both," she said. "Putting his child in danger to sell some goddam weed. He won't do that again. He won't have the chance."

A wave of guilt washed through me. "I should never have pushed you to let him see her again. That was wrong. I should have stayed out of it." Silence. "If he wasn't with Annie, he probably wouldn't have gone to San Francisco. Certainly not the archery range. He would never have been arrested; Annie wouldn't have been scared."

"You've got it all figured out, Harper. You're totally responsible for every fucked-up thing my husband does. He'd appreciate that. Maybe you could go to jail for him too."

She laughed again, but there wasn't much humor in it.

"I just mean I should have kept my mouth shut. I wanted to see more of you, and I thought—"

"I know. But I made the decision. I would probably have let James see Annie, regardless."

Our heads were touching while we talked. Danielle kissed me on the cheek.

"So your opinion is your opinion. Right or wrong, that's all it is. OK? I'm still responsible for Annie."

I was quiet. But I knew I'd advised Danielle out of self-interest. And nothing she could tell me would change that.

Danielle was talking again. I'd missed part of it, but started to listen when she said something about Annie being enraged.

"I can't stand it, her anger. It's like acid. She wants to see her father and I won't let her. So now she glares at me like I'm a child murderer. I explain it all, but she doesn't care. Annie wants to see him, period."

Danielle let out a slow breath. I could feel it on my mouth. A minute or two went by.

"I'm sorry," I finally said. "You're getting it from all sides."

"Not this side." She kissed me on the cheek again. And hitched her leg over mine.

Silence. After a while I touched her. Gently through the denim. Feeling her breathing change.

"Is this OK?"

Danielle didn't answer. Instead she pulled the zipper and wriggled her pants down.

But the mood changed—Danielle arched back to look at me. She said something I couldn't hear.

"What?"

"You wanted to do that."

I'd no idea what she was talking about.

"You wanted to do that," she repeated. "Undress me. I can feel it."

"You said not to. You were afraid—"

"I know."

She pulled me close to her again. Opening to be touched. No more words. After a time she shuddered and closed her legs. Then kissed me deeply.

"Would you," she started, "would you undress the rest of me?"

"You sure?"

"It's OK now."

I did it. And we made love. With a sweetness. Looking at each other. And afterwards slept, warm under the quilt. Letting the storm rage in a gray noon light.

When we woke up, it was one-thirty or two. If anything, the storm was worse, wind making a siren sound as it slammed between the porch posts. Danielle was quiet. And though I tried repeatedly to draw her into conversation, she seemed reticent.

We built a fire. Then made lunch. Eating slowly. Watching the angle of the snow change with the ebb and thrust of the wind. After lunch we sat in the living room, Danielle folded up in a wing-backed armchair. It wasn't till after three that she began to talk. She'd had a dream, she said, while we slept. Something sad. Something that had disturbed her.

Danielle watched the fire as she spoke. For some reason my eyes were drawn to knickknacks on a table at the far end of the room.

The dream was about two things Danielle did not want to see.

For one thing, it seemed to be an augury of some catastrophe. For another, it spoke of James's aloneness. His losses. And perhaps the sense that it was still in Danielle's power to rescue him.

The next day I wrote a poem about it called "The Speeches So Small."

I'm bound to report
the speeches, deaths,
the photographs so small
no book or newspaper
will have them.
And yet
they are the only news:

Gray dusk.
In a high-backed arm chair,
upholstered blue and white,
she has her legs drawn up.
A table by the window holds
the carving of a speckled shore bird,
wire legs stuck in a piece of bark.

"Now I understand the dream," she said.
"It was a seashore resort,
the carnival was on the other side of town.
This friend killed years ago helped with the rides,
so I knew both my girl and I were dead.
I thought: 'We'll go back for James because
he'll be lonely and

it's lovely here.'"

CHAPTER 37

n March 6, James hitchhiked to Oakhurst to rent a fire-red Malibu. He was quite particular about the color.

At five-thirty that afternoon, when Danielle returned from work, she learned that Annie had not been on the school bus. As usual, Mrs. Carver had met the bus to pick up Annie and her own daughter Cherie. Mrs. Carver was surprised to hear Annie had left school with a tall man in a red car. She assumed it was an arrangement her mother forgot to mention.

When Danielle got the news, she struggled for the breath to ask the next question.

Mrs. Carver offered Cherie's description of the tall man with the flashy car. "I assumed it was Annie's father and it was OK."

"It is her father, and no…" Danielle didn't finish. She was already getting in her Jeep for the short drive to Silvertip Lane.

Inside her cabin Danielle found evidence of packing. Some of Annie's drawers were open; a pink down jacket—her favorite—was gone. A few of her best-loved puppets were also missing, as well as Annie's toy binoculars. A check in the bathroom confirmed that McAllister had forgotten his daughter's toothbrush, barrettes, and skin rash medicine.

There was no note.

Danielle sat on her grandmother's chest. Through the window shone a three-quarter moon. And a single snow-clad bough. Danielle studied it, how the fir's up-turned needles captured the snow. How the moon lent a faint luminescence to the branch. She described it to me later as a scene from a Japanese print. And it felt strangely at odds with the fear tightening her chest.

"Where are you, Annie?" she said out loud. But the sound of her voice made the fear worse.

A sudden thrust of wind sent snow cascading down the tree. A moment's sibilance. Then again the quiet. Danielle was holding herself between the legs, like a little girl. She realized she needed to use the bathroom.

Five minutes later, Danielle called Tara. No answer. She called Fagan, letting it ring. The phone was cold against her ear, her breath a faint mist. Nothing. She could hear the roar of a snowplow working down on the highway. And the faint hum of the freezer clicking on.

In a moment, Danielle was running to the Jeep, gunning it. She skidded into the bend by the post office, turned at the gas station, and headed south on 41. Nixon was on the radio defending new bombing in Laos. A commentator followed, reporting on the effort to destroy staging areas of the Pathet Lao. Danielle changed stations, heard the conga roll in the middle of the Chambers Brothers' "Time." Which made her more anxious. She switched it off.

The sign for the Sugar Pine Railroad was crusted with snow. Danielle shot the Jeep into a hard turn, and descended the steep entry road to the parking lot. It was empty. Except for two black ribbons cutting the snow, suggesting a recent car. Danielle parked and began walking south along the rails. She came to a siding filled with derelict cars. Next to it, the moonlight caught boot prints in the powder. Two sets. Large and small. Danielle followed them all the way to James's caboose.

In the thin light, she could just make out *West Side Lumber Company* on the side of the car—its Tuscan red varnish turned gray by the moon.

"James?" she said, as she climbed the steps.

Silence. The caboose was dark inside.

"James?"

The door was locked. She shook it.

"Annie? Can you hear me, sweetie?"

Danielle stepped down from the platform. The snow next to the roadbed wasn't thick; she pressed her fingers into it. Tentatively. Then plunged in both her hands—feeling the ground below. A moment later, holding a large rock, she once more mounted the caboose steps.

In front of the door Danielle hesitated. Again she called her husband's name. Then smashed the window. The air was cold on the inside, smelling of mold and kerosene. Danielle spent five minutes searching the inner surface of the door for a latch. Nothing. No getting in.

"Annie." But it was a whisper now.

She smashed a second window. And a third.

Where the road cuts, I see how the land has been opened. Dissected. On one side is a high bank of shale. Up-thrust. Brittle. On the other is the Merced.

The shale seeps. Red moss softens the tilted blades. I climb a pile of loosened stones to touch the moss. The leaves of overhanging trees flicker.

Years ago I drove this road. Instead of shale, I watched the river weaving on the other side. White boulders. Water cut in lucent planes, fresh from the ice. I never stopped.

CHAPTER 38

anielle showed up at Wawona around seven. Her eyes were unfocused and frightened as she pushed into my room.

"Annie's gone," she said. "James took her."

Danielle sat on the bed and told me everything she knew. At the end of her account the room seemed compressed. As if Danielle's fear had saturated the air.

"You're quiet," she prompted. "Tell me what you think."

I touched her hand. "Let's make a list of places he'd be likely to go."

"I called Tara's house. No answer. I guess it's possible he's there and not answering the phone."

"But if he wanted to keep Annie—for a while at least—he'd need to go somewhere you couldn't easily find."

"I don't actually know where Tara lives."

"Could you find out?"

"Yeah, from Fagan. But I called him too. He's not home."

"Maybe they're all somewhere together."

"It's possible, but I don't think so. James was alone in a new red car when he picked up Annie.

"And here's something else. That red car has to be a rental. If James was doing this with Tara, why spend money renting a car? Why not use hers?"

I'd no argument for that, so I asked Danielle if she wanted some port. She did. For a moment we drank in silence, Danielle's eyes strafing the room.

"Let's keep thinking. Where else would he go?"

"San Francisco. His mother's house. He's taken Annie there to visit three or four times since we broke up. Of course, I always knew about it."

Danielle rubbed her lips with an extended finger. Circling her mouth. I noticed her hand was shaking. "I don't think there's any point in calling his mother yet. If he left Fish Camp at four o'clock, and made really good time, it would still take him four and a half hours to get there."

"Maybe we should call her anyway, see if she's expecting him."

"I don't know. She'd probably lie to me. And I can't read people very well on the phone."

"You might be able to tell from her voice. Whether she was upset or excited."

Danielle didn't answer. She was looking at the floor—a place where the building had settled, bending the hardwood.

"Jesus." She touched the sloping area with the toe of her shoe. Delicately. As if the slightest pressure would break through to the lobby. "I never noticed that before."

Danielle took a deep, stuttering breath, and let her body drop backward on the bed. She stared at the ceiling. After a moment there was a tugging at the corners of her mouth; tears welled in her eyes.

"Maybe I shouldn't have cut him off," she said. "Maybe that was a mistake."

"You had to. He was putting Annie in danger."

"I know, but I'm scared I made him crazy."

Danielle began to make a soft, high-pitched sound. Her lips stretched, baring her teeth. The caps she'd gotten after the accident, I noticed, seemed whiter than the rest.

Now Danielle drew up her knees, twisting into a fetal position. The sound got louder.

I touched her hand, oddly cold, and laced my fingers into hers. I said things I don't remember. Murmurs. All the while feeling detached. As if I were watching something in a theater. Something mysterious and foreign.

"Where are you, Harper?"

"I'm here."

"No, you're not."

"I'm sorry. I'm trying to—"

"Forget it. It doesn't matter."

I felt like I'd done something wrong. Somehow abandoned her.

"Let's call James's mother," I said. "If he's not with Fagan or Tara, it's the logical place for him to go. And if we don't like how she sounds, if she sounds the least bit cagey, we'll go to San Francisco tonight."

"You're trying to help," Danielle said. "But I need something."

"What?"

"You can't give it to me."

"What is it, Danielle?"

"I need you to feel like I do. About Annie. About her being gone. But you can't." She started crying again. "My girl is missing, and you're just glad to see me."

I didn't know what to say.

After a moment, Danielle rolled to the edge of the bed and stood up. She rubbed the backs of her hands across her cheeks, spreading the tears. A child's gesture.

"OK," she said. "Let's call Mabel. See what Flint Lips has to say."

"What?"

"I used to call her that. 'Cause her lips were thin and kind of gray looking." Danielle shrugged. "Forget it."

Danielle held the phone away from her ear so I could listen. It was ringing. When the connection finally clicked open, there was a long silence, followed by a deep female voice. Danielle identified herself.

"You don't have to say who you are, Dani. I know your voice." The woman sounded tired.

"Mabel, I was just calling because...James said he was heading down there. With Annie." Silence. "I wanted to leave a message for him to call me when he gets in."

"He's not here. What do you want to tell him, Dani?"

"I need to speak to him as soon as he gets there. It's important, Mabel."

"Like I said, he's not here. I don't know nothin' about him coming down. I guess you know more than I do." There was resentment in the voice.

"Didn't he call you, Mabel? Didn't he tell you he'd be there?"

"You sound nervous, Dani."

"I just want to get him a message."

"Well, tell me what it is and I'll give it to him. If I see him."

Silence. Danielle turned to look toward the trees.

"Mabel, I'm sorry for...what happened. You know? I don't feel like I chose any of it. Things got decided for me. But now I need your help."

"For what? I don't know nothin' about him coming. But if he shows, I'll tell him you called. After everything you did, Dani, I don't owe you more than that. You understand me? You stopped getting favors from me when you took Annie away from him." Her voice was croaking through the receiver. "You understand that? I got nothin' else to tell you."

The line went dead.

Danielle hung up the phone and traced the edge of the dial with her gloved finger. Our breath made frost, illuminated by the single bulb at the watch station. Wind was starting to shiver the branches of the sequoias behind us.

"What do you think?" she said.

"Flint Lips is lying. She's heard from James. Otherwise there'd have been more surprise in her voice when you said James was coming."

"Do you think Mabel knows he took Annie?"

"There's a good chance. I can't think why else she'd bullshit you that she hadn't heard from him."

Danielle nodded. Silently she dropped more coins in the phone. A sudden thrust of wind slashed at our faces.

Danielle hunched as she heard the pickup. "Lara, it's me...Yeah,

I'm at Wawona. Listen, I've got to come to San Francisco. Tonight...I know, but something's happened. James took Annie, ran off with her. He's out of his mind...He's doing stupid, impulsive things. He might...He rented a fancy car. I'm afraid he'll take Annie somewhere I can't find her. I think his first stop is his mother's house in San Francisco. I got to get there before he takes off again and I...Right, can we stay with you?...Harper and me...Right. I'll see you in about five hours."

She rang off, then touched my arm. "You coming?"

Twenty minutes later, we were at Danielle's house in Fish Camp. She packed a single bag including some underclothes and coloring books for Annie. And a red, leather-bound notebook that turned out to be her journal. Then we were back on 41, heading south through Oakhurst, Coursegold, and Madera. The Jeep's high gear roared when we finally hit the straightaway on 99. Wind ripped at the canvas, flapping the isinglass, finding open seams to press its way into the cab.

In Modesto, Danielle asked me to drive. She was too distracted, she said. Her head was filled with pictures of Annie—in some foreign, unreachable place. She wouldn't talk. Somewhere in the orchard country of the San Joaquin, Danielle demanded that I stop. She had to urinate. She ran into the dark corridor between a row of trees. Her jeans were wet when she came back.

As we pulled into Oakland, I asked directions to Lara's place.

"Just head for the bridge." Danielle pointed vaguely toward the windshield.

"And then what?"

"Is this fun?" she asked. "Is this an adventure?"

"I don't know." The conversation had suddenly grown dangerous.

"You're excited. I can feel it."

"I guess so. I was just sitting in my room listening to the radio. And suddenly..." I shrugged.

"Do you have any idea how much this is the *opposite* of adventure for me? How not fun this is? Can you imagine?"

Her voice was low, cutting. She looked at me like I was a stain on a new sofa.

"I'm trying. Annie isn't my child. But I'm here. Anything you need…"

I didn't finish. Because I couldn't do the thing she needed. To merge with her. To join her in that most lonely of all places: the fear of losing what you love.

"Do you want to drive by his mother's house? See if we can find a red car?"

"Yeah, OK." Silence. "Harper, look. I'm fucked up; I know it. I'm asking," she rubbed the fresh tears across her face, "I'm asking too much."

CHAPTER 39

here wasn't a red car. Not new anyway. And not anywhere near Flint Lips' place on La Playa. We drove the
streets by her house, windows open. The air smelled of
salt and kelp. Of rotting clots of jellyfish. And it was cold—not like
snow. Or mountains. But like the emptiness between planets.

It was sometime after one a.m. when we finally arrived at Lara's
address. Fog haloed the street lamps. The house was one of a long
row of narrow dwellings, all abutting wall against wall. Some stucco,
some clapboard. I couldn't see much, but I had the feeling I wasn't
missing anything.

The bay windows of Lara's house shone yellow through the
mist. Our feet scraped the terrazzo steps. Before we reached the door
it was thrown open, and Lara stood there in a blue kimono, smiling,
a finger to her lips.

"I have a little boy sleeping inside," she said. "Let's try not to
wake him. He's the son of a dear friend; he stays with me sometimes." Lara gestured toward a closed door, then led us down a narrow hall to the far end of the house.

We arrived at a sitting room, its dark windows giving on what
was probably the backyard. It was full of old-fashioned furniture—
a Morris chair with ottoman, a mohair sofa, a brass-base floor lamp.
Facing the window was an oak swivel chair, and a mahogany lamp

table swimming with notebooks and papers.

"It's a nice room when there's light," Lara said. "Otherwise…" She shrugged.

"Thank you for putting us up." Danielle took Lara's hand. "I'm sorry for getting here so late. We checked my mother-in-law's house first—looking for James's car."

"Did you see it?"

"No, but I'm not sure. I think he rented something. It was described to me, I don't know exactly what it looks like."

"What are you going to do?"

"Go there first thing in the morning and see if she'll let me in. If she won't, it could mean James is inside."

Lara nodded slowly. Creases appearing between her eyes. "And then what?"

"I don't know. Maybe the police."

"Maybe we should just go in and take Annie," I said, full of sudden bravado.

"I don't think so, Harper. He can get crazy. There's no predicting what he might do."

Danielle told Lara about James's weird display in the Snowflake Room. Lara apparently already knew about the incident where he cut himself with a knife, and there ensued a long discussion about what was wrong with the man. And what he might be capable of.

The room was cold. Lara kept rubbing her fingers and glancing toward the window. There was nothing to see outside.

"You look kind of upset," Danielle said. "This must be difficult with us—"

"No, I'm thinking about James. About what he has left to lose if he loses Annie. Is there any way to give him hope that if he cooperates—"

"I can't trust him, Lara. So I've got nothing to offer him. How can I promise James some kind of relationship with Annie when he does shit like this?"

Danielle was making chopping gestures with her hand; she dropped it palm down on the coffee table—with a bang. Even Danielle seemed to startle.

"I'm sorry, Lara. I can't think right now. I'm tired. And the truth is, I'm more worried about James *not* being at Mabel's house than what to do if he is."

Lara stood and smoothed her dress. "Then you should try to rest. There's a hide-a-bed over there. All made up." She pointed to a modern-looking loveseat shoved into a corner of the room. "Charlie and I got that when some friends came to visit a few years back. It was a mistake. Doesn't go with anything." She shrugged.

The loveseat had the distinction of being uncomfortable as well as ugly. The mattress, as I recall, was a relief map of Colorado. I spooned behind Danielle and rubbed her stomach. Her body felt dense. Rooted in place. I parted her thick hair and kissed the back of her neck.

I was trying to soothe her. But I have to be honest, I was excited to find her in my arms. My breath was a little fast, my heart getting ready for something.

Danielle grasped the hand I held on her stomach, kept it from moving. "You want to do something, Harper? More than this?"

I started to speak, but she interrupted me.

"I can't. Do you understand? I'm scared out of my mind and you…you're wondering if you can touch my ass. Don't. OK? I'm too frightened for that."

"It's OK, Danielle. Please. Just sleep if you can. I'm not trying to do anything."

I backed away from her slightly.

"Harper, look." For a moment she pressed my hand. "It's not that you're excited. It's not that you want something." There was a long pause and I wondered if she'd drifted off. "It's that we're in totally different places. Emotionally."

Danielle pulled her knees up. Tight. Huddling.

I didn't know what to do. I took my hand away, rolled on my back.

The next morning, Lara scrambled us some eggs and we met the little boy who was staying with her. John Madrone—serious, sad eyes. Already at ten a furrowed brow.

"How do you do," he said as we all shook hands.

"Not very well," Danielle told him. "My little girl is missing and I'm looking for her."

John nodded gravely, a reaction suggesting such things were sad but not uncommon. Nothing more was said.

It was about eight o'clock when we got to La Playa Street. Since it was Saturday, not many people were out. The fog was gone now, the air still leavened with ocean salt.

Flint Lips lived in a duplex. It was mustard color, with generous sections of peeling paint. Creaking outside stairs led to a green door, also showing the effects of salt air.

Danielle opened the letter slot and was staring inside.

"What are you doing?"

"Trying to see if a car's in there. But I can't tell; it's too dark."

At the top of the stairs Danielle paused once more, listening. She twisted the bell handle; a sound like coins rattling in a jar came from inside.

It took a long time for anything to happen. When the old lady finally opened the door, she kept the chain on.

I couldn't see too much of her. Long, gray braids were pinned across the top of her head. Her housecoat had big yellow daisies, and some small brown holes, thanks to cigarette burns. Her nose looked like she'd gone a few rounds with Joe Louis, and her lips— as reported—were a sickly blue-gray.

I find I am distancing myself from this. Emotionally. As if it is some-one else's story. Afraid to feel it. Afraid to do more than recite events.

The moon backlights the trees. Voices through the windows of the dining room stagger across the air. Broken. The lilt and lightness gone. Across a lattice of high boughs, a crow makes the last flight of the day.

Flint Lips didn't say anything. She pulled the housecoat around herself, protectively.

"I know it's early, Mabel, but I have to see James."

"I told you I'd call you if he came. You went to a lot of trouble for nothing."

"I wasn't home to get the call, so I—"

"He's not here, Dani. Is that plain enough?"

"Can we come in, Mabel?"

"Who's this? Your new boyfriend? You didn't wait long. You don't let no grass grow, Dani."

"It's cold out here, can we come in? There's something I want to talk to you about."

"It's not much warmer inside. And I'm not dressed to receive visitors. Why didn't you call first?"

Danielle didn't answer.

"So good-bye, Dani. Go have your life. I don't think we need to see each other again." She started to close the door, but Danielle shot her arm through the opening.

"I want to see James and I want to see Annie." A near shout.

"Get the hell out. Go pull your crap somewhere else."

She smashed the door on Danielle's arm. Then opened it, hoping Danielle would pull out. There was a scream. I put my weight against the door, trying to stop Flint Lips from slamming it again.

Then the old crone did something extraordinary. She bit Danielle. Hard on the knuckle. Danielle screamed a second time and pulled her hand back. I shifted my weight for a moment to look at the wound—in an instant the door banged and I heard the bolt shoot home.

We stood on the landing, Danielle crying with the pain. Bent over, rippling her fingers. Delicately touching where the teeth had broken the skin. I kicked the door. Several times.

What we didn't know during all that commotion was that James had carried a sleeping Annie downstairs to the garage—while we'd stood ringing the bell. He'd lain Annie in the backseat of the Malibu—out of earshot of the shouting and her mother's voice.

The police station was on 24th Avenue, off Taraval—a brick building sandwiched between stucco row houses, with a playground across the street. There were already children's voices coming from the swings. The sergeant seemed to take the matter seriously, ushering us through a gate to his battered steel desk. After several attempts, he was able to insert the complaint form in the typewriter.

Danielle was efficient. She explained that James, out on bail for a drug-possession charge, had just kidnapped their daughter.

"Do you have custody of the child, Mrs. McAllister?"

"Yes, she lives with me."

"Did a judge award you custody?"

"No. We're not divorced yet."

The sergeant looked at me. He scraped dirt out of one of his nails. "So there's never been a custody hearing? No visitation agreement?"

"No." Danielle leaned toward the cop. "But I told him he can't see her. After his arrest."

"I see." The sergeant, absently pressing the space bar on the typewriter, looked surprised when the bell rang. "But technically—legally—your husband still has the right to see his daughter?"

"What do you mean?"

"I mean the fact that he's awaiting trial doesn't take away his rights. Unless there's a court order, he can still see his kid."

"You mean he can pick her up from school and take her away somewhere and not tell anyone? You mean he has the right to disappear with my child?" She was getting loud, leaning with both arms on the cop's desk.

The sergeant held up his hand. While no picture comes to mind of the man's face, I can see his fingers—stubby and dark stained—waving like he was trying to flag us down.

"I want to help you," he said. "I will help you. I just need to get the facts straight."

"Then go to my mother-in-law's house. That's where I think they are. Hurry before he leaves and goes somewhere I can't find him."

The sergeant nodded gravely. For some reason, he reminded me at that moment of little John Madrone out at Lara's house. Both so serious. Both incapable of helping.

By the time the cops visited Mabel later that afternoon, James was long gone. Checked in, as it turned out, to the elegant and stately Mark Hopkins Hotel. A hundred bucks a night—which was a lot of money in those days.

The cops did do one thing that later proved useful. They gave Flint Lips our phone number at Lara's house so James could call. Which he did later that day.

CHAPTER 40

*A*round dusk, the phone rang at Lara's place. Little John Madrone answered it, advising the caller that it was "the Bordon residence," in a very serious voice. An English butler couldn't have done it better. After a moment the boy covered the receiver and pointed to Danielle. "It's for you."

The phone, as I remember, was on a delicate three-legged table edged with battered rosewood carvings. It wobbled when Danielle leaned against it. As she began to listen, her face clouded. Her body became dense.

"Where are you? Is Annie with you?" Silence. She began tracing invisible patterns on the phone table.

"I'll meet you if you bring Annie...No. Only if you bring Annie. I have to see her."

There was another long interval. Lara clicked off the television, and you could hear a clock ticking somewhere. The room had a penetrating quiet.

"Where?...Then I'll come without him...I don't know. He's just helping me, OK?...Look, I can't even think about that right now."

More silence. John picked up a peewee football and tossed it to Lara. She put her fingers to her lips and underhanded the ball back to him.

"OK, I'll listen to what you have to say. I've got no choice. But just bring Annie, OK? That's your side of this. You bring Annie, and I listen. And then we figure something out."

The football started up again—three-way this time to include me. It dropped with a thud. Danielle jerked up, startled. Without a further word, she hung up the phone.

The meeting was set for eight that night, in Sutro Park. Danielle had been told to come alone, but I was in the back of the Jeep, hidden by the canvas top. There was a cutting wind. Even though the Jeep was parked, air seeped through the edges of the doors and windows. The wind whipped the fabric with a whistling sound.

Danielle climbed to a small plateau that once held the gardens for the Sutro mansion. As instructed, she walked to the middle of the park and waited. She could hear the surf thundering 300 feet below, and the wind keening in the branches of nearby cypress. A rope made a hollow clanging sound as it whipped against a flagpole. No James.

Finally, on the east side of the park, at a place overlooking the street, a shadow detached itself from a row of bushes. James took his time, using sauntering steps to cross the open space, stopping twice to observe Danielle or check the dark borders of the park.

"Where's Annie?" Danielle's voice was high, angry.

"Safe."

"You were supposed to bring her."

"I know. But I didn't."

"That's not our deal. She's supposed to be here—so I can see her."

"I know."

"So what the fuck, James? What are we doing here?"

"Talking. You wouldn't talk to me before. You just walked on by, remember? Remember that, Dani? Now I've got something to say and you're gonna listen."

Silence.

"Are you gonna listen? Or should we just part ways, just say good-bye now?"

"I'm listening. But I'm not going to believe anything you tell me. Anything you promise. Because you didn't bring Annie."

"You're not running this, Dani. I'm in charge of this shit. And I'm going to say some things, OK?"

Danielle didn't answer.

"You need to say 'Yes, I'm listening.'"

"Yes."

"OK, good." He took a breath, staring for a moment toward the sound of the breakers. "OK, so now you're going to listen." He hesitated again. "You were a girl who was beautiful. To me."

He held his hands out, spreading them slightly, moving downward in front of her body. As if the gesture was a summation of everything he knew about her. "You were the girl I used to imagine when I was a kid. So when I met you, I knew we should be together."

James opened his arms, pausing. "Then this thing happened."

"My accident."

James pointed at her. "Yeah. We had something good and it changed everything."

"Are you trying to convince me of something? Because if you are, it's not happening." Danielle shifted her weight to one leg and shoved her hands in her pockets.

"Look, I gave it up already. Believe me. I didn't come here to convince you of jack. You've moved on. That's clear." He paused. "Are you screwing that guy? Harper?"

Silence. Danielle looked in both directions, eyes sweeping the edge of the park.

"I suppose that means yes." More silence. "But I didn't come here to talk about that either."

James took a step closer to Danielle. "That accident made you somebody else. A woman I don't know. But there was more than that. Afterwards you could see me. I realize that now. You could see what I want. Why I do things. What I fucking feel. *Everything*." He drew out the word like he'd just come down from Sinai and was reading from the Tablets.

"Here's the thing, Dani. The thing that kills me. You see everything." He ran his hands down his body. "You know me. But you can't forgive me. Do you understand what I'm saying? What that feels like? To know that you see everything in me—the good and the bad—and it all adds up to being…nothing. Thrown away.

"If you can see me, you know what a mistake I made. That I ache about it. You know how much I love Annie. How I can't stand not seeing her. I'm burning inside. You know that, but you have no feeling for me. It all adds up to being…" He shook his head.

"That's all. That's all I wanted to say."

She could feel his anger, and his hopelessness. But she didn't want to stay in that place inside of him. "OK, I heard you, James. I listened. It's sad, and I don't know what to do about it, OK?"

She waited a few beats and pointed a finger at him. "But I want to see Annie. I want to go where she is. Then we can talk some more."

"I said what I have to say. I'm done talking."

"Let's go see Annie then."

James shook his head. A foghorn bellowed up from Golden Gate Straits. And Danielle noticed the first tendrils of fog drifting high across the park.

"What do you mean?"

James turned and ran for the street. Danielle ran after him, but James's long legs easily outdistanced her.

Danielle screamed: "Annie needs me. Don't be selfish, James."

By the time Danielle got back to the Jeep, I was already behind the wheel, engine gunning. She was breathing fast. "Take a U-turn, head back toward Geary," she gasped. "Look for a red car."

And then we saw him, peeling out of a parking space near the corner. A fire-engine red Malibu, low, with a long hood and super-wide tires. James turned right on Geary, then right again on 45th. The Jeep, with its high center of gravity, leaned with terrifying indecision as we took each of these corners.

I never got close enough to read his license plate, and by 45th I was falling seriously behind. The big taillights of the Malibu looked nearly a block away. On Lincoln, James darted left, then seemed to slow down, perhaps playing with us.

As I began to catch up, he accelerated again, doing close to seventy. The dark trees of Golden Gate Park flashed by on our right, stucco-covered flats and apartment houses blurred in the left window. Ahead of us, James was weaving around slow traffic. Suddenly brake lights. The Malibu fishtailed and disappeared into the park.

By the time I got to the turnoff, the taillights were gone. We shot towards Stow Lake, careening through tight, tree-shrouded curves. Then up and down Kennedy Drive. All the way to the beach, where the fog was pressing through the cypress, then racing back the length of the park to Oak Street and the Panhandle. Nothing.

CHAPTER 41

*B*ack at Lara's place we sat stunned in the living room. Nobody had any idea how to find James. Danielle perched morosely on the arm of the Morris chair, twisting strands of her dark locks, glancing at the late news. Lara was in John's bedroom, reading to him. A story about hobos who hopped freights in the thirties.

I sat on the mohair sofa, feeling useless and incompetent. I should have kept up with James, should have run him off the road. I imagined Danielle silently blaming me for letting him get away.

After a little while, Lara killed the light in John's room and sat with us. Her first words startled me.

"His mother knows where he is."

"What?" Danielle jerked to full attention.

"James left his mother's house. He had to before the police got there. But you can bet he called to let her know all was well as soon as he settled in someplace."

"That's not going to do us much good," I said. "Flint Lips won't tell us anything."

Lara seemed very confident. "Suppose you're James's mother. He calls to tell you where he is. What do you do?"

"Probably write it down," Danielle said.

"Where?"

She shrugged. "By the phone."

The next morning we were on La Playa Street again—Flint Lips' stoop. Danielle turned the handle on the bell while I waited out of sight. After the customary delay, the door opened a crack. Before a word was said, Danielle wedged her foot in the jam and I stepped up with a long-handled metal-cutter.

The old lady started screaming, but it only took a few seconds to snap the chain and shove through the door.

"Shut up," Danielle told her. She dragged the old lady by her elbow in the direction of an armchair. "Sit down." With a little shove Flint Lips toppled backward into the cushions. Her hideous daisy housecoat opened on an equally ghastly striped nightgown.

"You're helping James take Annie from me. I'm here to find my daughter."

"She's not here. Get the hell out of my house. You're committing a crime, a break-in. I told you I don't know where she is." The old lady was making a lot of noise.

"There's been a crime, Mabel. You're right. It's called kidnapping. And when you phone the police, why don't you report that crime too. Tell them your son's a fucking kidnapper."

I called to Danielle. I was in Flint Lips' bedroom. From a nightstand spilling over with medicine bottles and old magazines, I'd picked up an envelope that had the words "Mark Hopkins" noted in spidery script.

"What?" she called back.

I was already on my way to the door. "Time to go," I said.

The trip to the Mark was largely in silence. Danielle drove: down the Great Highway to where it bends eastward at the Cliff House, then jogging left to California, which goes directly to the Mark. Danielle pushed it. Weaving around traffic, running the yellow lights, jamming the shift with quick, violent thrusts. Her face was compressed into a hard mask. I sat back and listened to the gears whine.

When we got to the hotel, Danielle slammed to a stop in front of the taxi stand. The doorman shouted at her, but we ran into the lobby before he could do anything. At the front desk, she quickly learned that no one named James McAllister was registered. Then Danielle did something I thought extraordinary: she climbed up on a bellman's cart and asked for everyone's attention.

Holding high a small photo of Annie, she said: "My little girl was abducted by a man staying in this hotel." She lifted up a second picture. "This is the man who took her. Please, will you look at these photographs so I can find my child? Can you tell me if you've seen her?"

Danielle stepped down from the cart and laid the snapshots on the marble counter of the front desk. The clerks, to my surprise, abandoned their posts. As they gathered near the photographs, the lobby erupted in a dozen conversations.

One of the clerks, a woman with thick, colliding eyebrows and a beehive, pointed to the picture of James. She said something to Danielle and walked over to an open file. At this point the manager showed up, trying to figure out what was going on. He was an officious, Ichabod Crane type, with a huge Adam's apple and a slight stoop. He glanced briefly at the photos and listened as Danielle explained again about the abduction.

The manager gathered himself for a brief moment of good posture, and told Danielle it was a matter for the police, that he couldn't release any information about guests of the hotel. Aligning his long, simian fingers on the edge of the counter, he asked if Danielle would like him to call "the authorities."

"Call them, then. Hurry up." She was in a rage. "I'm going to hold you responsible if he gets away while we're fucking around here."

Ichabod laced his fingers as if in prayer. Long pause. "There's no reason to speak in that manner. People are not used to that here." Another long pause. "Perhaps you should leave, and take it up with the police yourself. The Northern Station is on Ellis Street, I believe."

"No, I'm staying. Call the police now or the whole lobby's getting a lesson in sailor talk." She turned back to me. "Watch the elevators. Don't let him slip out."

Ichabod, walking slower than a bride down the aisle, headed to his office. Presumably to call the cops. As he disappeared, the clerk with the beehive came up to Danielle. She mouthed the words, "I'm sorry," and slid a piece of paper across the marble.

The note read, "He was registered as James Hutchings. He checked out fifteen minutes ago."

We were too late. Flint Lips had warned him.

The mood was funereal at Lara's house. Another visit to the police had proved unhelpful. It seemed there was nothing to do but wait for James to call again. Danielle sat on the swivel chair by the back window, staring into the neat rows of Lara's vegetable garden. I tried to comfort her—rubbing her shoulders, kissing the center part of her hair—but she seemed frozen, unresponsive to the sweetest touch.

The little boy went home. Picked up by his father. As he left, he shook hands very formally with Danielle and me. "I hope you find Annie," he told her, his sad eyes never quite reaching Danielle's face.

Lara hugged and kissed the boy. Very obvious affection. "I'll see you soon, my fine young man," she said.

Lara watched the child descend the front steps until he was out of sight. When she finally closed the door, her eyes were wistful. "I miss him when he leaves. Especially now. Now that Charlie's gone."

Long silence. Lara crossed the room to sit by Danielle. She took the younger woman's hand.

"I used to work for a man who was amazing at solving problems. In fact, there was only one problem in all the years I knew him he couldn't solve. Anyhow, he used to say, 'Lara, we'll find a way.' So now I'm saying that to you. We'll find a way."

Danielle nodded. "What was the problem he couldn't solve?"

Lara looked out the window. Into her garden. The wistfulness returned to her eyes.

"Me. That was the problem. We loved each other, but I was married to Charlie. I was committed to Charlie. So…we had to let go."

After that, Lara went down to plant some bulbs. But, before she got to work, I watched her walk the straight white paths between the beds. Slowly, trowel in hand. Pausing now and then, bending, then looking away into the distance.

Suddenly I felt afraid of her pain. Of those unknown losses.

An hour later—maybe around four o'clock—we heard Lara's feet scraping up the back stairs. When she walked in, the knees of her jeans were caked with loam. Her cheeks were pink from the sting of the March air.

"I've been thinking, and I may have a way," she announced. "Who's Hutchings? Why did James choose that name?"

Danielle shrugged. "I'm not sure. When we were first dating, I remember James got interested in stories of some of the early pioneers in Yosemite. I think Hutchings was one." Danielle frowned. "And his daughter was another. Floy Hutchings. He was quite obsessed with their stories. Read everything he could."

Lara held up her hand. "Wait. So it wasn't just an arbitrary name. It means something to him."

"I guess."

"So he'll probably use it again. He has no reason to think you know what it is." Lara smiled.

Nobody said anything. I'd no idea what she was getting at.

"We can find him. It's simple. We just call every hotel in the city and ask for James Hutchings." Lara spread her hands, like she'd just pulled out a rabbit.

Within half an hour we were working our way down the Yellow Pages' listings of hotels. Asking an endless string of desk clerks if James Hutchings had checked in with his daughter. After a while, Lara cut out some of the hotel listings and took them to her friend's house next door. She started making calls from there. Once we got a rhythm, Danielle and I could make close to thirty calls an hour. One of us read the number out loud, the other dialed. Every so often we switched off.

The desk clerks were polite, sometimes unctuous. But the work was numbing. And we hardly talked. I noticed at around nine o'clock that Danielle rarely looked at me; she stared at the phone or her hands. I felt as though our relationship was evaporating. Looking back, I suspect there was a sea change when Danielle found out that I didn't share her feelings, that Annie was someone I cared for only in the abstract, only because she was important to Danielle.

By ten, the switchboards of many of the smaller hotels seemed to have shut down. And we'd already called all the bigger places. So far there'd been no luck, so we made a list of the motels and small, down-and-out hotels we planned to call in the morning.

Again that night, we slept without touching. I asked Danielle how she was, but the response was biting.

"I lost my daughter. I'm doing great."

I persisted with questions.

Finally she said she was so scared, it was like a hot poker in her chest. Every second. And that she couldn't think about anything else.

I asked if there was something else I could do to help. She shrugged. That was it. No more words. We lay awake for hours, inhabiting our private anxieties: hers that she might lose Annie; mine that I would lose Danielle.

We started with the phone again at eight the next morning. Maybe my twentieth call was to a dump named Roberts at the Beach. James Hutchings and his daughter, Floy, had checked in yesterday afternoon.

We were there at nine. It was a triangle-shaped building wedged between converging streets. A trifle run-down, more than a trifle nondescript. James was still checked in, but there was no answer at his door. And the red Malibu wasn't in the garage.

As it turned out, James and Annie were eating breakfast at the Cliff House—maybe half a mile away. But we had no way of knowing that. So we parked the Jeep on another block—where he wouldn't see it—and hid behind an old delivery van where we could watch his room.

Hours passed. Danielle resided in some other place. Foreign and unreachable. There were desultory comments about the fog. The ubiquitous rust from ocean air. The fact that Roberts needed paint. The look of certain people as they emerged from their rooms. Briefly once, Danielle took my hand. "Thank you," she said without looking at me. Then returned to the vigil.

James and Annie never came.

Around two we called Lara.

CHAPTER 42

The news from Lara was at first encouraging. The police had called, and urgently wanted to speak with Danielle. A Sergeant Roca. Lara read off the phone number. Danielle made the call immediately, hoping the cops had located James. What she heard from Roca made her hand tighten on the phone. She hunched slightly, touching the wall for balance.

A man had jumped from the Golden Gate Bridge, a child clenched in his arms. Somewhere around eleven o'clock. The description might fit James, but the body had no ID when a fishing boat recovered it. So far, the child's body had not been found. That was the extent of what Roca knew. He wondered if Danielle would come to identify the John Doe.

The trip to the morgue was a nightmare. Danielle had me drive. She was shaking, shoulders crushed, hands clasping her knees.

She said several times, "It's not fucking true."

The air seemed viscous, thickening in my lungs. I breathed hard, a sense of starting to drown. I felt encapsulated. Danielle was gone. Only a few feet away, but consumed in a terrible resonance between fear and grief.

I waited, hoped she would say something. As if words could keep me alive. As if words were oxygen.

Danielle stared at the dashboard, eyes locked. Nothing.

The morgue was a nauseating expanse of white tile. To steady myself, I think, or perhaps to find some comfort in a place of death, I watched Danielle's lovely hips, the curving muscles of her buttocks as she pushed her body down the hall. But she turned to me, eyes crinkling with pain, and said, "Harper, no."

A soft voice. Not angry, but resigned. A blade of the sharpest metal.

It made me despise myself.

Danielle went in to view the body alone. I saw her lean for a moment on the gurney. There was no sound. And, as she turned, no change in her expression. But it was James. A moment later Danielle touched her stomach, asked directions to the restroom.

Oddly, I remember little of the next few hours. We were questioned by the police. Danielle phoned Mabel. There was shouting on the line—I don't recall now what was said.

I remember the smell of chemicals. Of decay. I kept watching a bird's nest through an office window—a dark clot among still barren branches. I remember the cop voices, washing over us in waves. At times resonant and sympathetic; at times probing, sharp.

When we got back to Lara's, she had a copy of the *Examiner*. The jump was headline news. Father and daughter, witnesses said, walked hand in hand on the bridge. He left a note, weighted on the sidewalk by a child's toy binoculars. It said: "This is my last selfish act."

That night, Danielle secluded herself in the bedroom. The one where little John Madrone had slept. I recalled his sad face, as if he somehow felt the loss coming. And helplessly shook our hands, knowing we'd be falling headlong into grief.

When the house was quiet in the early hours of the morning, I wrote a poem called "Your Father."

The morning sky,
empty and blue
above the clearing fog,
is letting you fall,

letting you fall
through cold bursts of air,
a wind that keens against your face
and takes your voice.

Your father dressed you for this,
he chose your coat and tights.
And held you, the *Examiner* said,
to his chest as he stepped off.

And as the water broke
you from his grasp
you became his last,
the most imperishable strike

against the ones who wouldn't love.

The gray waves take your trust.
In time police boats winch
his floating body up.
But you are lost.

Your hair moves now
in the drifting currents of the bay.

    Reading it now, it seems to stand at such emotional distance from the events that day. As if I had turned from the explosion, the flying glass. As if my back was to Danielle so I would not have to see it cut her. Or cut me.

CHAPTER 43

*T*he next morning the police had more details. The rented Malibu was recovered in a parking lot near the bridge toll booth. It contained James's wallet. A search of the room at Roberts yielded a partially unpacked duffel bag, some strewn underwear, and three puppets tucked carefully in one of the beds—just their heads peeking above the sheets.

A waitress reported serving breakfast to James and Annie on the previous day. At the Cliff House—a table overlooking the ruins of Sutro Baths. They had, it seemed, an animated conversation. Looking down at the rocks. Pointing. Laughing. James had a few glasses of champagne.

Witnesses on the bridge were impressed with how close they seemed, how comfortable with each other. Daughter and father stopped now and then as they strolled, looking over the rail, Annie trying to watch passing ships through her binoculars. At a point where there were no nearby pedestrians, James swung one foot over the guardrail and straddled it. He handed something to Annie. She put it on the ground and weighted it with the binoculars.

Then James reached for her—an inviting gesture. She hesitated, finally offering herself to his arms. He lifted her up and balanced there, pointing to something. He zipped her pink jacket. His longish hair was thrown across his face by the wind. He pushed it back.

He swung up his other leg, turning to face the water. And they were gone.

The witness, who ran to look over the rail, said he held her "till they hit." I don't know what that means. Whether it was the last expression of his instinct to protect, or he was holding Annie prisoner—all the way down—to his need for revenge. I wish someone would tell me, someone who understood the man.

As of Monday morning, Annie's body hadn't been recovered. The police told Danielle that as time went by, finding her was less and less likely. They were correct.

Over the next few hours, Danielle made obligatory contacts. She called her parents, who went into a righteous fury about how she never should have married James. Their conviction, formed during a few visits, stemmed from James's propensity to touch Danielle's ass. And worse, the suspicion that she enjoyed it.

Danielle called Mabel, letting the old lady know she could claim James's body and his effects.

"How could he do such a thing?" Flint Lips' croaking voice pushed through the receiver; I could hear it halfway across the room.

"Because he's James. Because you helped him." Danielle hung up.

Lara made us lunch. We ate mostly in silence. Danielle scooped tiny portions with her right hand; her left was in a fist. It was nearly twenty-four hours since Danielle had seen James's body—and known for sure that Annie was lost—and she had not yet cried.

The anger was a wall. Holding her up. Holding me away. Keeping the pain from paralyzing her.

I watched her nourish it. In the swivel chair, looking into the garden, I could see her lips compress suddenly, a word start to form. Her eyes would slide along the paths and planted rows, turning, circling, starting again to make another cycle. Then her body would tense—as if waiting for a blow. Or preparing to strike one.

Things changed at four o'clock.

Roca called again. He was finishing up, he said. Preparing a report. But he felt James's note was a loose end. What had he meant, "last selfish act"? Had there been other things he'd done—things Roca should know about? Had there been abuse? Or violence? Were other people involved?

A long time went by before Danielle answered.

"It was a message to me," she said. "I'd called him selfish, I think, the night before. And maybe other times. I don't know. I think he was saying…it was my fault."

"I see," Roca said. "So that's it, then. That's what I needed to know, and I guess that's it."

"That's it, then," Danielle repeated. And she dropped the phone.

Danielle sagged to her knees, hands flat on the carpet. The crying started slowly. High-pitched and soft. She looked like she was praying. A devout posture.

The crying continued, breaking into sobs. Deeper, deeper. Shaking her body. Making her gasp to get air.

I got down with her, my hand on her shoulder. Rubbing. Holding it. After a while, she toppled against me, her back curling against my arms. Hunching her knees until she was fetal. Alone.

Lara watched from the chair behind us. "She has to do this," she said. "There's no other way. It comes in waves, knocks you down and then it passes. Then another one comes to knock you down again."

I thought of what Danielle, herself, had said to me so long ago—the time by the fire when I'd cried about my father. "If you want to be alive, you have to feel."

The deep sobbing went on for a long time. Maybe an hour. Then Danielle started to chant Annie's name. Drawing out the vowels—A-a-a ne-e. Like she was invoking a spirit, trying to reach her.

When finally Danielle lay quiet, I kissed her cheek. Once. She twisted to look at me, dark hair spilling on the carpet.

"You're waiting for this to be over, Harper. I feel you holding on, hoping that it can end." Long pause while she pushed her finger into the nap of the carpet. "It will never end. Harper? Do you hear that? It won't end."

I kept my hand on her shoulder. I didn't know what else to do. After a while, Danielle rolled back on her knees and stood up. "I think I'm going to bed," she announced.

"Can I come?"

"No." She turned toward the hall.

I felt slapped.

"Why? I'm—"

"Harper, stop. Don't you understand after all this time? I know the truth. I know you didn't even like Annie. She was in the way, she was between us. And the first thing you felt deep down—when she was gone—was hope and excitement."

"No."

"That you would have me all to yourself."

"Don't say that. It's ugly. Why do you say that?"

"Because it's true, Harper. It's why I can't be close to you, can't touch you."

I felt flayed. Opened.

"If that's true, if I felt that, Danielle, it would be a small part of it. I would still love you, I'd still protect you. Still want to hold my body between you and anything that would hurt you."

Silence.

"If that's true, it's only part of it," I repeated.

"I realize," she said, "but I can't stand knowing it. I can't stand," the tears started welling again, "that you don't really care about her."

"But I care about you."

"I know." She shrugged. "I'm sorry."

Twin streams ran down her face. No sound. She stood there for another few minutes, looking around the room. As if she'd lost something.

"Do you need something?" Lara asked.

I'd forgotten she was there, watching everything.

"Nothing."

"He's a good man, honey. You know that."

"Yeah. I know."

She went to bed without me.

CHAPTER 44

t this moment I am thinking about the nature of sadness. How for some people it requires silence, and for others expression; for some isolation, and others a great reaching out. A joining.

I'm sitting by a tall stone hearth. Empty now. Walnut wainscoting runs high around the room. I'm in a Windsor chair arranged to look through the windows. But there is nothing to see. Just darkness.

Danielle taught me, in this room, how to put sadness into words. How not to be alone with it. I suspect we choose silence when the sadness is laced with shame. When speaking of it would expose some dark failure. Some damage we did by giving in to fear. By somehow serving ourselves.

Danielle blamed herself for Annie's death. And she couldn't talk about it.

On Tuesday morning I woke up tired; I had slept fitfully. I checked the bedroom, but Danielle wasn't there. The Jeep was gone from the driveway. I remained in Lara's house all day. Waiting. Danielle never returned.

CHAPTER 45

*I*t was sunny and unseasonably warm that day. Children were playing on the street—tag games like ice-and-snow. Throwing frisbees. Lara and I sat on the stoop and watched. The voices were high, ebullient.

"John's father grew up there." Lara flicked a finger toward the house across the street. "He and Charlie were great friends—always playing catch out in front here. He was a sweet kid, always doing things for people. Like you, Harper.

"But sometimes, no matter how much you try, or how much you love, you can't do anything for a person. They're beyond reach. John's father learned that with his wife. She's a real misery. Nothing's ever going to cheer that woman up."

"What am I supposed to do, Lara?" I felt suddenly angry. "Walk away? Try to stop caring about her?"

Lara began rubbing the fingers on one hand. I noticed they were chapped and red. "She won't be back, Harper. Everything here is connected to Annie's death. You, me. She's going to run to a place with no reminders. With strangers who don't know what happened here."

For a while we were quiet. I began to cry.

"Why did this happen?" I asked.

"Why did he do it?" Lara stopped rubbing, spreading her hands in a gesture of surrender. "Pain. Pain he couldn't stand. What else would there be?"

A kid wearing a watch cap threw a long pass that was caught with a running fingertip grab. Lara clapped. "Good one, Jerry. That was Pro Bowl stuff." Jerry waved to her.

Another silence.

"Go home, Harper. Go back to Wawona. Tend the greens and fairways. There's no fixing this. Annie is too big a loss."

My hand rests on Danielle's journal, left behind that day at Lara's house. The leather is dry and rough. I keep touching it, to finally let in her grief. The pain I was afraid to feel, or didn't know how to feel. The leather warms beneath my fingers, as if what's inside is making its way back to me.

I left the next morning. Train, then bus, then hitchhiking over Chinquapin Pass to Wawona. My room was cold. Full of dirty cups and glasses. Danielle's bracelet was on the bed. A single silver hoop, lost probably while she'd been curled up crying. I looked in my bureau drawer at my collection of notes from Danielle: "Meet me at…Annie will be overnight so we could…James has Annie at the caboose…" And the treasure of her condolence note after I lost my father. I read them over and over. Savored the peculiarities of her script.

Then I had to work. To be a night watchman stumping between Wawona's outbuildings. Turning the cold keys in my clock. I thought of Danielle walking these paths with me, how the key caught the moonlight as she pulled it from the box. I thought of her voice, asking questions that would end my invisible, ghost life.

I imagined the future without that voice. Without the warmth of her breasts against my body. I thought of Annie, drifting in the dark currents of the Golden Gate. Her small body bloating now. Beyond anyone's protection.

I felt leaden. Pressed against the cold planet.

When I slept that night I dreamt of my father. Sick, on the golf course barely swinging his clubs. I was carrying him from hole to hole. Trying to get him to talk to me. Instead he was singing to the dragonflies, drawing them near him. Like some kind of pied piper.

The next afternoon I hiked down to the south fork of the

Merced. It was still frozen, with a few broken places where you could see the current. I just started stabbing it with a long branch. Over and over. Making a hundred little holes until the ice cracked and broke up.

After that productive effort, I hitchhiked to Fish Camp and walked up to Danielle's house. I broke a window pane in the back door and let myself in. The place was freezing and dark.

I sat in a living-room chair, imagining the three of them. Their voices. The sounds of dinner being prepared. Annie playing with her puppets on the floor. James touching Danielle's body—casually as she passed. Momentary laughter. All gone now.

It was the most alone moment of my life.

After a while I found Annie's puppets and her puppet house; wrapped them in the grandmother's quilt. I lugged it all down to Highway 41, and hitchhiked back home.

To my knowledge, Danielle never returned to that cabin. So I feel good that a few months later I gave the puppet house to the daughter of someone who worked the front desk. I still have the puppets.

Over the days that followed, I made a dozen different narratives to explain what happened. Danielle and I had sinned, stealing happiness we didn't deserve, breaking up her family—and this was the punishment. I left my father to die alone—and this was the punishment. Those were the moral explanations, suitable for one who'd grown up in the Catholic church.

Then there were the psychological theories. That James was consumed by simple jealousy. Or depression because he'd been cut off from the woman and child he loved. Or he was overwhelmed by fear that he would go to jail and lose all hope of being a father again. The most elegant explanation was anger: his last words at Sutro Park, the note, killing Annie—these all seemed like an exquisite, planned revenge.

And then there was Frank Riles's suggestion: "The asshole probably drank himself to where it looked like a good idea. To where stupid shit looks fucking genius. Like getting even. Getting even always looks good."

He had a point. But I didn't know James had done that much

drinking. I hitched down to the Valley one day about a month later—in a particularly vicious period of self-hate. I was deep in the conviction that I'd reached for something that I had no right to. And reaped catastrophe.

It was dusk. I was walking in Stoneman Meadow—just released from the heavy snows. Hawks were looping between branches in the high pines, and I could smell the earth. In that moment something turned in me. I was suddenly not the architect of the tragedy. Of James and Annie's death. Instead I began to feel something I think James had craved—and never been given. That night I wrote about it, included here for whatever it's worth.

Half Dome Turning Pink at Twilight

The face that accepts scars
rises above these ages of ice,
rises sheer
and faintly pink above the meadow
rustling with the work of field mice.

Here is the place you agreed to come
where nothing is wrong,
nothing is human.

The granite becomes pink
as death comes for a day;
the day perfect in its dance and its disease,
perfect in love and love's denial,
ending in a meadow
of fern and grass and purple thistle.

No day left but a perfect lying down.
Oh field mouse, oh thistle, I give you everything I am—
All love, all shame.
You will take it and give it back
clean and just the same.
And I will not have to despise myself again.

To be forgiven. There is no explaining it. For me, it could not come from a person. It was not a decision. It was in the place, the moment. In the rocks, the inevitability of the changing season.

CHAPTER 46

When the golf course opened in May, my night watchman job ended. I was returned to my life of watering and mowing grass. In some ways my isolation was more pronounced on the fairways. For while a hundred golfers marched daily around the course, their presence made me acutely aware of how alone I was. Often they'd pass within a few feet of me, yet rarely spoke. Sometimes a complaint about the high cut of the rough, sometimes a wave and a generic greeting, but the aggregate experience was of moving invisibly through a crowd.

As I had the year before, I would occasionally join Frank Riles while he practiced his fastball. Sometimes I went to employee parties, or hiked with a few of the younger staff. But when I wasn't on the tractor, I was likely in my room. Reading. Drinking port.

During the day, I focused on the geometric patterns of watering, watched for brown spots, fixed cleat or ball gouges in the greens. The course, and the life of millions of blades of grass, held my attention. But at night my thoughts were often about Danielle. Imagining her in different places. Reliving holding her hand in the ambulance, or when we climbed the great rock on her birthday hike. Or seeing her lovely body as I washed her in the tub.

More than once I found myself replaying that brief walk I took with Danielle and Annie on the snow-covered golf course.

Remembering how anxious Annie was to get rid of me. And how resentful I was on that single occasion I met the little girl. To make memory more bearable, I sometimes revised the scene—being more attentive to Annie, giving her a ride on the tractor. It didn't work. She would always disappear with her mother down that road, to be swallowed by her fate.

In July, I think, I called Tara. She still worked in housekeeping for the Swiss Melody Inn, but was planning a move to Oakland when the season ended. We met in a Fish Camp bar called the White Chief.

We shook hands; she kept looking at the door as if longing to be on the other side of it. She began zipping her picture agate necklace up and down its chain.

"So what's up?" she asked. "You said there was something you wanted to know—about James."

I tried to strike the right tone. Nothing would come of this if I put her off. I started with chitchat, but she asked again what I wanted.

"I guess I think of us as being in the same boat," I said. "Our lives got blown up last March. I want to know why. Why it happened. Why we—"

I didn't finish because Tara had gone into a frenzy of chain pulling and looking around.

"Don't ask me. I didn't know shit about him. Obviously. If I'd known he was capable of something like that, I'd have kissed him off at the get-go."

She lit a cigarette, blew out the match in my direction. "I started smoking again—after what happened." She shrugged. "All I know is he got totally nuts both times Dani took his kid away. Fucked up behind it, like it was all he could think about."

"Do you feel that's why he did it?"

"I don't know."

We ordered beers. She clicked bottles. "Here's to the aftermath," she said.

I decided to take another tack. "What kind of person was James? I never got much of a picture of him from Danielle. But you saw him day in, day out. How he reacted to things."

She took a long drag and blew the smoke into our beers. "He had to be perfect. He couldn't stand being wrong, making a mistake."

She told me the stories—either then or later, I can't remember—of the collapsed bed, and the time he burned himself in the Shay's firebox. And how he blew up when Tara challenged his commitment to the relationship.

"The biggest mistake he ever made was me. That's the truth. Our relationship was long over. But when Dani found out about it, she kicked his ass out anyway. He couldn't get over that. The fact that she felt that way, that she wouldn't forgive him."

"What did that mean to James—that she wouldn't forgive him?"

"That he was fucked, a worthless piece of crap. There was no getting over that."

"So did he want her to take him back?"

"Yeah, he did. In the beginning. He tried to hide it, but I could see it plain as I see you." She flicked the cigarette around twenty times over the ashtray, took a puff, and started flicking again. "But later he wanted her…he wanted her just to be OK with him. To say 'OK, I know this man.'" She stopped, lost somewhere else.

"So he wanted her to still care for him?"

She looked at me. "Something like that."

"Is there more?"

"I think he wanted her to think he was good. To think he was a good man. And he tried. He stopped drinking. He tried to make the caboose cozy for Annie. Even though Annie treated him like shit sometimes, he was always very…steady in his love for that child."

Flecks of ash were collecting on the table around the ashtray. Tara tried to dab them with a wet fingertip. She wiped the finger on her pants.

"I feel bad for the child, for what happened. Believe me. But she wasn't an easy kid. She was angry. Maybe she was too much like her father."

"Getting angry when something hurt?"

"Yeah, maybe." Long pause. "He loved her though, that's for sure."

Tara took a deep, hesitating breath, and her eyes started to well. She brushed the tears quickly, smearing her mascara. After a minute she stopped because it wasn't doing any good. A single silver stream coursed down each cheek.

"Yeah, well," she shrugged. The tears were coming hard now. Dripping off her chin. "Yeah, well, I know he didn't love me. They were his 'baby girls.' Both of them. And I was...but I tried to stick anyway. Just to see, to see how things would turn out.

"But he was crazier than I thought. He left without saying anything." She lit a cigarette from the last one. "So he didn't love me at all."

We drank our beers in silence.

"So, is that it?" she said after a while.

"I don't know. It still doesn't make sense. He loved Annie. Why would he kill his own child? Was it like if he couldn't have her, he wouldn't let her mother have her either? Is that the 'last selfish act'?"

"I don't think so." She hesitated, started fingering her coat. Dropped some ash on it. Smeared it. "I think maybe he just couldn't leave her. He had to keep her with him."

"He was gonna keep her with him when they were dead? Did he believe in an afterlife?"

"I don't know. I don't think so. I think it was just too lonely without her."

We looked at each other.

"It doesn't make any sense," I said.

"I know."

We met three or four more times before Tara moved to Oakland in September. Always at the White Chief, always trodding the same ground. We shared a sense of having survived the same great wreck; Tara was as interested in understanding what happened as I was. And I think we helped each other mourn.

It was raining when we met there last. The White Chief was deserted. As was the custom, Tara toasted to the aftermath and raised her bottle. On this occasion, for some reason, I began talking about the meeting at Sutro Park—James and Danielle's last conversation. I told Tara the gist of what was said.

"Yeah," she responded. "To be completely known, then thrown away. It makes sense."

I shrugged. "To you, maybe."

"Isn't that what happened to you, Harper? Dani could tell you weren't touched by Annie's death, that you didn't care that much. And she took off."

I didn't know what to say.

When we stood to leave, Tara kissed me. Very sweetly on the lips.

"What happens now?" I asked, thinking that we might stay in touch.

"We forget," she said. "That's all, we forget."

I tried it. Forgetting. And I wrote about it.

> Daily now I bathe
> in the River Lethe,
> letting forgetfulness rush
> like water to the drowning lungs.
>
> How night descends for a family
> I can't describe. Men take
> what they want.
> They are afraid to scream and so
>
> are compelled to damage.

But the more I worked at forgetting, the more I found myself locked in a room with Danielle and the ghosts of James and Annie.

CHAPTER 47

I'm watching the falls. A man and a woman walk to the edge of the trail. The man is looking down, seeing the glistening spray collect on their hands, their fingers, the tattoo of wet beads on their faces. Now he reaches across to her as if the arc of falling water, felt equally, would make them, that moment, the same.

In November, Lara sent me a letter. She wished me happy Thanksgiving and asked how I'd been. Then came the shock: she had heard from Danielle. A postcard, which she included. The canceling date was November 10—Salt Lake City.

The card was an apology for leaving with no good-bye. And a thanks to Lara for "helping in so many ways."

> *I'm OK. Surviving. I work and live in a hotel. Fishermen in the summer, skiers in the winter time. A place almost as beautiful as Yosemite. I know I can never go back. I just wanted you to know how I was.*
>
> *Love, D*

"I wonder where she is?" Lara wrote. "Probably not Salt Lake—no fishing there." She signed off with, "Just thought you'd like to know."

Quite right—I did want to know. After getting her letter, I was consumed with nothing else.

CHAPTER 48

The next week was spent in research. I called a boatload of travel agents, learning about resort areas within 250 miles of Salt Lake.

My theory was that Danielle had gone to Salt Lake for a weekend of big-city life. Which meant, practically speaking, it had to be within five hours of where she worked.

The postcard suggested Danielle's hotel appealed to all-season vacationers. It had to be near lakes and streams, as well as ski runs. And the phrase "almost as beautiful as Yosemite" suggested more than a pretty resort. It implied a sense of grandeur.

There was another important factor about Danielle herself. She liked living in a town, having neighbors. She wouldn't have been happy in some isolated lodge, cooped up with a small cadre of permanent employees.

When all these factors were combined, it turned out there were really only a few places. And by far the most likely was Jackson Hole, Wyoming. Jackson is the gateway to the Grand Tetons, a range whose sawtooth peaks and sapphire lakes rival anything in the Sierra. It has nearby skiing, boating, fishing, and world-class hiking. And the town is quaint, with a variety of shops and restaurants all catering to the tourist trade.

I left on Monday, November 23. Took a 727 bound for Salt

Lake, and then an old prop job to the airport just north of Jackson Hole. As I stepped from the plane, I was facing a high, grassy plateau. Far to the east, you could see evidence of glacial moraines. And behind me, to the west, were the beginnings of the Teton range. The air was sharp and thin, with an undernote of smokiness.

The town had a few main streets lined with ancient buildings and boutique-type stores. That was for the tourists. Then there was the real town set on narrow lanes straggling into the forest. The smell of smoke was stronger there, plumes bursting from dozens of chimneys.

I stayed in a dive called The Bunkhouse on Gill Street—a simple room with the luxury of a TV that didn't work. Immediately I started inquiries.

By three o'clock the next day, I'd covered every hotel and motel in the immediate vicinity. No one named Danielle McAllister worked in any capacity for a Jackson Hole lodge. I suspected she'd stolen a page from James's book and changed her name. Which made my task immeasurably harder.

Over the next four or five days, I methodically staked out each of the lodges, watching employees come and go, occasionally asking friendly-looking housekeepers if they knew someone answering Danielle's description. The process was greatly hampered by the fact that I had no photograph.

It snowed. Then it rained and turned everything to slush. Then it snowed some more. I can't find words for the unpleasantness of standing on a street corner all day—freezing, wet—anxiously watching each passing face. I never caught sight of her; I hadn't a single lead.

On my sixth night in Jackson, I needed a drink. In truth, I'd needed a drink every night, but I usually sipped port in my room. On this occasion I stepped into a cowboy bar called the Rodeo Club. It was a big, smoky room with worn plank floors. The tables were old cable spools surrounded by short, rough-cut benches. There was a dance floor, a country-western jukebox, and a carved, nineteenth-century mahogany bar. They didn't have any port.

There were maybe thirty people in the place, mostly men. They all had cigarettes; they all had Budweisers. There was one barmaid, a good-looking blonde in a cowboy hat.

I drank my beer. Periodically someone dropped a quarter in the jukebox for some Johnny Cash or Tammy Wynette. The smoke got thicker. Maybe every third song, a couple got up to lean on each other for a few minutes on the dance floor.

Around nine o'clock, a blue floodlight illuminated a postage-stamp stage that was maybe four or five feet above the dance floor. Oddly, the jukebox was unplugged, and a second flood illuminated a list of maybe twenty-five songs—again mostly country-western, but including some Animals and Stones. A framed sign next to the playlist read "Two dollars per dance." Within a minute, a big lumberjack-type guy with a navy coat and silver belt buckle passed some money across the bar. The bartender put on an LP and gently eased the needle into the right groove. Loretta Lynn started blasting from the speakers.

Through a curtain behind the tiny floodlit stage, a woman stepped into the light. She was dressed in pseudo-western style, with a buckskin vest and skirt. The vest was open, revealing her torso and a fire-red bra. The skirt was so short that staring up from the floor, you could see her matching panties. The outfit was completed by a red cowboy hat she wore low, casting a shadow on her face.

The woman started to dance. A combination two-step/mashed potatoes. Bending, spreading her legs, turning so we could see her ass. The air filled with hoots and catcalls. I got swept up in it, shouting, "Yes," and getting aroused. When the song was over, the woman bowed and took off her hat. It was Danielle.

I watched in disbelief as she slipped behind the curtain. The crowd clapped. Someone ran up to the bar to order another song. This time, as the music started, the blonde waitress I'd seen earlier burst through the curtain with a two-step version of the bump and grind. More hooting.

I saw Danielle emerge from a door marked *Employees*. She looked the same, except now the vest was buttoned. She picked up a tray at the bar and started taking orders.

At the first table she seemed to be joking and laughing with the men. When Danielle bent to hear their orders, a thin, balding cowboy felt her ass. She smiled at him.

Whole armies clashed inside of me. Rage at the cowboy's familiarity, competing with relief at finding her at last. Horror that the anonymous dance had turned Danielle into a sexual object, fighting the intense arousal at seeing her lovely body. And there was fear that she would see me and run away. And a sudden, welling sadness for all that had happened, everything that was lost.

I moved into a dark corner. As soon as Danielle's back was turned, I escaped. Out on the sidewalk the snow was at it again, slicing into my coat with a nasty windchill. I waited till two a.m., stomping, blowing on my hands, running back and forth to the end of the block.

When Danielle hit the street, she was wearing sweat pants, a ski cap, and her gray down jacket. She carried a small duffel bag for her dance costume. She didn't scan the block, just kept her eyes down and headed south. I followed, maybe fifty yards behind.

We were heading down West Deloney when Danielle turned into an alley. I had to be careful and hung back. About midway to the next corner, she headed up some stairs—the back entrance to the Wort Hotel. Now I had to be quick. As soon as Danielle was through the door, I ran to get a closer look.

A minute later, a light appeared on the bottom floor—second window from the end. I was breathing hard. Frost pumped in front of my face. Now I knew where she lived. After eight months of waiting, I had seen her face, I had seen the light go on in her room.

When I tried the back door of the Wort, it was locked. I went around to the front on North Glenwood. The Wort is stately, by Jackson Hole standards. It has a muted, forties elegance. It's the kind of place where the staff falls all over you, trying to make up for not being the Sheraton.

The desk clerk raised his eyebrows when I came in. Just enough to suggest that two a.m. check-ins were not the norm in Jackson.

"I'm meeting my sister," I said. I gave her real name. "She's driving in late from Salt Lake—couldn't get away earlier. I got delayed by the snow myself. You should have the reservation under Kane."

He looked through some file cards and shook his head.

"Oh my God, I told her to book it and maybe she forgot."

He was looking at me like I was wearing a clown suit.

I ran my fingers through my hair, probably overdoing it. "Do you have any rooms?"

There was a long pause. "Where's your suitcase?"

"In the car. I'll bring it up later."

After more deliberation than Truman took to drop the bomb, the guy finally offered me a key. Third floor.

"I'm just going to check the room first," I said. "When my sister comes, send her up."

I did actually peek at the room, then snuck down to the first floor, back hall, and knocked on the second door from the end.

Danielle's voice, suspicious: "Who is it?"

"Police," I said in a deep voice. "There was a problem at the Rodeo Club."

When she opened the door, she didn't say anything. But she backed away. I walked in and gently closed the door, leaning against it. Danielle's face was dense, expressionless. A minute went by.

"I saw you dance."

She nodded. "It's my only relief," she said.

Silence.

"I missed you." I held up the postcard. "I had to find you."

She nodded again. The tears were starting, spilling to the edges of her lips. She didn't move.

"You are the person I love," I said. "I came to tell you that. I know now it's a selfish love. Otherwise I could have taken some of your pain when Annie died."

She had been looking at the floor, and, for a moment, she raised her eyes. "I know," she said. "But you couldn't have saved me...from any of it." Long pause. "I thought I'd never see you, that I'd just go on here."

She held her hands out to the side, fingers splayed. "I thought I would just go on here. Cleaning rooms. Dancing for...the men."

"I know."

She was still wearing her buckskin vest, and now she unbuttoned it. The tears fell steadily. She untied the string of her pants and let them fall. In a moment Danielle was standing before me as I had seen her that first night in Moore Cottage. Lovely, without caution or defense. Yet now shimmering with grief.

"What do we do?" I said.

"The only thing we can. What we have left."

We did it. She didn't stop crying.

CHAPTER 49

I'm on Big Creek, where the old stage bridge crosses. The place where Annie and Danielle used to fish. The leaves tremble above the water, shrill in the light. Gray in the shadows of pine.

There's a faint wind, the sound of water falling on water. Sun touches the moving shadows of trout.

I dip my hand in the water, feeling the weight of the current, the chill of the snowfields. Sand glitters with mica in the deep pools, the surface a Janus of shadow and light.

It would be a perfect stream except for the memory. Danielle and Annie on their way to an afternoon that should have been lost in the ordinary, the unnoticed march of days. I witnessed the moment they were snatched from it. When the course of things forever changed.

While Danielle lay unconscious, bleeding amid the glitter of broken glass, while Annie ran across the fairways to take refuge in the woods, a life ended. And another one began. In this other life, Danielle was given sight and knowledge—a gift so powerful that it blew everything apart.

I watch the stream where they were headed, where they would have talked in the desultory way people do as they cast and reel in. Talking about nothing, every word a strand that connects them.

It's lovely here; Annie would be forty now.

On March 8, 1985, exactly fifteen years after James eased himself over the rail, I got a call from Tara. I was living in San Francisco; she'd remained in Oakland. I hadn't talked to her since we said goodbye at the White Chief so many years ago.

We agreed to meet at a pub on Geary Street called the Edinburgh Castle. It's a quaint place with a bagpiper strutting through the bar each hour, and a seventy-five-year-old parrot named Winston, whose job is to outlive the customers.

Tara still looked good at thirty-eight. A slender gym junkie. Long black hair that seemed like it had been ironed. A touch too much makeup. Brown eyes that held the sadness of a recent divorce.

After a half hour or so of catching up, she got to the point:

"I told you on the phone there was something I wanted to show you. I should have looked you up years ago when I found it, but…" She smiled, made a dismissing gesture. "I discovered it in a book of wildflowers I used to look at quite a bit. When I was in Fish Camp."

Tara retrieved something from her shoulder bag. "I didn't use the wildflower book in Oakland, so I didn't find this till seventy-one or seventy-two. When I was moving, I think. And by then I didn't want to remember about James anymore. Or anything that happened, so I just put it back in the book."

She was waving an envelope back and forth while she spoke.

"But I think it tells something—about James."

She placed the envelope in front of me. Making fussy adjustments till it was straight. On the outside it read: "For Annie on her 18th birthday." I opened the flap. It was a letter.

Dear Annie:

By the time you read this I'll have been gone a long time. Twelve years. I doubt you remember much about me. Your mother may have told you things that aren't true, or maybe just said nothing. Maybe just let the past die.

That's why I left this letter with Tara—because I think Dani might not give it to you. So if you're reading it, it's because Tara kept it all these years and got it to you.

Anyway, the first thing I want to say is I love you. You are my baby girl, more precious and special to me than anything. Do you remember when we used to catch frogs by Big Creek? Do you remember skipping stones? Do you remember me coming to your bed when you cried at night? Do you remember us practicing bird calls? Or looking at the snow fall from the top of my caboose?

It breaks my heart to think maybe you don't. That you're reading this and thinking back, but you can't remember.

I just want you to know that right now your face is in front of me. I can see you as clearly as if you were here. I can see your shiny blonde hair, done up in pigtails. I can see your new big front teeth. Your little freckles. And it makes me miss you so much. I want to hug you. I want to walk with you down one of our trails, and carry you when you're tired. I want to lift you to your bed after you've gotten sleepy.

I want to see you grow up, baby girl. But I can't. Your mama won't let me. She won't let me see you anymore, and I can't stand that. Can you understand what I'm saying? Because your mama doesn't. She thinks I can live without you, baby girl.

[There were some smears on the paper at this point. Oil or grease maybe.]

So remember that I love you, OK? Because it's important to know that your daddy thinks you are the best girl in the world.

I'm trying to imagine you at 18. I don't know what you'll be like all grown up. I'm trying to think what else to tell you.

You have to take care of yourself, baby girl. You can't depend on people. They change. They do things for themselves. Don't ever count on anybody but you. I mean that. If you depend on people, it makes you weak.

When I was a kid I knew a boy who had a dog. A big Labrador. And that dog followed him around all day, and just waited to be played with. They used to run a lot on the beach.

The dog would jump into the waves to fetch for him. One day that boy went swimming in a high surf and drowned. The dog was desolate, just wandering the street, the beach. He never got over it.

Don't be like that, baby girl.

And don't believe anything anybody says about me, OK? Just believe this letter. Believe me that I love you. Always.

Daddy

When I finished reading it, Tara clicked my bottle with hers. "To the aftermath," she said. "You can keep the letter if you want it."

We drank in silence for a while.

"So he was planning suicide, but alone," I said. "When he slipped this letter into your wildflower book, he expected Annie to live."

"Yeah. He's trying to tell her all this stuff, sort of rambling. It's kinda pathetic, all the weird advice."

"Maybe he's the dog," I said. "Maybe that's what happened to him."

Tara extended her fingers in front of her, studying them. "Maybe."

"But why did he change his mind? What made him decide to jump with Annie?"

"He loved her too much."

"That's no reason."

Silence.

"What are you going to do now?" I said.

"Lick my wounds. Keep fucking up my life." She looked at me searchingly for a moment. "You're one of the good ones. I never go for that kind of man."

On that, we clicked bottles one more time. I never saw her again.

The wind is getting stronger. Sliding among the ragged branches. It comes in waves—each made out of stillness, each whispering like a final breath.

Annie cast from this spot on the bridge, standing on Galen Clark's toll road that once thundered with stages and teams of six. She cast from this spot, where countless tourists have dangled their feet, eaten their sandwiches.

I try to see her, but she is not here. The dead are not allowed this beauty.

CHAPTER 50

*T*he porch slopes gently toward the edge. Gray floorboards, warped here and there, bear scratches from the ceaseless shuffling of the wicker chairs. Glossy white paint coats the balusters and railings. Below me, children play in the pool. Shrieking. Splashing. People in recliners have arranged themselves in the shadows of pines. Spray from the old stone fountain, illumined by the afternoon sun, drifts over the lily pads.

To the west is a chalk-dust sky, overcast slipping across the fading gray of distant ridges. Above me the sun has broken through a seam in the clouds. The air is thick with the scent of pitch and new-mown grass.

I tell myself that I am finished now, but I do not stop. As if the act of putting down words keeps open the possibility of some final understanding. Some yet unrecognized truth. I imagine James at that last breakfast with Annie. A few hours from death. Smiling. Lighthearted. About to betray his child.

I wonder what he saw when he looked at Annie, or whether she had simply disappeared beneath his brutal plan.

Tara said he loved the child. And was disturbed both times he was forbidden to see her. What does "disturbed" mean? That something which belonged to James was taken away? That he couldn't control Danielle? Or that he unbearably ached to see his girl?

I find myself returning to that picture of James at the Cliff House. Laughing. Pointing at the sights. Who is he there? It occurs to me that he may be relieved. The pain will be over soon.

And the pain that gives death a good name, that makes it attractive— what is that? I'm not sure I have the words. I can sense a turn in James's relationship to Danielle—long before the end. From being her teacher, the strutting master of her world, to a man who became oddly dependent, who needed Danielle more than she needed him. Only in the mirror of her eyes was James good.

He had never been real. He was a fabricated man, invented to win a woman's love. And when Danielle turned away from him, love became impossible. But worse, he was stripped to a barren core. Without the one person in the world who could make him believe he was OK.

Of course, that's wrong. There was another person who could give James love. Annie. And he would lose her too.

A familiar car is pulling into the carriage drive of the hotel. It parks on the far side, by the squat gray building that was Hills Studio. Danielle gets out, stretches for a moment in the hard light. Her dark hair is shorter, salt and pepper now. But she is still lithe and strong looking. To me, still lovely.

She pulls a wheeled suitcase from the trunk and begins to walk, cross-ing in front of the main hotel. Where I used to live; where she first came to me. Danielle hasn't been here in thirty years, yet she looks straight ahead. At the ground.

She was given too big a gift. A world undressed, without artifice or pre-tense. It seemed ugly. Wrong. The more she saw, the more blind she was to James's wretchedness. To the lacerations of his shame. Her gift destroyed him.

In time the unforgiven man becomes capable of anything. Suicide of course. But really any act the mind can conceive to stop the pain.

James found—after he wrote the letter for Annie's eighteenth birth-day—that he couldn't kill himself as planned. Perhaps because it felt too lonely an act. Or it seemed somehow an insufficient answer to his suffering. Death alone could not heal what had gone wrong for James.

I don't know. I still do not know.

Danielle is coming toward me down the wide verandah. Her suitcase trails, making rhythmic clacking sounds. Now she waves, gives her lovely downturned smile. The architecture of her face is the same—the high cheeks, full lips. The same brown eyes regarding me.

"How has it gone," she says, "three days here alone?"

"I've enjoyed seeing all the old places."

She nods. Fusses with the handle of the suitcase.

"So that's what you've been doing?"

"Yes. And writing…about what happened."

"Oh." Creases deepen around her mouth. She looks down at the children in the pool. "Did you learn anything?"

"An inkling of something. But then it's gone."

"So nothing came of it?" Her face seems to relax.

"Not really."

Silence. She pushes open the door.

"It's cool inside. Nice."

"Sometimes I start to see…"

"What?"

She pauses mid-motion. Looks back at me, lips tightening again.

"I don't know. I can't seem to finish that."

She drags the case into the room. The spring door closes.

"Is it really all right?" Soft, muffled voice.

I poke my head inside. I smile.

"I'm going to take a bath, then," she says.

"Would you like me to wash you?"

Her eyes search my face. She nods.

"Yes."

What is at the end
of this mystery of fate?
We do what we have left to do.
We touch the weeping shale.
We hear the wind
scrape the granite.
We watch the orange light
walk up the mountain.
We lay with each other
all night
in the hands of the moon.